© Carlo Dalla Mura

Mariolina Venezia was born in 1961 and has written poetry as well as for television and film. She
lives in Rome.

Been Here
a Thousand
Years

Picador

—

Farrar, Straus and Giroux
New York

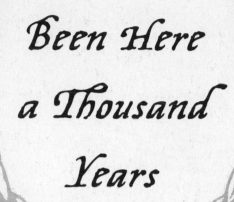

Been Here a Thousand Years

Mariolina Venezia

TRANSLATED FROM THE ITALIAN BY
MARINA HARSS

www.picadorusa.com

For information on Picador Reading Group Guides, please contact Picador. E-mail: readinggroupguides@picadorusa.com

Designed by Gretchen Achilles

The Library of Congress has cataloged the Farrar, Straus and Giroux edition as follows:

Venezia, Mariolina, 1961–
    [Mille anni che sto qui. English]
    Been here a thousand years / Mariolina Venezia ; translated from the Italian by Marina Harss.—1st edition.
    p. cm.
    ISBN 978-0-374-20891-2
    1. Basilicata (Italy)—Fiction. I. Harss, Marina. II. Title. III. Title: Been here 1000 years.

    PQ4882.E47M5513   2009
    853'.92—dc22

                         2008047164

Picador ISBN 978-0-312-42978-2

Originally published in 2006 by Giulio Einaudi Editore, Italy, as Mille anni che sto qui

First published in the United States by Farrar, Straus and Giroux

First Picador Edition: August 2010

10 9 8 7 6 5 4 3 2 1

Been Here
a Thousand
Years

You need to draw me a picture, because I can't remember anything any-
more. Write down the names of my children, and who my father was. I'll
carry it in my pocket.

All right, I'll draw it for you.

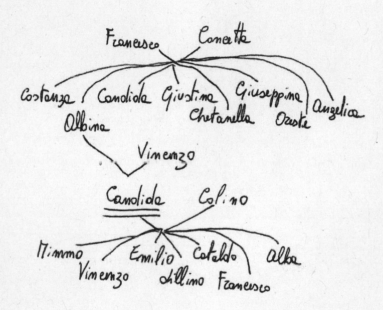

The underlined name is you. And me, well, I'm not there yet.

Part

I

Some days a colorful wind would blow; it lifted up the dust and everything would begin to rise like bread dough under a kitchen towel. Events from the past would return again and others in the future would become visible. On these days, drafts crept in under the doors, like the giggling of children not yet born; they wound themselves around the ankles of the women like intangible threads, tripping them as they walked.

Even Gioia could feel it, no matter where she was. She felt like laughing and crying, and became distracted in midthought; then everything would return to normal, as if nothing had happened.

This is how it always was. And how it had always been, back when Mammalina folded a handkerchief into the shape of a mouse and made it hop across the palm of her hand, as if it had a life of its own. When Gioia was a little girl, this trick always had the desired effect; it amused her and distracted her from the terror of insect bites, the unpleasant surprise of shiny golden coins that melt in your hand, from long afternoons in her sickbed, when the covers formed hills and valleys, frozen pools, and deserts where she sometimes got lost.

Gioia's sadness came from far away. It would surprise her in the subway or at a bus stop, or when she crossed the street in a crowd. Sometimes she could hear it rumble almost imperceptibly in the night, like the pounding of horses' hooves as they approach, ridden by bandits in black cloaks. Their hooves beat like a heart, like a drum, filling the darkness with whispers, then with screams. Gioia drove away the feeling by blinking her eyes and staring at herself in the mirror. She fixed her hair. Sprayed on some perfume.

Happiness too came from far away. Farther, even, than the sadness.

Chapter One

At around three o'clock in the afternoon of March 27, 1861, in the town of Grottole, which is in the part of Basilicata that lies about one hundred kilometers from the Puglia coastline, an event took place that would be the subject of stories for years to come.

In the hours that followed, the inhabitants of the town discussed all the possible meanings of this event, weighing every potential explanation. To some, it was a miracle, to others, witchcraft, or, if seen from a slightly more orthodox angle, a temptation of the Devil; only to a select few, the most educated residents, did it seem like a simple natural occurrence.

Perhaps it was somehow the fault of Zí Uel the Potter, but given how things turned out, no one dwelt on this notion for long. Sometimes, when a nodule in the clay was not completely ground down, the jar would develop cracks. But this hardly ever happened with his pots. His hands worked quickly and precisely on the potter's wheel, and his singed fingertips delicately caressed the rounded sides of the pots and pitchers, just as God's hands must have caressed Eve's flanks on the day of her creation. He kneaded, modeled, baked. His kiln produced lamps, crocks, jars, which he marked with concentric circles like the ones used long ago to communicate with the dead in a language no longer spoken by the living. His delicately resonant terra-cotta pots were porous and damp, oozing moisture. His pitchers kept water cool. His pottery was so perfect and so delicate that a scream could have shattered it.

On the same day that the city of Rome, which had not yet been conquered, was chosen as the capital of an Italy that was finally united, the first person to notice the aforementioned event—altogether different, but no less prodigious—was the little Della Rabbia boy. When it happened, he was wandering around the old neighborhood known to locals as "S'rretiedd," a tight maze of streets and houses that the sun could not penetrate; he held a string attached to a sewer rat. His stomach rumbled with hunger.

He was pulling at the rat, who did not want to follow, when he saw a yellow liquid slowly cascading down the Saracen Straits; it gathered in small pools between the paving stones, and then descended, step by step, slithering over the stones that had been worn smooth by the hooves of mules and making its way down alleys and passageways until finally it plunged over the edge of the escarpment. At first he thought it was mule piss, but no mule he had ever seen, or even Totonno's cow, could piss for so long. Nor could it be the contents of Don Filippo Cocca's bedpans, because no matter how many guests his son, a student at the University of Salerno, brought home, it would have taken a battalion to produce so much urine. The boy was so intrigued that he did not even notice when his pet rat scampered off. He bent down and stared at the rivulet, his face so close that his nose almost touched the yellow liquid. It was still cascading down. It came down, its consistency fluid and viscous, limpid and golden in the sunlight, forming thick bubbles here and there, its flow increasing as if the source was growing rather than diminishing.

Finally, Rocchino stuck his finger in the liquid, sniffed it, and put it in his mouth. He made a face, whether of pain or pleasure it was unclear.

At that time of day, there were only women, children, cripples, and crazy people in the town. All the men of sound body were working in the fields. Rocchino began to lap up the liquid, immersing his face, then his entire body, in the current, rubbing his feet, hands, and even his bare head, and finally rolling around like a pig in shit. It was oil! Olive oil!

The ringing of the town bells boomed in his ears as he felt life flowing into him, thick and unctuous, and the aridity and brittleness of death released its hold. People said that during a particularly deadly winter, the Della Rabbias had eaten one of their own children at birth, grilled. A deliciously unforgettable aroma had lingered in the town for days.

As Rocchino growled with pleasure and almost suffocated with gluttony, the second person to encounter this extraordinary phenomenon was Felice la Campanella. When he saw the Devil's piss pouring down the muddy lane that led to Zí Titt's orchard, he was sitting absolutely still on a stone bench, waiting in vain for the afternoon sun to warm his heart.

He was roused momentarily from the image that had filled him for the last twenty years: that of his wife's ample body cut down by thirty stabs of his knife.

By the time he had returned from the Royal Prison in Naples, he had lost the power of speech, except for the curses he mumbled like Ave Marias. The nightmares that tormented his soul seemed to have surfaced on his skin. From his neck to his waist— and surely also over the rest of his body, including his hands, the tips of his fingers, and perhaps even his private parts—he was covered in a snarl of devils, broken hearts, naked women, and obscenities. When he was younger, the figures came to life when he flexed his muscles, but now they seemed to conceal themselves beneath the graying fur that covered his upper body.

Devoured by his solitude, he wandered around the town with his hands behind his back, his black cloak fluttering in the wind. In a hopeless attempt to stave off bad luck, he made horns with his fingers and his waistband jangled with the sound of countless horn-shaped amulets of all sizes. Only children paid him any mind; they threw rocks when he wasn't looking, and then scampered off to hide behind a wall or in a doorway.

When he noticed the oil, Felice la Campanella took it for the Devil's bile, convinced that the Evil One had finally come for him. He blurted out a tremendous oath and prepared to follow, almost with a sense of relief.

A WOMAN IN THE TOWN had the bright idea.

Comare Teresa, or Cumma Tar'socc', as she was known to all, was sneaking furtively along the cracked walls, diving into shadows and then emerging cautiously into the sunlight, wrapped in a brown shawl under which she hid a stinking bedpan that she was planning to dump out onto Largo Sant'Andrea. At that time of day, no one would see her; anyone who was not working in the fields was surely sleeping. She emptied the pot furtively onto the stones, worn smooth by cart wheels, just across from her sister-in-law Agnese's house. Imagine her surprise when she saw the turds floating in a yellow lake much larger than anything the members of her family, numerous as they were, could have produced.

She stood there, trying to make heads or tails of what she was seeing, teetering on her tiptoes, her neck stretched and tense as a chicken's, the bedpan resting on her hip. Suddenly her sister-in-law's scream sliced through the stagnant air of the early afternoon, waking clouds of flies and the rest of the dozing town: *"Ca pzz scttà u' sagn'da n'gann!"* ("May you vomit blood!") The prolonged ululation of the *a* in *"n'gann"* ricocheted against the stone walls and reverberated threateningly from street to street through the warren of alleys, and finally dissolved in a shower of echoes in the valley's ravines. Women emerged from their half-open doors to watch the fight, but what they saw was even more captivating. Seventy years later some of them would still remember the events of that day and recount them to their grandchildren, along with stories about Saint Peter, the Devil, and the woman with the white pig who appears at the crossroads whenever a person loses his way.

Agnese and Tar'socc' were just beginning to pinch and shove, their nails bared like cats, when Tar'socc' stumbled and fell. She found herself with her backside on the ground, her bedpan broken, and Agnese on top of her, grabbing, pushing, and choking her, as their skirts, drenched in the viscous liquid, stuck to their legs.

The two sisters-in-law grabbed hold of each other's necks as if to wring the neck of a chicken. Agnese's hair was standing on end, her eyes were beginning to roll around wildly, and her face was turning purple, when she finally managed to grab hold of Tar'socc's face and submerge it in the liquid. Tar'socc' lay still for a moment, then came up for air; something was gurgling in her throat. She licked the hair that stuck to her lips, and mumbled: *"Iè iuogghj!"* ("It's oil, olive oil!") The women looked at each other, convinced that the lack of air had deprived Tar'socc' of her senses.

There was a moment of silence, broken by Lucietta, Peppino Paglialunga's eldest daughter, who had drawn closer and cautiously stuck her finger in the liquid, inspected it, and finally given it a lick. "It really is oil," she said in perfect Italian, articulating the words clearly in her prim little voice, because she had gone to school up to the second grade.

The group began to buzz. One of the women started to tell a story about the time a spring of pure mineral water had suddenly appeared under Nascafolta's bed, but no one was listening.

Was this the fruit of the prayers recently introduced by the new parish priest, a miraculous spring gushing forth to deliver the impoverished town from hunger? Cumma Caniuccia, with the authority of her ninety-nine years, commanded the women not to touch a single drop of this strange oil, which, sure as death, had overflowed from the cauldrons in which the damned were being boiled in Hell. But the women left her croaking like a Cassandra and threw themselves on the miraculous fluid.

Lucietta removed her scarf and dipped it in the oil, and then carried it gingerly, like a baby, to her house, where she squeezed it out into an empty crock. The others did the same with their aprons and handkerchiefs, or brought copper and wooden bowls from their houses, dipping and squeezing the oil energetically.

As the women followed the path of the stream to its source, they came to the foot of Don Francesco Falcone's house. The youngest among them, Ninetta—Zica Zica's daughter—noticed that oil was pouring out of openings at the base of the walls of the storeroom beneath the house. She turned to the others, as if wondering what to do next, and then the church bells began to ring as if it were a feast day.

DOWN THE HILL from them, the miraculous stream had produced a variety of reactions: quarrels, shock, and heated discussion. Don Valentino Blasone, the elementary-school teacher—as well as the recipient of a Certificate of Merit and the author of a general history of the literature of Basilicata, in addition to being the doctor's assistant and an honorary citizen of the town of Miglionico—had taken great pains to explain that there was nothing supernatural about the phenomenon. This was no miracle, just a question of chemicals, an accumulation of molecules. By some fortuitous confluence of circumstances, certain natural elements had come together in an underground stratum of the earth to produce the fluid otherwise known as olive oil. Before ingesting any of the aforementioned liquid, however, he recommended that it be observed under a microscope, to check for microbes.

Echoes of what had taken place had even reached the ear of Don Antonio, the young parish priest from Salerno. It was he who had decided to ring the church bells, just in case, either to thank some generous saint or to frighten away the Devil.

The last to hear about the event were those most directly affected, in other words, the Falcone family, and the very last was the most directly affected of all: Don Francesco Falcone himself.

In the uppermost room of the house, Concetta was once again in labor. The pain was so intense and her screams so loud that the vibrations had apparently cracked the large jars of olive oil in the storeroom, one after the other. At least that was what people said. The oil had then poured out of the round holes that were used by the cats to go in and out of the storeroom. Fifty *quintali* of oil, enough to supply every member of Don Francesco's family and all their dependents for an entire year.

The first person in the household to hear about what had happened was Licandra, Don Francesco's thirteen-year-old daughter by his former farmworker Concetta. Licandra was with her sisters at her mother's bedside as Concetta went into labor for the seventh time, not counting four spontaneous—and five provoked—abortions.

No one, except Concetta herself, held out even the slightest hope that the Virgin might grant them the blessing they had so insistently prayed for all these years. The disappointment had been bitter on the other occasions—six in all—when Don Francesco and the members of his household had hoped that the longed-for male would finally arrive. This time, Don Francesco had refused to have anything to do with the matter. Even though Concetta had experienced her first labor pains during the night, he left for the fields at first light in a rage, growling at her to hurry up and get on with it and insisting that none of this had anything to do with him. Concetta hadn't been hurt by his attitude; she was in too much pain to think of anything else. Besides, she had the strength of a mule, the docility of a lamb, and the lightness of a butterfly, qualities without which she would not have been able to survive for long with Don Francesco, who was by nature as stormy as the Maestrale wind, and who was not even her husband. This was why he could threaten to throw her out every time something made him angry, in other words every time she bore him another daughter.

Don Francesco had not found it opportune to formalize a contract for the ownership of that which was already his to do with as he saw fit, in other words Concetta's body, along with her good will, devotion, and something that he took for love but that was instead a kind of pity, a deep compassion that Concetta reserved for injured animals, beggars, and for him. It was unclear why she felt this, since he was rich, healthy, strong, and it was he who put food in her mouth.

The only thing that might convince Don Francesco to marry her was the birth of a son, but this event, so keenly awaited by their six bastard daughters, had not yet come to pass and its like-lihood seemed to decrease with each passing day.

BEFORE TAKING IN CONCETTA, Don Francesco had been married to Donna Nina, a woman from Grassano selected by his father. She was already somewhat advanced in age when they married, yellowish, and a bit soft around the edges, with small, hollow bones like a bird's, but she had brought with her several pieces of land—Arsizz', Mazzam'pet, and San Lazzaro, as well as the farm at Serra Fulminante, which brought in over a thousand ducats every year.

Donna Nina had been educated at a convent in Naples, where she learned the lives of the saints, how to hem handkerchiefs, and above all, how to look down her nose at those whom she considered beneath her—and particularly at Don Francesco—as if they might infect her with smallpox at any moment. She and Don Francesco despised each other. After their wedding night, during which Don Francesco had done his duty, delivering the blood-stained sheets to his mother, he and Donna Nina, by mutual agreement, had continued to sleep in the same bed, but facing in opposite directions. After a year of marriage they were still childless.

Donna Nina spent her days wrapped in an air of rancorous dissatisfaction, hardly setting foot outside her marriage chamber, usually stretched out on the canopy bed suffering from one ailment or another. The air in the room was so stale that Don Francesco felt faint as soon as he set foot inside. There was a stench of death, augmented by the insistent fragrance of the lilies and candles that guarded over a prissy-looking Virgin to whom his wife was devoted.

Lying next to Donna Nina, Don Francesco was unable to fall asleep unless he was completely exhausted, perhaps out of fear of waking up in Heaven, his arms and legs bound by the slender cords of envy, haunted by his wife's mummylike charms. But he dared not ask to open the window to let in some air, or to leave the room. Nor did he dare to abandon his conjugal bed because of the scandal it would cause.

BUT ON THE EVE OF THE FEAST of San Giovanni, an early, suffocating heat wave had made Don Francesco's blood boil in his veins. He could hear the muffled sound of singing in the streets. Finally, he had to leave the room to get some fresh air, with the urgency of someone who has been buried alive.

Around the twenty-first of June—the summer solstice—the days are at their longest before beginning their gradual decline. In the town, the farmworkers would build piles of brooms in the streets and piazzas and light bonfires to help the sun light up the sky. Then they would take the ashes home to drive away evil spirits and bring prosperity. There was singing. The men jumped over the embers, always with the same look of astonishment, hoping to find a wife with whom to share the joys and suffering of life.

Don Francesco opened the window and the night wind swept in and caressed his dark hair and beard, making him feel young and vigorous. But for the first time in his life, along with this sensation, he was struck by a thought, or a kind of dark foreboding, that no matter how things turned out, even if he avoided the traps of the evil eye, spells, envy, wars, and contagious diseases, sooner or later he would die, and there was no way to escape the fact that this great strong body of his, which seemed hewn out of the wood of an olive tree, would grow soft and dissolve like the corn husks and leftover food flung into pits to make fertilizer. The noise that came up from the street, mixed with these thoughts, made his head spin. He leaned against the windowsill. The arms and eyes of the girls shimmered in the shadows. He heard someone laugh; it started down low, like the sound of the *cupa cupa* drum, and then rose, clear and clean as a bell, distinct from all the other sounds. Don Francesco Falcone peered into the darkness. In the light of the moon and the glow of the flames he realized that something extraordinary was taking place.

She had bloomed overnight, her lips red as cherries, her hair still loose around her shoulders, her body small and round, shapely and dark as a grape, with breasts that seemed to blossom before his eyes.

Not that he hadn't seen her before; that would have been impossible in a town where everyone was a relative, or a godparent, which in some ways was a tie even stronger than blood. But some girls blossom from one day to the next, like roses, which bloom one night and by the next are already withered.

He stood there, bewitched, watching that miracle, tortured by the desire to go down and join the carousing countryfolk, as he had always done before he married Donna Nina, longing to mix his flesh with that of this young girl who was becoming a woman, to feel the life blossoming in her body drive away the death that advanced inside of his.

The touch of a limp hand on his shoulder made him jump. It was Donna Nina asking him to close the window because the draft was coming into the room and she couldn't sleep. Don Francesco obeyed, docile, and followed his wife to bed. He feared her because she knew how to read and write and her blood was as cold as a reptile's.

When they turned out the light, Nina said that it is a sin to be married without children. Don Francesco knew it well, and secretly it tormented him. He said that they had time, but she had decided that the time had come. She made the sign of the cross twice and then held out her cold, dry hands to him. Don Francesco, who was strong and vigorous but often felt as lost as a child without its mother, had been unable to turn away and had consummated the act, while inside of him he felt clear waters turn cloudy and roses fade, night vanquish day, and life surrender to death.

At dawn, while Nina watched him through half-closed eyes, like a cat, Don Francesco dressed and left for the fields.

It took a long time to vanquish the disgust that had overcome him during the night, the nausea at the sensation of taking a woman by force, the sense of foulness on his skin produced by the absence of desire. And it took even longer for him to find what he was looking for, because his lands were so vast that the hours between dawn and dusk were not long enough to traverse them all.

It was the harvest. In the late morning he ate bread and fried blood with the other men who had come from the coast to work in the fields, and he felt better.

He found her at Ai Mar, gleaning, as the sun was beginning to set. He watched her with sad eyes, like a bird of prey, then abruptly asked who had given her permission to do what she was doing; he was a man of few words and had not been able to come up with any other words with which to court her.

As soon as Concetta saw him she knew that what had happened to her mother, her grandmother, and to most of her cousins, the subject of whispered conversations with her friends when they went to fetch water, was about to happen to her. The idea of running away did not cross her mind. She left her little brother, still in his swaddling clothes, under an oak tree and walked toward Don Francesco. He felt her heart beating as he carried her away on horseback.

But when they reached the shed at Santa Lucia something strange happened, something that had not happened to her mother, her grandmother, or her cousins. When he took her by the waist to help her off the horse, Concetta was overcome not by the quality of his clothes, or the virility of his hands, but by the power of his melancholy, and she decided to give him an additional gift, of the kind the poor usually give to the rich. Along with her body, she gave him something of herself that she would not have known how to describe or name.

He took her on a bed of corn husks in the shed. Concetta's skin tasted of grain. The blood of her lost virginity mixed with that of her first menstrual cycle.

The harvest at Calvarès and San Lazzaro was not yet finished by the time Concetta's belly had become round as a full moon, which made him desire her even more. Nina's belly was growing, too. After they aired out the house Donna Nina took to her bed for good because of morning sickness. They were planting the fields when she suffered her first threat of a miscarriage, and the fields were green when she went into labor. It lasted through a night and the following day, and it was night again when she gave birth to a monster with a head like a fish that survived only a few hours. She did not survive, either.

And so Don Francesco took Concetta, who was about to give birth, into his house to be his servant and his whore, swearing to himself that if she bore him a son, poor wretch that she was, he would marry her. After all, his father was dead and he no longer answered to anyone. But it was a girl, and they called her Costanza.

After the birth Don Francesco observed a strict period of mourning. He became even more insufferable and ill-tempered and, ironically, only Concetta, the one responsible for his ill humor, knew how to calm him down.

Once he had recovered from his disappointment, Don Francesco became much more attached to little Costanza than anyone, especially he himself, could have predicted. When she ran toward him, toddling along and crying out, *"Pappà,"* his eyes would light up and his heart would melt like a child's. Costanza was allowed to get away with things that no one else had even dared to imagine possible: she pulled at his beard, stuck her fingers up his nose and ears, flung his hat from the balcony, and dug around in his pockets for presents.

Sometimes, in a sudden flash of lucidity, Don Francesco would try to impose discipline on his imperious bastard daughter, but she had become so spoiled, and was so stubborn and despotic by nature, that there was nothing to be done. Don Francesco could only console himself with the thought that she took after him. Instead, he took out his frustrations on Concetta.

He would tell her—after making sure Costanza was out of range—that if her bastard daughter tried his patience one more time he would kick them both out without even a shirt on their backs, and that he could easily marry whomever he pleased and still had favorable prospects. But these threats went in one ear and out the other. Concetta knew that no one had ever burrowed as deeply into Don Francesco Falcone's heart as she had, and that though he was as skittish as a racehorse, as well as misanthropic and ill-humored, he was in great need of love. Emboldened by this secret knowledge, Concetta lived in his house without worries beyond the usual ones; she always made sure that there was a pot of chickpeas and one of fava beans on the stove for the poor, and she thanked the Madonna every day for giving her and her daughters bread for their stomachs and something to eat along with it, besides.

. . .

AFTER COSTANZA, came, in this order: Albina, Candida (known as Licandra), Giustina, Gaetana (known as Chetanella), and Giuseppina. Their arrival had brought tempests, tears, and regrets, but after the birth of each daughter, again and again, Don Francesco's heart had softened, though none of the girls occupied as large a place in his heart as Costanza.

To make up for his perennially thwarted desire for a son, Francesco had decided to educate his illegitimate daughters, imbuing each of them with an aspect of the virility that their household lacked.

He had taught Costanza mathematics, and in fact during the time of the events described here it was she who, at the tender age of seventeen, kept the accounts to her father's holdings and farms, and kept track of all that was owed to him by his tenants, as well as all the unavoidable expenses.

Albina's masculine qualities—inherited directly from her father—were her inability to express emotion and her frank, cold, and tough nature, in other words her obstinate pride, which meant that she would implode rather than openly reveal her passion or yield to another's will.

Licandra could shoot a rifle. In every other way she was pretty, sweet, and feminine, and she died at a young age of malaria.

Giustina decided she wanted to go to school, and later when she was forced to earn her own living, she did so by teaching.

Even as a little girl, Chetanella could ride a horse like a fury, with her legs astride the animal and not, like most women, together and to one side.

Giuseppina had the most unseemly masculine trait: she inherited her father's passion for women, and when this tendency became an embarrassment, she was kept in a back room where she was eventually forgotten by everyone and where, once her sensual excesses had been placated, she lived out an interminable existence as an unobtrusive old maid.

On that March afternoon in 1861, which history would make famous for a very different reason, it being the date of Italy's unification, Concetta was giving birth without the help of a midwife. Comare Rachele, the *mammana* who had assisted in the births of all the children in Grottole and had returned many others to their Maker through the application of her special infusions of parsley and knitting needles, was now too old to do the job and only showed up in the most desperate cases.

Between one scream and the next, Concetta called out instructions to her daughters. By now she knew exactly what had to be done, but this time things were complicated by the fact that it was a breech delivery. With all Costanza's pushing and pulling, Concetta's belly had become one big bruise, and Albina, who never missed an opportunity to criticize her sister, said it was all her fault that things were not going as they should. Amid her mother's screams and her sisters' reproaches, Licandra had heard strange voices coming from downstairs. At first she thought there might be bandits; their terrifying, glorious feats were recounted high and low. The idea filled her with excitement, because in her heart of hearts she was on their side. As soon as the people outside told her what was happening, she went down to the storeroom, where she was able to judge the undeniably serious nature of the situation.

IT WAS SUNDOWN when, just as every evening, the farmers returned from the fields, some on the back of a wagon, some by mule, some hanging on to the tail of a donkey, most on foot, while in Turin the master pyrotechnician that had been brought in especially from Naples for the occasion was preparing the fire-works. Don Francesco came last, on his black horse, followed by his two helpers' nags.

The bells were ringing the Te Deum. The farmers, exhausted from toiling from dawn to dusk, paused momentarily as they climbed up the hill toward the piazza wondering whether the new priest had gone mad, was simply confused, or whether something truly unexpected had happened, which in their minds was synonymous with disaster.

Wrapped in his black cloak, sporting an upturned mustache, gun tucked under his arm, Don Francesco was thinking about Concetta, hoping with all his might that things had gone for the best, but he would have confessed these feelings to no one, not even to himself, not even under torture. He was approached by Tommasino, one of the innumerable children of the many women whom the foolhardy Concetta allowed to scrounge around in his kitchen.

Tommasino had been chosen because he could run fast, to be the first to tell Don Francesco the news. When Don Francesco saw him, his heart stopped. If Concetta had given birth to another girl they would not have dared send someone to meet him on the corner of the Via Nuova. It must be a boy! This was the only possible justification for such haste. He felt himself go weak with joy but his sanguine face did not betray the least emotion. Tommasino explained in a whisper that the jars had burst and that the oil had been lost, all fifty *quintali*, down to the last drop. At first Don Francesco could not understand what he was hearing.

Tommasino repeated the news three times. He watched as Don Francesco's face darkened like the ocean, which he had never seen, before a tidal wave, or the sky, which he had seen many times, before a storm, and then he scampered off with all the strength and speed he could muster on those skinny legs of his, and disappeared into the dark, narrow alleys of San Nicola, where the horses couldn't follow him.

Back at the house, Concetta was crying. Partly because she was so grateful for the grace the Madonna had bestowed on her, partly because spilled oil brings bad luck, and partly because for once she had no idea what Don Francesco would do. She cried and laughed and held the child to her breast. It was a boy.

Earlier, when Licandra had returned to the room where Concetta had been in labor for several hours and had described the events below, Concetta had become so agitated by the news that she felt her insides churn and the wretched boy finally turn over. In a few minutes he was out, pulled by Albina, who, before even cutting the umbilical cord, cried out in disbelief: It's a boy! It's a boy!

Don Francesco entered the room with a tempestuous stride, his face like a hurricane, his gun still slung over his shoulder, and his cap pulled down low on his brow. Enough! They should all just get out, all of them, every last one of them! They were all bearers of bad luck who had brought nothing but ruin to his house, a bad lot, and this time he didn't want to hear any arguments. Nothing those simpering, insolent, louse-infested girls said or did would move him, nothing, they should just get out this instant and don't take anything with you, I've already spent enough on the clothes on your backs, I don't even want to hear your names, just get out and that's it, as if you never existed. Fifty *quintali* of oil! Spilled onto the streets like dishwater, like mule's piss, that's what happens when you keep too many women in the house!

Concetta pushed away the bed sheet and scooped up the newborn, who had not yet been swaddled. She raised him slowly, by his armpits, with his tiny manhood exposed. Don Francesco stopped cold, like a devil before the consecrated Host. He took a few steps back and dug in his heels, like an old broken-down horse. He looked more closely at the tiny, limp penis, the little undescended testicles, and all the rest, and he couldn't believe his eyes. His face trembled like a mountain just before a landslide. He pressed his lips together to keep himself from crying. He picked up his gun, walked to the window, and shot into the air for a long time out of sheer joy.

Chapter Two

The preparations for the wedding of Concetta and Don Francesco lasted a year. First came the celebration for the newborn; chickens and roosters were slaughtered and distributed to tenant farmers, laborers, and customers, and to various people to whom Don Francesco was more or less related, in other words, practically the whole town. There was a massacre of lambs and kid goats, of rabbits and game, and the women made dough for *foccazzole* and rolled out the pasta for *cavatelli*, kneaded it for *ricchitedde*, and coiled it for *screpelle*, served with honey and *vincotto*. They stuffed *calzoncelli* with chickpea paste or sour cherry marmalade, as if that year Christmas, Carnival, and Easter had all come at once.

People feasted for days, as the baby boy whimpered in his wrought-iron cradle, a cradle fit for a nobleman. Concetta never left his side and his sisters rushed over at the slightest sound. There was dancing to the music of the barrel organ; more people were betrothed during the festivities than at all the weddings for over a year. Don Francesco was so happy that for a period he agreed to a weekly day of rest for his laborers, and provided dowries for at least two or three girls from poor families who would otherwise have become old maids.

"È nat u patrun de scuppiett'," "The gun has a new master," he would say with a wink to everyone who crossed his path. He went around with a beatific expression, as if the knowledge that someone would inherit his name and land had begun to alleviate his obsession with death, which had sometimes made him unapproachable.

It was as if a decentered universe had suddenly found its sun. Everything in the house began to orbit around the boy.

No one cared anymore if Costanza had a tantrum or Albina was tormented with envy toward her sister. Now, each person had his rightful place and that was the end of it, because their world had a single purpose: to be passed down to this whimpering infant who had learned to give orders even in the cradle, sending people scampering in all directions. He was so demanding that his own mother grew to detest him, even as she became his servant. She breast-fed him until he was four. But from then on, and for the rest of her days, she felt only contempt for him.

ONCE THE POMP of the christening was done with and the afterglow of the feasting had worn off, and all the members of the household had grown used to the sleepless nights imposed by the whimpering baby and Don Francesco had secretly become disillusioned by his son's unpleasant nature, a period of dreaming began. They all felt as if they had escaped the whims of destiny, and could now begin to imagine a reassuring, even somewhat tedious future, like a desire that has been nursed for too long.

Concetta felt a new peace in her soul. In all those years she had never forgotten for a single instant that she was living in sin. Now she could finally put her house in order, even in the eyes of the Almighty.

Gazing at the wheat as it sprouted in the fields, Don Francesco lost himself in reveries in which he imagined the future of his descendants, picturing what would become of his seed, his land, and his name, which would now be passed on through the generations. Already, he was making plans for his son's education, imagining what he would make of him, and to whom he would marry him off.

Finally at peace with life and death, he made plans to expand his house and his family grave. The Falcone burial chapel, built on the crest of a hill in the new cemetery, became famous for its beauty and its imposing black and rose-colored marble, as well as for the tender expression of the angel who watched over it, whose features were based on Licandra's. The house, on the other hand, became a never ending construction project, a pile of luxurious rubble through which the Falcone family would wander for years, lost in the dust of its broken dreams.

ALBINA WAS HAPPIER than anyone with the way things had turned out.

As far back as she could remember, perhaps before she had developed the power of speech, or even before seeing the light of day, Albina had been tortured by envy of her older sister, Costanza. Perhaps even her own birth had been the product of her envy. Whatever her sister said, ate, or even glanced at became a vice that gripped her heart and twisted her insides into knots. If Costanza was sick, if she got scarlet fever or scabies or diarrhea, Albina felt herself dying because she had not been infected as well. All the injustice that had inhabited that land from the beginning of time, the rage of the forlorn peoples who had crowded together and perished there, seemed to nest in Albina's heart and give rise to the extreme envy she felt for her sister.

Costanza knew nothing of all this. She was growing up imperious and boisterous, her flesh glowing, firm, and shapely, with a face like a full moon, bright eyes, and voluptuous lips, at ease in every situation, a light breeze trailing behind her as she walked by. Meanwhile, Albina grew thin and a bit stringy, as if a solitary worm were digging its way through her soul.

Despite her thinness—which at the time was a symptom of poverty and as such an undesirable characteristic—one could not say that Albina was ugly. She was tall, with a broad forehead and severe features, like a Byzantine Madonna in one of the nearby grottos, half covered in vines. She never smiled.

At her brother's christening, Albina met Aurelio, the son of the Baron Lacava from Montescaglioso. If Don Francesco had not had a son, and had not decided to marry Concetta, his daughters would have remained illegitimate. Even though they were a good match, financially speaking, the best they could have hoped for was to marry a moderately successful artisan or a small landowner. But now things were different. Aurelio had come forward during the dancing.

After hesitating briefly between Albina and Costanza, his choice fell upon Albina, not because he was seduced by her stern beauty, but rather because the other's radiance seemed to promise much anguish and torment, while his main concern was the restoration of his family's financial situation as quickly as possible. Albina could not believe that a baron would choose her over her sister, and was prepared to swear eternal faith to him even though he was short and unattractive and had to tilt his head back in order to look her in the eye.

As Ciccillo the barber played the accordion somewhere between the large pot of pasta and a platter of goat chops, Aurelio did his best to advertise his family's noble ancestry, delicately introducing it into the conversation wherever he could. Feigning indifference, he listed his family's properties, I Tre Confini, La Difesa, Rivolta Sant'Angelo, more than twenty-seven hundred *tomoli* in all. Of course, he was careful not to mention that most of it was uncultivated land, huge expanses of scrubland and slugs, nor did he point out that the few families who farmed it eked out a miserable existence.

The trays of sweets and glazed *taralli* were being passed around when the two of them went out to talk under the light of the moon; Aurelio recited a few love poems, which Albina could make neither heads nor tails of.

They promised to see each other again.

Now and then he would travel to Grottole by gig. In order to avoid being seen, he would wait at the drinking trough down by the Via Nuova, which was actually the Via Appia, built in the time of the Romans. There, he and Albina would meet in secret. They would spend an hour together, watched over by the bored Giustina, who, sitting a few steps away behind a bush, fashioned carriages and corteges of ladies-in-waiting out of thorns, their skirts made from poppy petals. Beneath the shade of the branches, Aurelio whispered words of love borrowed from someone called Byron, to which Albina paid no attention at all. She was thinking of how her sister would envy her the suitor she had found.

In truth Costanza was the only one who hadn't noticed Albina's courtship, even though Albina did everything she could to bring it to her attention, and by now even the stones were well aware of what was happening. Don Francesco's firstborn continued, undaunted, to pursue her own affairs, which—given all the family's worries—no one bothered to investigate.

AFTER AN APPROPRIATE PERIOD of courtship, Aurelio came to ask Albina's father for her hand and the two became officially engaged. Now their meetings no longer took place by the shady drinking trough, startled by every rustling branch, but rather on the equally uncomfortable settee in the front parlor, with its broken springs, among piles of plaster left by the Neapolitan workers Don Francesco had hired to renovate the house. One of the younger sisters, either Giustina or Chetanella, was always there to keep an eye on them, eating cherries preserved in wine until she was tipsy.

Aurelio's conversation had become less romantic, to Albina's profound relief. The talk was now of hectares and linens to be included in the dowry. Albina's joy was so overwhelming that at times she forgot to feel envious for half a day.

But this unexpected stroke of good fortune could not save her from her destiny, and Costanza's shadow loomed once again, like an oak that towers over a shrub as it struggles toward the sun.

When Aurelio asked for his daughter's hand, Don Francesco's sole condition was that they should respect tradition, in other words that Albina's wedding should come after that of her elder sister. But Costanza was not even engaged. She had received many offers but continued to play hard to get; she was fussy and evasive, and it was unclear what exactly she was looking for.

Concetta quipped that she should go to Zí Uel the Potter and have him make her a husband-to-order out of clay from the river. He could fashion one according to her many specifications, put him out to dry in the sun, and bake him, and if she was lucky, this custom-made man might just be able to tolerate her as well. The joke stayed in the family for generations, because there was always someone who couldn't find a match, as if the good Lord had sent down an odd piece, a single sample, costly and useless, like a shoe without a pair.

Costanza's inability to find a suitable match kept Albina awake at night. She tossed and turned as if her bed had been sprinkled with thorns from the crown of Our Lord, and at times she even dreamed of killing her sister. *"Sorella mia sorella mo si arrotano li cortella, li cortella so arrotati e l'ora mia è arrivata."* ("Sister, the knives are being sharpened, the knives are sharp, and my time is come!") *"Ammazzala, ammazzala pure! Subito."* ("Kill her, kill her now!") Then she would repent. A boat floated downriver, carrying her toward Hell. Her dreams were filled with sharpened knives, the swishing of donkeys' tails against her forehead, like in the old folk tale, and bones poking out of the ground. She could hear women speaking in toad voices. On Saturday evenings, she was forced to confess her evil thoughts, as Costanza blithely went about her business and continued to dither, a heroic smile on her full moon of a face.

THE PREPARATIONS for Don Francesco and Concetta's wedding also dragged on because of the renovations.

Don Francesco had a rustic soul that rejected luxury, but in a moment of folly he had decided to bring an architect and a group of specialized workmen from Naples to renovate the house. He wanted them to convert what was a comfortable, large building at the highest point in town into an aristocratic mansion, ornamented with friezes and coats of arms, like the ones he had seen on his only trip to Naples, so that it could accommodate his children and grandchildren and their descendants—which he hoped would be plentiful—in a suitable manner.

Concetta was completely opposed. She feared the envy of her neighbors and anticipated misfortune and the destructive power of the evil eye, which strikes down those who display happiness and prosperity. Had he forgotten how they concealed their daughters' rosy cheeks under scarves so that the malevolent eyes of the hungry would not scorch them? From the moment she entered Don Francesco's household, Concetta had perched on the edge of her chair, made the sign of the cross after every bite, and asked the Lord for forgiveness because she lived in the midst of abundance while her brothers and sisters starved.

But there was nothing she could do. A man with a straw hat arrived one day, smoking smelly little cigars, and began to pace around the house, studying every inch with a clinical eye and the enigmatic expression of a doctor auscultating a patient who is gravely ill. He knocked on walls and listened with an air of discouragement, took measurements, decided to tear down some walls and build others, and brought his sketches to Don Francesco, who could make neither heads nor tails of them but was quick to approve so as not to appear uncouth. When Concetta asked him to explain the details, he raised his voice as he always did when he felt cornered or confused.

The master builders from Naples slept on a mezzanine from which one could reach the roof of the house, an area that for generations had been used as storage and a place to put guests, and there they piled their belongings—trunks, letters, and photographs—where Gioia would find them many years later when she clambered up while Mamma, Grandma, and her aunts weren't looking.

The hardest thing was keeping the workmen away from the girls; having them under the same roof was like keeping wolves with sheep, or fire with straw, and Concetta kept guard day and night to make sure none of her daughters wandered in unprotected. She was able to contain the damage to one or two of the neighbors' daughters who came to help around the house.

Local workmen were also hired, and a rivalry soon developed. Then it became a war, which eventually ended in a truce, and in turn evolved into a pact to get as much money out of Don Francesco as they could, by doing as little work as possible. But even then, the Neapolitans concealed their secret techniques for molding stucco and creating ornamentations, and the Grottolesi protected their methods of drying clay and transporting rocks. But from then on, they got along famously.

The Neapolitan architect left a week after he had arrived, with the excuse of an unforeseen emergency and a promise to return as soon as possible. Instead, a correspondence commenced between him and Don Francesco, detailing every catastrophe, aggravation, and obstacle imaginable to man, until one day Don Francesco stopped all communication. The mere mention of the architect's name would cause him to rant like a madman.

Meanwhile, the Neapolitans set up camp in the house. They had brought with them a whirlwind of high spirits that would be remembered in the town long after their departure. The surly Grottolesi watched them with curiosity and diffidence, as if these were animals of the same species but an utterly distant race, until finally the ice was broken and a period of feasting began. Many years later when their stay had been forgotten, now and then someone would cook a recipe or pronounce a word that could be traced back to their visit. And then there was Ciro, the much-loathed master builder; the reputation of his mother, Assunta, was the only thing that was completely finished by the time the workmen left town.

WHEN IT BECAME CLEAR that there was no chance, none whatever, that the house would be ready in time for the wedding, Don Francesco and Concetta decided not to wait any longer, and turned to other matters.

Concetta went to Matera to buy the material for her dress. It was the first (and last) time she left the town where she was born.

To her, it was like traveling to Rome or even New York—a place she had heard of once or twice—and she was gripped by a powerful homesickness, a combination of loneliness and vertigo that was alleviated only when, on her return, she caught a glimpse of the stones of Grottole's broken-down church from the Via Nuova.

Her heart thumped in her chest as she asked for directions. She had never seen so many unfamiliar faces, and she did not know how to behave. She would tell stories about this voyage of hers for years. She described the cavelike houses of the Sassi district, which she had seen from above, and the people moving about like tiny ants. She spoke of an elegant funeral she had seen, with music and a carriage drawn by six black horses. And she described how she had seen her first photograph in the window of a shop and had been so frightened that she ran away, afraid that it might follow.

She chose a length of silk in a color as changeable as the March sky, so beautiful that when she took it to Poltina the seamstress to make her a dress, women filled the shop day and night, hoping to see the material and the amazing nuances of its color. For her daughters, Concetta selected a bolt of blue velvet so ample that she was able to make a dress for each with some left over, to be stored on the mezzanine amid all the other objects they had no use for; Gioia discovered it many years later and in her hands, depending on her mood, it became a queen's cape, a shroud, or the sea.

Don Francesco was in charge of the banquet. He told the shepherds to set aside their best animals and ordered honey for the sweets. The whole family was so busy that no one noticed Costanza's transformation.

For some time she had been attending church services more assiduously than even the most pious old women. Between Masses she attended novena, vespers, and prayers for the dead, and took confession every blessed day. Albina came to the conclusion that Costanza had decided to become a nun and was so grateful to Our Father that He had finally decided to come to her aid, that she almost promised to do the same.

But when Concetta noticed what was happening she became suspicious, because Costanza did not have the pale, confused look of those who have decided to give their lives to the Lord. Quite to the contrary, she had become even more beautiful and full of color, with bright eyes and a smile that made her dimples quiver; if one paid attention one noticed that the slight breeze that accompanied her wherever she went had become a kind of zephyr, and if one listened closely one could hear a faint ringing of bells.

When the situation had almost reached its inevitable dénouement, Concetta did nothing to avoid it. Since the day that the renovations had begun, she had been expecting the worst.

On the eve of the wedding, Don Francesco slept at his property at Mazzam'pet to avoid seeing his future wife's wedding dress. That evening, surrendering to the instinctive partiality of her maternal love, Concetta called Costanza to her room and, without asking for any explanation, gave her a belt into which she had sewn ten gold coins. She knew Costanza would need them. The next day Costanza ran off with Don Antonio, the young priest who had come to Grottole from Salerno, but the gold coins were practically an afterthought because she also took with her the entire income from the sale of the harvest.

What followed was like a plague of grasshoppers, or a late frost that kills the young leaves on the trees. Everything that had begun to grow and prosper was reduced to dust and devastation. The wedding was canceled once and for all and Don Francesco felt as though he had been stabbed in the heart. For a long time it was as if he had died. When he finally recovered, his hair had turned gray and he was so weak that he no longer even had the strength to threaten Concetta and her progeny with banishment.

In a kind of empathetic reaction, Concetta suddenly became an old woman. After resisting the devastating effects of repeated pregnancies while retaining enough allure to inspire her husband to impregnate her again and again, she dried up and began to shrink, a process that would continue for decades and end only with her death.

Don Francesco no longer thundered; instead, he muttered and whined. He seemed always to want to be somewhere different from where he was, and so he roamed his properties like a soul in torment, inspiring compassion in the laborers who had once feared him.

But it was Albina's soul that was the most shattered by the turn of events. An oppressive weight, heavy as a tombstone, bore down on her. She never dreamed of revenge; she merely hated Costanza with all her might, and her hatred grew each and every day she spent on this earth, and was revived years later by the sight of the gold coins, pinned to the vest of Costanza's sons once they had grown older and walked around town with their happy faces. Her hatred was so powerful that it did not die with her, but was transmitted to future generations like a memory that chills the blood on long sleepless nights.

The marriage between Albina and Aurelio was not to be. On the day after Costanza's flight, when he came to call, Albina sent word that she never wanted to see him again. She returned his engagement ring and his love letters without explanation, and no one would ever know whether on that day Aurelio had come to take his leave or whether he might have been willing to turn a blind eye, if not for love, at least out of self-interest.

An obtuse sense of honesty drove Albina to find refuge in her rancor. Not long after, she married a cobbler, Vincenzo, a good-looking man who might even have loved her had she not made his life hell from their first day together. She became high-spirited, always ready with a cutting remark and a quick laugh. Wherever she went, she was followed by a cold wind, the kind that turns the leaves yellow and causes sore throats. Nothing ever seemed to impress her, not even, years later, what happened to her husband.

Chapter Three

On September 13, 1862, a group of bandits showed up at Serra Fulminante and completed the cycle of devastation. They set up camp in the ancestral house that had once belonged to Donna Nina's father, and gorged themselves for weeks on the provisions in the storerooms: wheels of provolone, wine, chickens, and kid goats. They got drunk on blood and danced, wrapping themselves in the damask silk curtains, with the fatalistic joy of the damned. They left nothing behind and destroyed everything in their path, as if wreaking their fury, not so much on their masters, but on the objects themselves, because until that day their lives had been worth even less than a pitchfork, and now they were worth even less.

Rocchino, one of the Della Rabbia boys, was among them. He had been called up for military service and at first he was elated because the army fed him twice a day and dressed him from head to toe in a new uniform and a beautiful new pair of shoes. Not even in his rosiest dreams had he imagined he would one day possess a pair of shoes made especially for him. He gazed at them, caressed them, and was even tempted to talk to them, but as soon as he put them on his feet the torture began. The shoes squeezed, pinched, and cut into his skin. They gripped his feet like a vice. He could feel his feet swelling, ramming into something, rubbing. They were covered with blisters, the blisters burst, and then the exposed flesh became inflamed; the pain was so excruciating that it shot up his back and exploded in his brain. Finally he wrenched off the shoes. Trembling and with a sigh of relief, he asked himself why on earth he had so ardently desired shoes all these years.

When the sergeant, who was from Turin, reviewed his troops and saw, amid identical rows of shoes, a pair of bare feet with blackened toenails and calluses as thick as a mule's hoof, he had to look twice to make sure he had not made a mistake. He felt a wave of rage rising: Could it really be that he, one of the best students at the Royal Academy in Milan, had been saddled with a band of louts who couldn't stand in straight lines even if you beat them? Could he really be expected to lead such men into battle, especially in a war where it was unclear just who was the enemy?

Even though Rocchino could understand animal sounds better than the sergeant's Piedmontese dialect, it was not difficult to imagine what the sergeant was shouting about, staring down at his feet as if they were criminals, blasphemers, or perjurers.

But Rocchino had no intention of squeezing his feet into those traps ever again and instead had tied the shoes around his neck; they dangled on his chest, swinging proudly. Seeing that his shouts had no effect, the sergeant from Turin became even more enraged, and Rocchino found himself surrounded by soldiers from the Guardia Nazionale who wanted to shoot him for insubordination. He understood this just from looking at their faces, without need for translation, and he decided to do what he had always done in such cases: he ran.

Even though there were thirty soldiers chasing after him on horseback, he managed to escape, because he could run like a hare and climb like a cat, and if it was required he could slip through a crack like a mouse.

He wandered around the countryside for days, sleeping under bushes and in trees, eating baby birds he found in nests and roots he pulled out of the ground, until finally one night, half dead from a combination of exhaustion, cold, and hunger, he saw the glow of flames in a clearing in the forest of Lagopesole. His curiosity drew him toward the light, and he peered at it through the branches of a bush.

He could see dark figures around a fire; they had long hair and shaggy beards and were adorned with human bones, horns, and communion wafers set in silver. There was a woman, too, with a childlike face and curious eyes. He thought he recognized Mastro Paolo the woodcutter, who had disappeared a year ago; people said he had been pushed down a ravine by one of his creditors.

Rocchino felt his arms and legs go limp. It was all clear to him now: these were the souls of the damned, who sometimes escape from Hell and gather aboveground to entrap the souls of baptized Christians. He recognized them from their sunken cheeks and feverish eyes. Those who saw them never returned, and the few who did went completely gray, like Teresa's mother, who had become an old woman at the age of eight, and developed a stutter.

But in addition to the fear that paralyzed his legs, something else held him there. It was the delicious fragrance of roasting meat that wafted in and out with the wind, teasing his newly awakened sense of smell. They were roasting a sheep on the fire.

Rocchino came to an instant decision: even at the risk of eternal damnation, he would sink his teeth into that succulent flesh. He advanced toward the clearing, his eyes, full of desire, fixed on the mutton. Someone held a switchblade to his neck.

Several men grabbed him and dragged him before the chief among the damned, who stank of wine, even more than the others. The man began to interrogate him.

Rocchino mumbled, terrified, but he was glad that at least these souls from Hell spoke a language he could understand and smelled like the people back home.

He tried crossing himself and reciting an Our Father to see if they disappeared, and wondered if they would take the mutton with them. They stared at him, filled with curiosity and amusement. Finally, Rocchino got up the courage to ask what things were like in the land of eternal suffering. They burst out laughing. All, that is, except for the leader. He was silent for a moment, and then he said that the real land of suffering was where they came from, where children died of hunger before reaching adulthood, where the downtrodden broke their backs working land that belonged to strangers. "You're right," he said, "to take us for dead men. Today we fill our bellies, but tomorrow Tata Vittorio"—he meant Italy's new king, Vittorio Emanuele II—"will take our bones and crush them into little pieces to make buttons."

The men exchanged disconcerted glances. The leader of the damned looked Rocchino up and down, noted his ragged uniform, and invited him to sit down next to him. "Our Lord and Master the Government," he said, "isn't interested in whether the sons of its peasants live or die, but if by some miracle they grow up to become men, he comes for them, every last one, and forces them to give their blood . . . for the Fatherland!" A faint murmuring rose around them. "I am a serpent," he told Rocchino. "My blood is poisoned. My mother died in the nuthouse at Aversa, my father was thrown in jail even though he had committed no crime. And all because of a dog. Don Vincenzo's dog." He laughed. The men began to join in. "We'll tear those gentlemen to pieces," they cried out menacingly, "for the Madonna and for Franceschiello!"—meaning Francesco II, King of the Two Sicilies.

The leader of the damned turned toward them, then back to Rocchino. "See here," he said. "Yesterday they shouted 'Long live Vittorio 'Manuele, long live Garibaldi, long live the unification of Italy!' Today they want Franceschiello, tomorrow who knows. The masters stir them up, the government sends the harmless little garden snakes off to war and clutches the vipers close to its heart."

His eyes paused on one of them, a thickset man with a yellowish complexion who was cutting up the sheep. Then he seemed to lose himself in his thoughts. For a moment it seemed as if he were about to add something, but he remained silent.

Rocchino, who had finally caught on, bowed his head in a sign of respect. This was Carmine "Crocco" Donatelli, general of the so-called Bourbon army, leader of all the bandits in Basilicata. The woman with the strange eyes was his lover, Filomena Pennacchio. When Rocchino told her the story of his shoes, Filomena began to laugh, and the longer she laughed, the louder her laugh became, and the harder it was for her to stop. She ordered that he be fed, and for this Rocchino worshipped her to the end of his days, which were not many. He died one year later, hanged from a walnut tree on the road between Grottole and Ferrandina.

TO DON FRANCESCO, the bandits were proof that bad luck always comes in threes. By then, he had accepted his misfortune, so he did not lose his calm when he heard the news. He simply became even more somber and did not speak for days. He worked frenetically, and the women of the house were afraid that the blows of misfortune had driven him mad.

Over the course of a single night he stuffed all of Donna Nina's dowry, the income from the olive harvest, and his mother's jewels and other valuables—including the red-gold earrings and ring he had bought for Concetta when she bore him a son—into barrels. He sealed them as if he were about to send them on a long sea voyage. Then he put the idle laborers to work. Without a word to the women—he trusted no one, not even his own shadow, which was female—he began to conceal the barrels in secret hiding places around the house, which was still a construction site, in walls, under the floor, and inside columns, and all the while he remembered Concetta's dark words before the building began, and felt them burn into his heart. When the laborers finished walling in, burying, and plastering over his treasure he sent them all away.

The house remained unfinished. In the middle of the parlor, the skeleton of the architect's grand staircase twisted and curled like a woman of easy virtue, and the upstairs rooms were left empty.

Everything was patched up and cleaned. Curtains were hung to hide passageways that led nowhere. Armoires were used as partitions, pots concealed gaping holes, and the family resigned itself to living on the battlefield of a war that had never been fought.

Amid all this disappointment and confusion, a new love blossomed between Don Francesco and Concetta—the surprising fruit of chance and distraction. Now that there were no more interests at stake or conventions to be observed, Concetta, who suddenly discovered that she was old and truly free, realized with a sense of relief that she had nothing to lose, and gave herself as she never had before. Don Francesco received the gift, astonished.

While the others drifted through the house, lost, he and the woman who would never be his wife would slip away to their bedroom, which had been left untouched by the Neapolitan architect, sometimes even during the day, and abandon themselves to a foretaste of death, which now seemed sweet. They mingled their dilapidated bodies, consoling each other, discovering together what they had become, with more passion than when they were young and their fresh bodies were like so many others. And thus, unexpectedly, Angelica was conceived; she was surely the most beautiful of Concetta and Don Francesco's daughters, just as withered grapes produce the sweetest wine.

It was 1864. For three years the bandits had stood their ground against the Piedmontese army and had come to embody the hopes and dreams of the poor.

Between 1861 and 1863 the newborn Italian nation deployed almost 120,000 soldiers, in other words half of the newly created national army, to execute a massacre that would be described in the rest of Europe as equal in magnitude to that of the native peoples of North America: the elimination of outlaw bands in the southern provinces. More people died in this carnage than in all the battles of the Risorgimento put together, but there is almost no trace of it in the history books.

Garibaldi's march northward from Sicily and that of the Piedmontese army southward took place at a time of great social upheaval regarding the division of state lands.

From his exile in Gaeta the deposed Bourbon king, Franceschiello, promised concessions to farm laborers at the expense of landowners. People dreamed of his return to the throne, as if in anticipation of the Kingdom of Heaven. The dons, on the other hand, took the side of the new king, Vittorio Emanuele of Savoy, and thus became "liberal" out of self-interest.

During those years, the new government instituted the draft and tormented the farmers with taxes that reduced them to penury. A strong movement rose in opposition to the new state. An army of the poor, led by bandits, held its own against the Piedmontese army until 1864, the year in which General Crocco, who had by then been abandoned by his supporters, was betrayed by a lieutenant, the gang leader Caruso, and captured. He spent the rest of his days in prison.

Even a few of the landowners supported the Bourbons and aided the bandits. They were called *"manutengoli,"* "abettors," and if they were discovered they were immediately shot.

Don Francesco Falcone did not choose a side. His concern was keeping his own land, and he was indifferent to all else. But when the bandits finished off his provisions and demanded that he supply them with food, it sounded like a death sentence. If he helped them, he risked being considered an abettor by the Piedmontese, and if he didn't, the bandits would wreak their revenge.

It was the only time in her life that Concetta refused to accept her fate. She had paid enough, in her opinion, and so she came up with a plan. They decided to make two of everything: bread, sausages, cheese, butter, and everything else. When the Piedmontese officers arrived to oversee the insertion of the poison, they followed the soldiers' orders precisely, with the intention of switching everything at the last minute.

The food was prepared, after which Concetta swiftly made the substitution, but something went wrong. No one knows exactly what happened, but there were many in the town who were envious of the respect that Don Francesco enjoyed from all parties, due to his loyalty.

Chetanella traveled into the countryside with baskets full of bread made with durum wheat, chains of sausages wrapped around her like serpents, and butter hanging on ropes like cow's teats. But her heart beat heavily when the bandits encouraged Saetta, Ninco Nanco's dog, to try the sausage, cheese, butter, and homemade bread.

When he dismounted from his horse, the terrifying Ninco Nanco was just a shy farmer who stammered and blushed as he asked her to wait. The other gang leader arrived, and Chetanella gasped. She would never, for the rest of her life, forget the beauty of his face. This was the son of the Madonna, the infamously bloodthirsty Giovannino Coppa, the bastard son of a noble-woman and a baron, raised by beggars only to be dispatched by members of his own class, a few years later, to his final barony in the sky.

After a moment Saetta began to run around, and then stopped in his tracks, his eyes bulging, foaming at the mouth, his greenish, swollen tongue hanging out as he gazed at his master, begging for mercy. Ninco Nanco finished him off with a shot from his double-barreled gun and climbed onto his horse, followed by Giovannino Coppa and the rest of the men.

Don Francesco was alone with Concetta, celebrating their narrow escape. He was so confident of the successful outcome of the switch that he had told the Piedmontese soldiers he did not need their protection.

Before the bandits dragged him off, Don Francesco tried to say something to Concetta. Not that he had always loved her, but rather where he had hidden the barrels of money. He never got the chance. The bandits barely gave him the time to say good-bye before tying him to his horse by his feet.

His whole life, Don Francesco had been tormented by the thought of death, but in the end, when he saw it before him, he discovered that he had already made its acquaintance and went toward it with courage.

The bandits dragged him all over town. He could hear children screaming as his bloody body went by. He felt his bones breaking against the rocks, and the thorns tearing his skin. They dragged him down to the fields. He left a part of himself on each of the fields that he had owned and cultivated, a piece of skin, a bit of flesh, a small trace of his body. As the race continued he felt the fury that had always possessed him slowly fading away. Memories floated through his mind, mingling with images and thoughts that were new and surprising, and then everything flowed away like dry leaves floating down the Basento River.

It took a long time for him to die. They dragged him beyond the Cugno del Ricco field. He saw the oak where the Puglian farm laborers ate their lunch and sang songs in the torrid afternoon. He saw the shed where he had first made love to Concetta, and the sorb apple tree where he gathered fruit for Costanza when she was a little girl, and the Ai Mar property where the wheat was still tender, and the cracked clay of Serra Purtusa, and the riverbeds, and the bushes fading with the sunset, until everything became confused and he didn't see anything anymore.

Storie e mamorie
e lu culu de zí Vittoria
e lu culu de zí Marí
e buonasera signrí.

Stories and glories
and the ass of Zí Vittoria
and the ass of Zi Marí
and good night Milady.

Chapter Four

"omo, pansy, butt boy, cuckold, son of a whore, retard, dickless wonder . . . come on, let me hear you say it."

"Homo, butt boy, cuckold, son of a whore."

"That's right. Now, moron, dumbass, monkey brain . . . Say it."

"Moron, dumbass . . ."

"Goddammit, Vincenzo . . . the child!" Albina pulled Candida away from her father, who .was holding her contentedly on his lap as she played with the adhesives and awls from his shop. "What are you teaching her?"

"They're back," answered Vincenzo. There was no need to specify whom he was referring to.

They had announced their arrival in the square. "Hear ye, hear ye, Minguccio the Merchant's back in town, and he's got all the quality merchandise you need! If you want the good stuff, the really good stuff, then step right up, ladies, they're not selling it, they're giving it away—morons—step right up! For your wedding day, your funeral, and your trousseau! Fine beaver cloth, plush fabric, fustian, tartan, double-woven marghera cloth, flannel and imitation flannel, velvet for ladies and boys, satin and cashmere, poplin for Sunday shirts and broadcloth for mourning." The women went weak at the knees.

Across from the church, Minguccio the Merchant, also known as "the Pugliese," laid out the fabrics he carried in his truck, unfurling them before their eyes. The women caressed the cloth furtively: smooth percale for sheets, tartan that flew off the shelves for shirts and tablecloths, flannel and imitation flannel for underwear, the heaviest flannel for underskirts, velvet for the ladies and corduroy for the men, brown or lilac-colored beaver cloth, dark and heavy, for wedding dresses—even in the summer—felt, white and thick, for tablecloths and mattress covers, black satin for fancy aprons, and cashmere or other types of light wool for kerchiefs, gabardine for men's summer suits, and vicuña for the bridegroom, so fine that if it was accidentally packed with the other merchandise it would get crushed and by the time they pulled it out it was ruined.

"What use is all that stuff? It's just a waste of money," Vincenzo would say. "Damn the lot of them for coming here!" He had always worn homespun cloth, thick enough to support its own weight. It was good for tablecloths and even sheets—if you could stand it—and it was woven by local women, who exchanged it for shoe leather, lamp oil, rope, and soap. As far back as he could remember, that's how it had been, before Minguccio the Merchant arrived from Puglia, uninvited, to ruin the piazza and spoil the women. They succumbed to the spell of his singsong and his fabrics, which were as smooth as babies' bottoms and rustled like temptation, filling their heads with God knows what thoughts.

The first to betray him, it goes without saying, was his wife, Albina, who never missed an opportunity to show her defiance; she had bought a kerchief decorated with lacework and wore it on her head like a battle flag. When Minguccio the Merchant rented a room with all the money he had squirreled away, a place to store his merchandise and take naps with his wife, Albina was the first to pay him a visit, with all the usual niceties.

SINCE THEIR WEDDING DAY, Albina and Vincenzo had been locked in a mute, deaf war, fought with low blows, vendettas, and spite, because Albina could not accept that she had married a cobbler when she might have netted a baron, and so she was a thorn in his side, provoking him at every possible opportunity. She had wrapped herself in an obstinate devotion to the life she should have led, rejecting the small portion of happiness that was within her reach, and cultivating the arrogance of an illusory nobility.

She had never given her husband the satisfaction of sitting down to eat at the table with him. When Vincenzo came home from the shop she would claim she wasn't hungry and serve him at the table, yanking away the dishes the very instant he lay down his fork. Vincenzo trembled with rage and hurled all the curses he knew, which were many, but Albina's only response was the almost imperceptible raising of an eyebrow; by now, her heart was pickled in vinegar. Vincenzo would erupt with rage, yelling and screaming, but he did not dare strike her, as another would have with much less provocation.

There were too many people in the house, all of them his wife's relatives. There was her mother, Concetta, small and silent, who skated around noiselessly and showed up where you least expected it. She watched them with those girlish eyes of hers, set in her deeply wrinkled face, without uttering a word. And then there was Albina's sister Angelica, a great beauty with pale, rosy skin, big eyes, and dark, curly, silky hair with coppery highlights who matured day after day like those pale-red and straw-colored apples, perfectly round, slightly larger than other varieties, with smooth, smooth skin, and a delicate fragrance that intensifies with each passing day, delicious, so delicious that at first one is afraid to take a bite and then, suddenly, no one wants them. And there was her brother, Oreste, who almost never left the house and was served and revered like a pasha; he was lazy and mean and spent hours arranging his thin, curly whiskers, now and then exploding in a blast of unjustified rage. And her sister Giuseppina; no one ever knew where she was, and she had yellowish skin and two prickly whiskers.

Vincenzo felt like a cat trapped in a pack of dogs, always on his guard. What a crummy deal he had been dealt—one must take the good with the bad—when he married Don Francesco Falcone's daughter! Now he had to support Albina, her mother, her sisters, and her brother, because when Don Francesco died no one knew where he had hidden his barrels of money, and the ignoble government had appropriated a portion of his lands with the excuse that he had aided the bandits. May they all rot in hell! They were forced to sell the house and it had become a card-playing club, with tables set up in the rooms decorated with half-finished Neapolitan stuccos. Vincenzo spent his Sundays there, and that was where Albina went to look if she needed him.

Whenever she entered those stinking, smoke-filled rooms, her stomach tightened at the sight of the plaster peeling off the walls, the spiderwebs, the hall filled with chairs in various states of disrepair, and, peeking through the wine-and-filth-stained sawdust, the flower designs on the floor that her father, Don Francesco, had had put in back in the days when he still believed in the future.

Each time she reached the final room, the one overlooking the valley, which, when they were children, was used only when there was an important visitor, she would stop, as if to catch her breath. In the center, twisting upward like a bad omen, stood the Neapolitan architect's useless staircase. Vincenzo was always in that back room, playing *briscola* and cursing. She would look at him and be filled with hatred as if all this were his fault.

And yet, he was the one who broke his back to feed them all. Many times he had considered saying to hell with all of them and going off to seek his fortune in America, a beautiful and immoral land that, he had been told, gave herself to anyone who desired her. If he stayed in the town, there was only one reason, and a surprising one at that, for it was the same one that often drove him to flight: his wife.

Unlike· her sister—who was like an overripe apple—Albina was like those small, tart apples that give you goose bumps but make you want another and yet another until your stomach hurts. She provoked him, she mistreated him, but when she brushed by him he felt weak at the knees.

The children born of their union had all perished, either when they were still breast-feeding or later, of typhus or malaria: one died of tuberculosis, another was poisoned with verdigris when he ate meat straight out of the pot on the Feast of Sant'Antonio. He was a sweet and lovely boy by the name of Francesco.

Every summer in the town children died like flies, of diarrhea. "The thresher came through town," the women would say.

But Albina was sure that their problem was of a different nature. "How many blessings do we need," she would say under her breath, "to make up for one honest man who cuckolded God with 'her'?"

Only their youngest, Candida, survived. She was born delicate and sickly and fell ill every other day as her brothers and sisters returned to their Maker, but she stayed alive. Albina was moved to compassion by her little girl, and whenever she saw Candida playing with her father's adhesives and awls, she shook her head as if the child were half-witted, or afflicted with an incurable disease.

AS SOON AS HIS WIFE AND DAUGHTER were out of sight, Vincenzo sought solace in his usual manner. He would stand at the window and let out a long, shrill whistling sound. Rosina Mastro Pietro never kept him waiting. She was curvaceous, all strawberries and cream, wore brightly colored clothes, and had a brood of boys who resembled all the healthy men in the town. Without her, Vincenzo would never have been able to withstand the life his wife subjected him to. With her, he could lose himself and find peace in the generous curves of her body. Albina's angular shapes, on the other hand, made him feel feverish.

One day, Albina and her daughter had passed the town square and had practically reached the house when Candida realized she had left her rag doll behind in the shop and she made such a commotion that her mother let her turn back.

The door of the shop was locked, as always, but Candida knew how to get in. She had learned a few days earlier when she was playing with the boy who worked for Mastro Vardın, the carpenter. He had proudly displayed all the carpenter's tools and let her play with them, enjoying the game even more than she did. Now, she borrowed the magical tool he had shown her, the one with a sharp point that drew perfect circles, and played around with the hole in the lock. When the door clicked open, in the semi-darkness inside, she saw a churning of white flesh, a fluttering of clothing, an undulating of hair, and her father's backside. She left without a word. That night the yelling could be heard from the middle of the Via Nuova, and from that moment on, Albina finally had an excuse to deny herself to her husband every night.

It was a time of sorrow. Vincenzo stood firm, taking up residence in the cellar, where he passed the hours slowly and venomously, as they both cultivated their bitterness, disappointment, and resentment, barricaded in their failure like a noble family in its ancestral castle, dreaming of what might have happened to the barrels of money buried who knows where. They began to doubt their existence; they appeared only now and then, in dreams. Almost half a century later, Gioia played a game with her cousins: on rainy, windy days, they would pretend to look for the barrels in all the forgotten corners of the house.

Like a curse, or an embodiment of the injustices of the world, Albina encountered her sister Costanza's many children at every turn. She recognized them by their happy faces and the gold coins pinned to their vests, whose glint pierced her eyes and her heart.

Meanwhile, Angelica steeped in her exuberant femininity, like a luscious rose. Oreste longed for the empire that was rightly his and had been stolen from him. He, who had represented the family's avenue to the future, was in fact nothing but a dead end, a lifeless tree trunk. Nothing was known of the intimate life of Giuseppina. Candida was growing up sweet and mischievous, and it seemed that evil could not touch her: neither her parents' arguments, nor her own illnesses, nor even the times when Uncle Oreste stuck his hands up her dress to see what she was like down there and paid her to keep quiet. Just as poison produces its antidote, she seemed to have been born with the ability to turn all wickedness into goodness.

Nothing had been easy for her; many times she had been ill, close to death, but she always recovered and landed on her feet like a cat. Every time she wanted something, destiny seemed set on taking it from her.

Her first playmate had been a little boy with a gold coin pinned to his chest. They had played together for a whole day, digging holes in the garden in search of the treasure that she had been hearing about ever since she was born.

Toward evening, as a pledge of friendship, the boy had given Candida a little robin. It had black wings, a yellow breast, and a round, downy head.

When Albina arrived they were patting down its feathers. She yanked the bird out of Candida's hand, stared at it for a moment, and then flung it aside. Candida watched as it flew farther and farther away, until it became a tiny spot in the sky, smaller and smaller.

A change took place within her at that moment, without which she would not have survived, something with no precedent in her family, which she transmitted to her descendants like a gift or a curse, depending on one's point of view: it was the ability to change her mind. As the little bird disappeared she murmured softly, through her teeth, "Fuck it," and instead of breaking into tears, she exploded with laughter.

From that moment on, this became her reaction to everything. Her laughter began softly, in little hiccups, a dull sound like the first, slow drops of a summer storm.

In fourth grade she was pulled out of school because the few girls who still attended had been mixed in with the boys, among whom there were no less than two with gold coins pinned to their vests.

Another girl might have been crushed, for there was nothing she liked more than tracing letters with her little pen, in orderly lines on the white page: *ameno* (agreeable), *recondito* (recondite), *anacoreta* (anchorite), words that were never used in daily life, like jewels to be brought out on special occasions. With these and other words like them, she could create things that became real simply because they had a name. And yet, even on this occasion, Candida took the injustice with grace and found other ways to fill her time.

Since there were no little brothers or sisters to look after and Aunt Angelica did the chores, she enjoyed more freedom than most girls her age and was able to dedicate herself to what would become her two great passions: romance novels and talking to Christ, to the point that she began to confuse the two.

Her passion for romance novels came from her aunt Angelica, a fervent reader of them; in fact, this was the main reason for her aunt's difficulty in finding a husband. In her crepuscular years, Don Francesco Falcone's most beautiful daughter still hoped, imperturbable, filled with these mawkish notions, for a pilot to come down from the sky, or a ship's captain to sail in from a distant ocean, and sweep her off her feet. She scorned the less glamorous but much more real farm laborers who, with decreasing frequency, came a-courting.

As soon as Candida was capable of deciphering words on the page, she began to read stories about the burning love experienced by devout young girls who were unfailingly compared to roses, lilies, and violets.

In her innocent mind, sacred and profane love fused to become a sublime mishmash, and as a result she developed a serious crush on Jesus. Not the abstract and divine concept of Jesus, but his chest, his hips, and his legs, as embodied by the statue in the local church. Christ descended from the cross, the Pietà.

The statue stood, alone, in a rather dark chapel, where the whiteness of its marble surface glowed sinfully beyond a wooden balustrade. He was a beautiful man, with elongated limbs and well-shaped muscles sculpted under the skin. There were no men like that in the town. The wounds in his marmoreal flesh released a great sensual power, and Candida developed the habit of spending hours each day in contemplation of them. As she knelt, she felt a mysterious fire within her; perhaps it was sanctity, coursing through her delicate body and exploding between her legs. On Sunday, when she took Communion, she played with the Host in her mouth, taking great care not to touch it with her teeth, because it was the body of her beloved and she did not want to hurt him. Then she swallowed, feeling the communion wafer melt inside of her.

Her infatuation became so intense that she spent every free moment in the church, always wearing her best dress. She could not understand why one day her mother came for her in the dark chapel, where she had spent many sublime hours, and dragged her away, calling her vicious names and forbidding her ever to return except in her company, on Sundays and religious feast days. Candida did not rebel, but she promised Christ that one day she would be his bride, and in a certain sense she succeeded in doing so, though she did not become a nun as she had initially intended.

She was twelve years old when she caught her first glimpse of the man who would become her husband.

You couldn't call her beautiful. When she was little she had suffered from a slight case of rickets, and she was a tiny little thing, light as a doll one might place on a bed. She was slender, with a narrow chest and shoulders, a slightly larger than average head, gentle eyes enlivened by a mischievous look, and soft lips. She inspired a variety of reactions in men, ranging from brutality to tenderness, and at times verging upon unconditional love. There were always, everywhere, men who lost their heads for her, as a child, as an adult, and even as an old woman, when she continued to receive marriage proposals from the hospices in the nearby towns. She turned them all down with coquettish disdain.

The first signs of her mysterious charm had surfaced during

the visits of Angelica's suitors. Even as they stood before this great beauty they could not help but steal a glance at the young girl serving the rose liqueur. After exchanging just a few words with her they fell shamelessly in love.

Finding a husband for Angelica had become Oreste's driving mission; he exhibited her like a bear at a town fair, and was dead set on marrying her off. When Angelica was young, men had come from across the province to ask for her hand, but they were never good enough for him. One was too tall, another too short, yet another had a crazy cousin. A prosperous landowner was eliminated from consideration because, just as he was about to leave the house, he had blown his nose into a red handkerchief with a joyful trumpet sound. One might have thought it was Oreste who was supposed to marry him, not his sister.

At first Angelica was impatient, but eventually she let things take their own course, putting her fate in her brother's hands and finding consolation in romance novels. The rest of the family were too distracted by their own difficulties to pay attention, but once the tempests had passed, everyone suddenly realized that the family beauty had become an old maid, and everyone did his best to remedy the situation.

The marriage brokers plied their trade from Grassano to Miglionico and Salandra, in search of a good match, and later, even an acceptable match. As time passed, they had to go farther and farther afield to seek out foreigners who did not know her real age. In this they were aided by the fact that Angelica, in part because of her lack of vitality, hid her age admirably; her beauty had lost only its flavor, solidity, and reality. More and more she came to resemble the perfectly crafted and odorless wax fruit that Albina exhibited on the linen chest, her only token from their paternal home.

When a man actually seemed ready to come forward, Angelica would refuse him angrily, and if her family tried to push her
to accept, it was easy enough to find a way to discourage these
already hesitant suitors. She did not want to ruin the chances of
meeting her pilot. It took all of Candida's stubbornness and love
to alter the course of events.

Chapter Five

*I*n mid-October there was a week-long fair in Grottole. It was the last fair before the one in Potenza, which marked the end of the season, and it was so big that people came from all over the district. It started with a clamor in the piazza when all the tinsmiths arrived from Puglia and Matera with their copper pots, laundry tubs, and sundry kitchen implements. Meanwhile, down the road that led to the fairground, the animals began to arrive. This was the time of year when the Gypsies celebrated their betrothals.

It was during the fair that Candida had caught her first glimpse of Colino.

She would have preferred to forget that day. The fair had begun the day before. That morning, while her father stood among the tables selling odds and ends and her mother went off with one of the Gypsies who was a friend of hers, Candida left the house. She zigzagged her way through the tables of shoes and linens. Without stopping at the piles of hazelnuts or the barrels of cured olives, or pausing for an ear of roasted corn, which she liked so much, she went straight to the stall belonging to Gennarino the Wig Man.

There, amid the usual merchandise—ribbons, hairpins, and

perfumed soaps—sat a Spanish doll with a painted wax face, body stuffed with sawdust, with a frilly red satin dress. Since the day before, when it had first appeared there, it had become the forbidden desire of all the little girls in town. In order to take it home, Gennarino said, one of them would have to patiently comb out her hair with a thin lice comb—the kind that scraped your scalp till it bled—and then gather, one by one, the hairs that were left on the comb. This would require a seemingly infinite patience. But Candida decided to take a shortcut.

That morning she had found the scissors they used for gutting chickens and with one clean swipe she sheared off her braid, which came down to her waist, just as a few years hence women would be doing on the other side of the world, albeit for different reasons.

When Gennarino held the braid in his hand, wrapped in a piece of newspaper, he shook his head as if he had already seen this many times before. He couldn't use hair that had been cut off with scissors! The hair had to be intact, with the root. In exchange for the braid—he could see the girl was upset—he offered her a noisemaker. It was there with the rest of his junk. He shook it so it would make a noise. It croaked. Candida said nothing. She left without even taking back the braid and started to wander around the tables, her eyes welling up with tears.

Colino was manning the stand next to his father; when Candida's eyes rested on him he was unrolling a bolt of taffeta the color of ripe prunes, which rustled so vividly that later in her memory Candida could still hear it sing.

He had the dark, languid, Levantine eyes typical of men from the coast, more caressing than even the most expensive fabric sold at the stand, the silk-blend velvet. His lips were shapely and his teeth were white, straight, and healthy. He had long fingers and in these and other ways he reminded Candida of the Christ descended from the cross that she had loved as a child, as if the marble had somehow suddenly become flesh. At the time, Colino was eighteen years old.

He had been away for ten years, during which time he had lived with his uncle Cataldo, a textiles salesman in Bari. Now he had come to help his father at the fair, and business had never been so good. Because of him, the women crowded around the stand, feigning interest in the fabrics that Minguccio the Merchant unfurled as he filled their heads with his chatter. Provocative glances were fired at the boy from all directions, but none had ever struck its target. To the great satisfaction of his mother, who was jealous and proud of the miracle she had produced, Nicola, or Colino, as she called him, was still a virgin. Despite many opportunities, he had never been ensnared by one of these widows or women of easy virtue, nor had he stained the virtue of any young girls. A roguish innocence protected him from temptation. He emanated a sweetness that verged on deceptiveness. He had become used to all these women surrounding him like flies around a steer, and if he couldn't drive them off with a placid whip of the tail he would drown their ardor in his limpid gaze.

Colino was in the process of measuring a piece of fabric with the palm of his hand when he looked up and, in the trajectory of his gaze, came upon Candida.

At first his attention was aroused by her strange, choppy haircut. Then her eyes met his, and something strange happened. It was as if a door had opened. Filled with wonder, Colino walked down corridors and through rooms, some of them filled with light, others dark and heavy with secrets, passing hidden corners, closets, sunny terraces . . .

"Wake up!" He was startled by a smack on the back. His father, Minguccio the Merchant, had followed the direction of his gaze to see what could possibly be distracting him, but saw nothing. Just a little girl with skinny shoulders and a flat chest, hair chopped off at her chin, tear-filled eyes illuminated by a smile at precisely that moment.

Once again, he asked Colino to wrap up the velvet from Tricarico. Colino pulled his eyes away from Candida's face to complete the order. When he looked up again she was gone.

For the rest of the time the fair was in town he hoped to see her pass by their stand again, and as soon as he had a free moment he went looking for her among the stands, amid groups of people haggling over merchandise, in the corner where the barkers sold soapwort and licorice root, even over where the Gypsies told fortunes with cards. He looked everywhere and asked everyone, but was unable to give a precise description. Then he went to Gennarino's stand.

Candida was at home cleaning *lampascioni,* hyacinth bulbs, to make soup with. Her father had walked by just as she and Colino were gazing at each other and she stood, mouth open, before Minguccio's wares. Without a word he took her by the arm and led her home. He gave her a good slap and pointed at a mountain of *lampascioni* to clean. Candida did not protest. That way she could dream about Colino in peace. As she picked up each bulb she went over the details of his face. His cheekbones, his eyes, the arch of his eyebrows, the curve of his lips, and every proportion assumed multiple meanings, hidden or evident, but she would have been unable to explain even one of these meanings.

Lost in such thoughts, time passed, full of promise, until she found herself once again standing in front of the real thing. Her father had left the house with a basket full of *lampascioni* and she suddenly realized that it was the last day of the fair and she had not yet seen him. Without hesitation, she betrayed her father's trust and went looking for him.

There was only a smattering of people on Largo San Rocco. As the day waned, many had left and others were packing up their wares. The air resounded with greetings and guttural cries to encourage the mules: *Ayhhhhhhh*. Wisps of dust and hay floated in the air, making Candida sneeze. As her heart beat furiously, she made her way among the people loading merchandise onto carts until she reached the spot where Minguccio's stand had been. She found only hazelnut shells and seeds, mule dung and hay.

A wind began to blow. The air was crisp and sharp, cold for the season, and it picked up scraps of paper here and there, spinning them in the air for a moment, then letting them flutter to the ground. Someone informed her that Minguccio had left that morning. She pretended not to understand, unable to believe her ears. Suddenly everything went cold and dead. She thought that her life, what was left of it, had become a useless burden.

A figure emerged out of the darkness of the midwinter day to meet her. It seemed to come from a different time, more joyous or more sad, she couldn't tell, but distant nonetheless, a time when she was still a child who played with dolls. She recognized Gennarino the Wig Man waving wildly to get her attention. When she drew near, he handed her the Spanish doll. She held it awkwardly. "It's yours," he said, as if to reassure her. She looked at him in disbelief. "And many greetings from the son of Minguccio the Merchant," Gennarino said with a smirk and a wink, before walking off, because he had to finish loading up before it got dark. To Candida it felt as if the sun had risen at that very moment and everything around her were coming alive.

A FEW DAYS LATER Colino told his mother that he had found the woman he wanted to marry. He pointed her out one day when they were walking down the road; his mother was carrying a bas--ket of eggs that for a moment were in danger of becoming an omelet.

"Her?! But she's still in diapers!" Diodata said mockingly. She had little desire to hand over her beautiful boy to anyone, and now it' was evident that he understood nothing about women. She would have to find him a good wife. But for once Colino wouldn't budge. He wanted this one.

When Vincenzo saw Minguccio the Merchant walk through the door, the first thing that occurred to him was that he had come to make him an offer for the shop, and he decided on the spot that he would not sell it to him at any price. But instead Minguccio wanted his daughter. No less. "My daughter, my daughter, Candida," he said over and over under his breath as if trying to grasp the situation. The nerve of that prick!

During Minguccio's visit, Vincenzo took the opportunity to nose into his business and satisfy his curiosity on a few points that had been bothering him all these years. He asked how many bolts of cloth they had stored away in Puglia, and how much cash, and how many carts, and if they owned any houses, mules, donkeys, or chickens, as if he were actually evaluating his offer. Minguccio did not want to reveal any of this, but he had to say something, so he fell back on his famous gift of gab. But Vincenzo would not let him off the hook.

Colino answered all of Vincenzo's questions, because he did not want him to get annoyed, as his father looked on angrily. Vincenzo repeated everything Colino said as if reflecting. "One donkey, one mule, two carts, one dog, one house in Monopoli, and a property in Grottole, an inventory of four hundred pieces in a warehouse in Puglia . . . you can stuff all of it! I wouldn't give her to your son for any price, not even if she were dead! I'd rather drown her with my own hands, twist her neck like a chicken, starve her to death, or let her die of a broken heart, and you, you son of a bitch, if I ever see you get near her or even think about her I'll wring your bloody neck, I'll beat you to a pulp, you and all your family, too, you and all the rest." Minguccio the Pugliese and his wife and son were seen walking slowly down the long descent to the piazza, while Vincenzo stood in the doorway of his shop and cursed at them, furious and satisfied.

From that day on, Candida was not allowed to set foot outside the house.

She whiled away the hours holding up a hank of wool for her grandmother Concetta, who wound it at an amazing speed. Every so often Concetta would look up and shake her head as if she had always known how this story would end. Then, to console the girl, she would tell a story from the old days, whose moral was always that when something is supposed to go wrong nothing can make it right, and the proof was what had happened to their family: just look at Aunt Costanza—may the Lord forgive her—and Grandpa Francesco, may he rest in peace, and at her own poor mother.

But Candida bridled at the notion, and decided that she would write the final chapter of this story, just like when she wrote compositions at school.

Since she did not know what else to do she turned to the only influential person she knew: Jesus Christ. As one does in such cases, she promised something in return for his help. She pledged her first child in exchange for the man that her aunt had stolen from him. Perhaps the Good Lord appreciated the gesture, but he was not the only one who helped bring about the successful outcome of the love between Candida and Colino.

. . .

ALBINA WAS IN SHOCK. There must be some mistake. How could her scrawny little runt of a daughter have caught the eye of the most handsome young man anyone had ever seen in Grottole, the one everyone wanted but none had been able to catch? But there was no mistake, Colino wanted her and no one else; even his mother, her friend Diodata, had said so, and Albina couldn't help but agree when Diodata exclaimed that her son had lost his marbles. She felt that she had to act on this unexpected turn of fate before her luck changed. And Mastro Vincenzo, her husband, would just have to grin and bear it.

In February a meeting was held at Nascafolta's tavern and there the issue was settled. Even Vincenzo attended. Nascafolta's wife invited the neighborhood women over for *coratella* (innards) and they ate in the cellar.

That night a series of events took place that for one reason or another no one would ever forget and which went on to enrich the repertory of stories that would one day help Gioia pass the time when she was hovering between life and death.

There was a lunar eclipse.

Candida had her first period.

For the first time since Colino had asked for her hand, Candida was allowed to go out with her aunt Angelica, but while they were out walking by the wall Candida felt unwell and had to return home by herself.

Behind the partition Concetta was already sleeping; Candida could hear her snoring softly. Quietly, she went down the stairs to the basement where she shared a bed with her aunt. There was a sudden flash. She opened the curtain and saw her uncle Oreste lying in a languid pose in front of a camera mounted on a tripod, wearing her aunt Angelica's clothes, as well as eye shadow and rouge on his cheeks.

He threatened to strangle her if she told anyone what she had seen and she swore she never would. She kept his secret for years, at first out of fear, then out of indifference. She had almost forgotten it when, years later, suddenly it became useful to her.

That night, while they discussed women and hunting at Nascafolta's tavern, Vincenzo drank half a demijohn of wine, with some sense of guilt and much satisfaction. He wasn't supposed to drink because of his heart.

He had suffered from a heart condition for a long time, more or less, he calculated, from the time his wife began to turn away from him every night. The doctor told him not to drink alcohol and gave him some foul-tasting drops which he forgot to take most days. But he never forgot to throw back a little glass of wine on the sly, or even two or three. He would drink it all down in one gulp, checking for witnesses, and if someone caught him he would mumble something about how it really didn't matter, after all the doctor couldn't see him.

When he went home that night, he could barely keep himself from singing.

His wife had just arrived.

Back in the tavern, as the disk of the moon went dark and some of the old women began to worry about bad omens, Albina had laughed so hard that her stomach ached. When she went home, something else happened that hadn't occurred in years; she made love to her husband.

She was undressing in her room when he came in. The others were all asleep.

Vincenzo watched her for a moment, in silence, and then pounced with the fury of a dehydrated man lost in the forest. Albina had a strange thought and let him have his way.

Vincenzo took her vigorously, feeling his heart leap out of his chest as he entered that which had long since become a mirage.

Albina felt him pounding down against her thorax, beating hard, hard, hard, until she suddenly felt him shudder and collapse.

For a moment, she did not move from under him, enjoying the weight of his body. With some effort she slipped out from beneath the heavy mass. She turned him over. His face had a beatific expression, suffused with the same joy that for a moment had invaded her as well, despite her efforts to the contrary. She caressed him, quickly, perhaps because in all those years spent making his life difficult she had developed a feeling of tenderness toward him, but never enough to convince her to make him happy. Then she quickly closed his eyes in order to block out the thoughts that were entering her mind.

This is how Candida's prayers came to be answered. The engagement was celebrated as soon as the strict mourning period had come to an end.

Civl Ciavl sceva a l' uort
la malombra sceva appress
si nan era p'a muss tuort
Civl Ciavl saria mort.

Civl Ciavl went out to pasture,
a dark shadow followed right after
if it weren't for his ugly face,
Civl Ciavl'd be dead, without a trace.

Chapter Six

You know when you fell in love with me?" Candida would sometimes say to Colino, flashing her mischievous smile. "When I was born, your mother sent you with some chicks for my mother. As you were leaving, my mother called you back: 'Don't you want to see the baby?' She lifted me out of the crib and you gave me a kiss. From that day on, you never forgot me."

Colino looked at her, perplexed. "Get out of here," he would say, giving her a little shove, his eyes smiling.

They had to wait for Angelica to find a husband before they could get married. Oreste had laid down the law, as he sometimes did, emerging from the shadows of his wasted life to exert his sterile tyranny. Their hopes of marrying Angelica off had long since faded, but Candida worked so hard that in the end there was not one wedding, or even two, but three, turning the town head over heels.

JUST BELOW THE HOUSE that had once belonged to Don Francesco and that now housed the local club lay the Della Rabbia home. They had been multiplying for generations in that gloomy shack like weeds, which when you yank them up always come back stronger. They were resistant to illnesses and fires, to typhus and cholera, to hunger, floods, lice, and scabies; they concentrated on reproducing, fathers coupling with daughters, brothers with sisters. They no longer knew each other's names, and could barely speak. Some uttered couplets, others could only snarl like dogs.

But once in a long while, by error or by some random genetic combination, a girl was born who was a notch ahead of the rest on the evolutionary ladder. And for this reason she would be particularly unhappy. Lucrezia was the most unhappy of them all.

She didn't eat grass without distinguishing it from chicory, nor did she wrestle with the pigs for a pear core; she had never eaten a freshly killed cat or a fish out of the Basento with all its scales. And at the age of twelve, by some miracle she was still a virgin. She combed her hair, and when she had the chance, she even washed. She had learned to speak at a decent age and because she was ashamed of her family's dismal poverty, she told a heap of lies.

She constantly made up new details about her house, describing her brother's beautiful crib, the jar brimming with oil, the cupboard full of bread, the storeroom filled to overflowing with grain, pots crammed with coils of sausages. She did not care that everyone knew the truth. When people offered her some food she would always say that she had already eaten. But she would take the food. It's for Antonino the pig, she would say.

She was well liked in the town because whenever there was work to do she did not hold back. When she could barely speak she already went out to feed the pigs and gather water at the fountain, standing on the tips of her toes.

When Giuseppe set eyes on her, Lucrezia was washing the floor in Albina's house. Because of her, Candida almost became an old maid.

GIUSEPPE AMODIO, ROCCO'S SON, had left for America when he was just a child. He saw the sea for the first time when he went to Naples, to board the ship. When he was gazing out at that incredible mass of water—constantly moving in all directions, with an odor unlike any he had smelled before mixed with the stench of coal tar from the ships—all the hair on his body stood on end and his legs dug into the ground as if they had suddenly sprouted roots.

He had to be dragged onto the boat like a mule. His family had paid one hundred and fifty lire for the ticket in advance, plus one hundred for the middleman, so there was nothing to do but shove him into the hold.

He threw up during the entire journey. Innards spinning and stomach jolting, he would stare out of the porthole at that detested substance that turned bloodied twice a day, at dawn and dusk. He imagined that it was populated by horrible monsters that would drag the ship down at any moment, but he could not share his terrors with anyone else on the ship because no one understood his dialect and because his sense of bewilderment had rendered him solitary.

As he twisted and turned in the night, unable to sleep, he asked himself what sin he had committed. He could not believe that a God-fearing Christian who had done nothing wrong could be sent to Hell while he was still alive.

The only thing that kept him from losing his mind completely was a little bag of black salted olives that his mother had given him before his departure. He ate one every evening, chewing it slowly along with the bread he set aside at lunchtime. The flavor of the salty flesh reminded him for a moment of who he was, helped him to recall the faces of his family, the warm breath of the brothers who had shared his bed, the noises of the animals, the smells and sounds of his family home, and turned his fear into nostalgia, his dismay into regret, his madness into resignation.

One tempestuous night, as he was tossed around by the waves while vomiting from the balustrade, he wondered how he had let himself be reduced to such a state and was so ashamed that for a moment he wished he could lose himself forever in the black water that filled him with such terror. But then he had an idea; it felt like a hand reaching out to him in the midst of the waves for him to grab onto. He swore that if he survived this nightmare, his son would never have to suffer a similar fate. His son would keep his feet planted firmly on the ground, and no one would ever force him to go to a place that no Christian man should be forced to see, even in his dreams. His son would never be obliged to sign his own death warrant with an X on the dotted line.

Giuseppe managed to escape his worst nightmares, but he would never again be the boy with the oversized jacket whom he had left behind at the port of Naples, the boy who had walked down to the harbor eating a rum *babà*. Its sugary and unfamiliar taste seemed to contain all the promise of "'Merica," the land of plenty where cheese rained down on plates of *maccheroni* and carts propelled themselves forward without the aid of mules. That was how the middleman had described America to his father, who had broken his back to put aside enough money to feed the family for six months, all to send him over there like a message in a bottle.

On the day of his departure the whole town came down to the Via Nuova to see him off. As he climbed onto a cart a few people asked him to carry letters for relatives, others gave him their blessing, and some asked him to remember them, as if he had already made his fortune. When the ship left with its human

cargo—the company was called La Veloce—the wool thread that
an Abruzzese farmer on the ship was winding snapped, and at
that moment everything seemed to come to an end.

It took three weeks to reach New York. One morning, he
heard someone cry out, "La 'Merica!" Climbing up from the
hold Giuseppe saw seagulls circling around gloomily between
the leaden sky and the leaden sea, and soon after, an unimaginable
vision exploded before his eyes: the skyscrapers of Manhattan.

Two days later, after the paperwork and the formalities, and
after fourteen hours of waiting, cold and hungry, on the ferry, he
was unloaded, along with a thousand other people, at Ellis Island,
the island of good fortune for some, and for others, the island of
tears.

They were lined up under a metal roof and pushed into a
redbrick, glass, and steel building, as big as all of Grottole.

In the atrium he was confronted by a tumult of voices and
faces of all different colors, some with beards, others with tur-
bans or hats. Beneath the arches, people shouted orders in incomprehensible languages, and sobs echoed. A woman next to
him struggled as if possessed by the Devil because a policeman
wanted to separate her from her luggage, which consisted of a
wicker basket and two bundles, in which he could make out a
wooden spoon and a ball of wool. In another spot, a little girl in
her First Communion dress looked around as if in a daze.

They removed his clothes and explored every millimeter of
his body; they pulled back his eyelids with a buttonhook and
asked him questions that, then and there, made no sense to him.
Someone told him that they didn't want any rejects in 'Merica:
no epileptics, dimwits, cheats, consumptives, anarchists, polyga-
mists, or beggars were welcome.

A man with a thin mustache and shiny eyes standing next
to him had an X marked on his back. He broke free and would

have flung himself in the frigid water if they hadn't held him back.

A policeman suddenly called out his name, and he panicked. Who had told this man his name? They had never seen each other before, of that he was sure. It seemed to him that the man was looking at him strangely. Maybe he had inadvertently committed an offense and now they were coming to throw him in jail, or worse. Far worse. Instead, the doors of 'Merica were cracked open and he was shoved inside on a cold January day.

Years later when he was a barber with a little shop on Mulberry Street in Lower Manhattan who wore a clean white shirt and a starched suit on Sundays to go to Mass, he tried to forget all of this, as well as what followed. Had he thought back to those times he would surely have been moved to tears, but he could no longer cry because he was a grown man. When he turned thirty he decided to go home and find a wife.

He was not as terrified on the return trip, not because he had become more courageous or because he had grown accustomed to such things, but because something inside him had snapped during his first crossing, like the Abruzzese's thread. When he arrived, he described America as if it were all honey and roses; he was dapper in his starched suit and a hat with a name that no one had ever heard in those parts, Borsalino. He reminded them of the swallows caught by the local children, who would clip their wings to fatten them up.

Angelica was put forward as a potential wife. Her family tried to pass her off on anyone who had been away long enough to forget her age.

Giuseppe sat with her in a darkened parlor, a place that protected her from the noise of the outside world and concealed the slight thickening of her figure that was the only sign of her advanced age.

They sat together on the sofa, she stiffly upright, he at a loss for words, feeling intimidated despite his starched suit, every so often blurting out something in a hybrid dialect spoken only in one particular corner of New York, or to be more precise, in that particular form, only by Giuseppe himself.

The whole family waited expectantly outside the door to hear the result of their meeting. For once they all agreed: Angelica could not do better. They would have accepted any conditions.

But as chance would have it, Giuseppe, feeling awkward and intimidated, knocked over the bottle of rose liqueur with his elbow. The crystal shattered and the sticky liquid spilled onto the carpet. Angelica told him not to worry and sent for Lucrezia.

Since she had learned how to walk, the Della Rabbia girl had spent all her time in other people's houses, and when there was work to be done, she was always more than willing to do it.

On this occasion she once again threw herself into the task. She put her head down and scrubbed, her chest pressed down toward her waist, her arms outstretched and her posterior bobbing up and down like a mule's behind as she scoured the carpet. It was a truly shapely posterior, candid and round as the full moon.

While Angelica continued her insipid chitchat, Giuseppe's attention was gradually captivated by the undulating movements of that posterior, by its perfect proportions, its exuberance, its hunger for life, until finally he was unable to look at anything else. The feeling of oppression that had filled him when he entered the room began to dissolve, and all the sadness of his life seemed to find consolation. The meeting came to an end and the family accompanied him to the door. Giuseppe swallowed hard a few times, pulled himself together, and, as the entire family looked on expectantly, asked for Lucrezia's hand in marriage.

Lucrezia's, Angelica's, and Candida's weddings were all set for the same day.

WHEN EVEN CANDIDA was beginning to lose all hope, a blind man arrived on the scene. He had been a forest ranger and had lost his sight in an accident one day when he was cleaning his regulation firearm. He had stayed on in Perugia, where he could live well on his pension. Candida decided that this was an occasion not to be missed. He would not reject Angelica, as by this point even the least attractive and poorest callers did. The important thing now was that Angelica not reject him.

Candida was the only one in the family who was privy to her aunt's secret life, her rose-colored dreams, her florid fantasies. She decided to take advantage of these senseless confabulations to make sure that her plans succeeded.

First, she spoke with the blind man. She described Angelica's beauty, basing her descriptions on memories of her appearance when she was young and with the help of a photograph taken when Angelica was eighteen. Her immaculate skin, the copper reflections of her hair, the liquid gold of her eyes, the nobility of her carriage. Candida transformed her aunt into a heroine from a novel, the unfortunate heiress of a great fortune, barrels full of lost riches, a princess without a kingdom, dispossessed but not defeated. The words came to her as if Don Francesco's daguerreotype had come alive and Don Francesco himself were whispering them into her ear.

The blind man let himself be seduced, fascinated by Candida's voice and by the words with which she wove her stories. Little by little he fell in love—though he wasn't sure exactly with what or whom, because the creation had become confused with its creator, reality with dreams. But still, the confusion was pleasing; the enforced immobility of his condition had taught him the value of fantasy and Candida exploited this in order to advance her plans.

Now she had to make Angelica fall in love. She began to instruct the blind man regarding the character of his future wife and the best manner in which to win her over.

During long afternoons spent sipping liqueur on the couch with the broken springs, the blind man told Angelica the stories Candida had fabricated for the occasion. He spoke of his experiences in Tripolitania, of the colorful costumes of the Moors, of the fertility of the lands he had once lorded over, and described in minute detail his past as a pilot, and what it felt like to float among the clouds. He described the feeling of the wind washing over you, dense as the water in a stream, and how the earth looks like a colorful piece of cloth when seen from the air, the fields like little squares and the houses like polka dots.

Angelica was won over, and when the blind man told her the story of the battle he had fought in and the moment his plane had been shot down and how he had lain for three days like a corpse, and how he had lost his sight, she began to cry quietly. Her cheeks, no longer as full as they had once been, were bathed in tears, just as they always were when she reached the climax of one of her novels, when the protagonists' love affair was in serious danger. Impulsively, she took his hand. No longer willing or able to distinguish reality from fantasies—their own or those of others—Angelica and the blind man swore their eternal love.

ORESTE LED ALL THREE women to the altar. His whiskers were so stiff with pomade they could have pierced the clouds. He was brimming with pride, just as Don Francesco had imagined him even before he was conceived. The first to be led down the aisle was his sister Angelica, adorned with length upon length of lace, like the Madonna of Pompeii.

But there was no one waiting at the church doorstep to take his place at the beauty's arm. Oreste's face turned a reddish shade of purple and looked as if it might explode in a ball of fire at any moment.

When Cacalenzuoli's nephew came to inform Candida, who awaited her turn at home, of the situation, she remembered what her grandmother had said: When something is meant to go wrong nothing can make it go right. She felt ill and almost fainted.

In the churchyard, people were whispering. "A blind man can smell whether a piece of meat is fresh," Luigino La Ciminiera, the butcher, said, with the air of an expert. Concetta made the sign of the cross three times and said, "Quiet! Quiet!" She had always known how this story would end.

But somewhere, something was fighting to exist. It battled against the cold and darkness. It did not want to become something else, one of many possible outcomes. It wanted to be what it was and nothing else. It dug in its heels and in the end it got its way. That thing was, or rather would one day be, Gioia.

The blind man was standing in Zucculecchia's shop, still in his underwear, with one foot stuck in a trouser leg. "You kept saying make it smaller, make it smaller," Zucculecchia said without panicking, marking the spot where he would have to let out the fabric. He always left more fabric on the inside than on the outside, to account for changing styles, regrets, growth, and widening girth, without worrying about the lumps or folds this might cause.

He would ask his customers to arch their backs a bit, or pull in their stomachs, or bend their arms or hold them out straighter. "There!" he would say, satisfied with his work. "It fits you like a glove." He sewed clothes for contortionists, or people with a willingness to adapt.

The wedding feast was held at the farmhouse at Serra Fulminante, the one that had once belonged to Don Francesco Falcone and where many years earlier the bandits had set up camp. Someone had carved a rough design into the bark of an ancient olive tree; if one looked closely, one could just make out the Bourbon coat of arms.

One week after the wedding—long enough for Lucrezia to become pregnant—Giuseppe returned to America. His plan was to sell the barbershop and use the cash to buy a house and a piece of land.

Angelica and the blind man left for Perugia, where they would embark on their semi-imaginary life, each filled with illusions about the other and consequently able to give each other complete happiness. On the few occasions when they came to visit, Angelica did not seem to have aged at all; she simply appeared more and more unreal, as if by living in an imaginary world for so long she had herself become part of that world.

Chapter Seven

O n May 24, 1915, Italy officially entered the war. In the rest of Europe, the conflict had already been raging for a year, but for the inhabitants of Grottole, the war still felt very far away. At the club the conversation was still about the weather and the harvest, the same discussion as every other year. Now the news arrived that all able-bodied men would have to leave for the front. It was a terrible blow for all those who had something to lose. For the others, it seemed like a stroke of good fortune, because they imagined they might be able to help maintain their families with the meager pay. There were lame men who attempted to walk, and men who were blind in one eye who pretended to see perfectly so as to be called up. Colino, on the other hand, would have given an arm—as some in fact did— to stay home. When war was declared, Candida had just given birth to her first child. She named him Domenico (known as Mimmo), in honor of Minguccio the Merchant, who sometimes came to visit.

Just after the wedding, Candida and Colino were swept up in an ecstasy of love that would last for the rest of their time together.

In the morning, when Colino woke up to go to the shop,

Candida would stay under the covers. He made coffee and brought it to her in bed, a strange habit that caused benevolently incredulous whispers in the town. The time it took Candida to drink her coffee was all she needed to induce her husband to rejoin her under the covers. Sometimes she would surprise him with a kiss that made him blush. "You little . . . ," he would murmur. Meanwhile Oronzio, who was waiting for him in the square, passed the time getting drunk.

No one in Grottole had ever been happier than they were. As the town prepared for war, Candida and Colino abandoned themselves without remorse to their conjugal love, and Albina muttered quietly to herself, shaking her head, because such happiness had never been approved of by the good folk of the town. After all, unhappiness was more stable, more secure, and more decorous. But she couldn't complain openly because Colino brought home the bread, and sometimes even some meat, which he hid under his coat so as not to offend the neighbors.

But earthly paradise was never meant to last, and one day the letter came calling Colino to arms. Candida's milk dried up and Mimmo almost starved.

That was when Mammalina appeared.

Oronzio's unfortunate wife had two children, but more important, she had a wretched husband who spent all the money she earned working as a servant and wet nurse on drink. Colino gave him work out of compassion, but most days Oronzio didn't bother to show up. When Mammalina complained he hit her, but she didn't let him have his way and defended herself like a tiger. Her screams were audible from the town square.

When war was declared, Oronzio was one of the first to sign up, enticed by the rumors that the government would take care of soldiers' families and even give them land when a soldier died in battle. The notion that someone would do so much for a drunk like him sounded like a fairy tale. Land . . . Even if he had to pay for it with his blood, it seemed like a good deal.

When Mammalina found out that he had joined up, her attitude toward him changed. It was the first time since he had made her pregnant at the age of fifteen that he had tried to do something for his children.

The day before Oronzio was to leave home, Mammalina went over to Candida's house, but she had trouble formulating the words she wanted to say. She would open her mouth and then pause, hemming and hawing until finally Candida began to lose her patience. "Comare, can I ask you for a favor?" Mammalina finally blurted out, looking penitent. She asked Candida for a little money so she could buy a lamb's head to cook for her husband who was leaving for the war the following day. Then she went around town asking one person for a potato, another for an onion. In the end she cooked a meal unlike anything her family had ever seen.

That evening she put on her good clothes, dressed up the children, and set the table. The lamb's head stew gave off an irresistible fragrance. She had to watch the pot like a hawk to keep the children away until Oronzio came home. But it grew dark, and Oronzio still hadn't appeared. The children were hungry. They got on her nerves, and she slapped them and pinched their arms to keep them away. She waited as long as she could, until they fell asleep with their heads on the table. She sent them to bed with empty stomachs, which was nothing new.

Oronzio returned at dawn, so drunk he could barely stand. Mammalina was waiting for him with his bag packed, all his clothes ironed, and a package with the lamb's head inside. She handed it to him and said, "The first bullet will be for you."

About a month later Candida received a postcard from Oronzio, written out by a fellow soldier, in which he apologized to his wife for all she had suffered because of him, and begged Candida to speak to her on his behalf so that she would believe that this time he would change. What he said was true. By the time the postcard arrived Oronzio was already in midtransformation, chemically speaking, at the bottom of a crevice on Mount Cosich. He had been killed in the battle of Isonzo, the first of the war. He became one of the many unknown soldiers who would be celebrated in Italy's main squares.

The piece of land he had dreamed of, which had driven him to sign up in the first place and for which he had given his blood, turned out to be a myth, but with his pension, meager as it was, Mammalina was able to raise her children. She was even able to educate them at a boarding school for war orphans. The girl became a nursery-school teacher, and came back with a northern accent. The boy finished his agronomy degree, but died on the Russian front during the Second World War.

Every day, Mammalina thanked her husband, Oronzio, for having finally decided to do right by her. She honored and adored his image more than the man when he was alive.

One day in 1971, when Gioia was playing with her friends in an abandoned lot near the sea, President Giovanni Leone conferred the honorific title "*Cavalieri dell'Ordine di Vittorio Veneto*" on the veterans of the First World War who were still living. The first monthly pensions were paid around 1980, and consisted of eighty thousand lire a month, nonretroactive except for a hundred thousand lire granted to cover all back pay.

COLINO DID NOT GO TO WAR. The night before he was supposed to leave, he realized that Candida would not survive if something happened to him. So he went to his shop, and there he tried several different combinations of ammonium nitrate and calcium nitrate—highly volatile substances used for fertilizing the fields. When he came home he was deaf. He didn't go to war, but from that day on in order to have a conversation with Colino one had to stand directly in front of him and yell. This never bothered him. It kept him from hearing slander, troublesome noises, and useless chatter. He only heard what he needed to hear, the crème de la crème, and anyway, he didn't need words to understand most things.

After the war, the town was filled with cripples and widows. Of the few able-bodied men who were left, many emigrated. The bandits returned to the streets of Grottole and the neighboring towns, as well as to the Via Nuova, Ai Mar, and Cugno del Ricco, where Don Francesco had died. But General Crocco had not returned from the dead, as the song said; these weren't legendary heroes whose exploits could be recounted in front of the fireplace. They didn't fight for a mysterious kingdom situated who-knows-where, maybe in Tripoli, maybe nowhere, like the Garden of Eden. These bandits were hungry and prepared to kill for a handful of flour.

Colino had to defend his home from them several times. In the impoverished town, he was the one who kept the economy going.

During the years of his engagement he had set up a shop, little more than a hole in the wall, which had quickly become more important to the town economy than a bank. Besides fabrics, he sold food, fertilizer, sulphur, and copper for the vineyards. He bought wheat from the farmers and sold it wholesale to the millers. He sold flour, chickpeas, lentils, beans, pasta, and corn. He sold *lampascioni*, ricotta, feather dusters, and soapwort. Olives and eggs. Orzo and bran. Buttons and cotton thread to make lace. And anything else that could be bought or sold.

He sold merchandise on credit, with accounts that ran from August to August, supplying entire families with everything from fabric for their clothes to disinfectant for the vineyards, keeping track of the accounts in a graph-paper notebook covered in scrawls that only he could read. During the harvest, people brought their wheat to pay their debts, and the cycle began again when they acquired seed for the next year's harvest, plus fertilizer and sulphur, and then eventually wheat and olives bought on credit when their own stocks ran out. During bad years, when there was no harvest, Colino did not deny credit. The cycle simply began again, and lasted until the following August. He never tormented people for the money they owed, nor did he ever forget a debt. In the end he always collected.

He did not ask for interest, not even what a bank would have charged, or even the equivalent of the interest he would have received if he had deposited the money himself. If he had, he might have become rich. More likely, he would have gone out of business in a few years. No one ever knew whether he behaved this way out of honesty or good business sense. But there was no other way to do business in a place where it was a miracle if the farmers made it from one year to the next. Little by little he had built up a modest fortune and a reputation. After a few years he had been able to buy back Don Francesco Falcone's house, one of the most beautiful in town, and hired laborers to make it fit for habitation after being used as a social club for many years.

He had them knock down the spiral staircase that still stood unfinished, intending to use the rooms on the second floor as storerooms. To reach them, they had to climb up a simple wooden stepladder, the kind that had been used for generations and that didn't play dirty tricks on their owners. They whitewashed the walls to erase the shadows of the ghosts some claimed to have seen wandering among the card tables, suggesting bets that always lost.

One morning during the renovations, a workman began to scream as if he had lost his mind, claiming he had found a lost treasure. They all thought he was drunk; it was no secret that he liked to raise a glass before breakfast. But when they went to see for themselves, they discovered that it was true. Don Francesco's decaying barrels, filled with jewelry and old ducats—now corroded and worthless—had resurfaced.

When she saw the barrels, Albina cried for all the poverty she had seen in her life, for her husband the cobbler, their mended clothes, and her dead children. Oreste puffed up with rage like a toad. Concetta put on her jewels and refused to take them off again.

The corroded coins were stored away in the attic as a souvenir. Many years later, little Gioia had the luxury of playing shop and pirates with her cousins using real ducats.

GIUSEPPE DIED, but not in the war. When the conflict started he was still in New York, trying to get a good price for his business, a process that turned out to be more complicated and drawn out than he had expected. His draft card arrived at Spring Street, where he was living at the time with five compatriots. A few days earlier, he had received a letter from Lucrezia, which someone had written for her. She had given birth to a boy who looked just like him.

She wasn't just saying that. When Giuseppe saw the photograph of his son, even if he was only a newborn in swaddling clothes, he recognized his own serious-looking eyes, his nose, his forehead, and even the furrow between the eyes, the mark of an obstinate nature. Here was a chance to begin everything again. He had been offered the opportunity to erase all of the errors and injustices that had marked his existence, even his first ocean crossing, when the waves had shaken him and soured his soul.

His son would have a straight road ahead of him. He would not be forced to learn strange, blasphemous words; he would not become familiar with blonde, shameless women; he would not see vast abysses opening overhead between steep walls of sky-scrapers. He would grow up in Grottole, get married there, and have a decent house, a house firmly planted on the earth, and in that house his children would be born. For love of this child, Giuseppe became one of the 470,000 draft dodgers of the First World War.

Lucrezia waited for him, in Grottole, and raised the boy on her own. The remittances that Giuseppe sent disappeared into the hands of intermediaries and the vagaries of the conflict. Lucrezia had to work as a day laborer and was forced to take the boy into the fields with her.

Rocco was four years old when he saw his father for the first time.

In 1919, Giuseppe boarded the *Regina Giovanna*, a ship whose motor was almost 8,000 horsepower, even though there were no horses anywhere to be seen. The ship weighed 22,500 tons, was 210 meters long and 25 meters wide, and it could carry almost two thousand passengers on its route from New York to Naples. The third-class deck, where Giuseppe traveled, was filled with celebrations. There was singing day and night, accompanied by harmonica or snapping fingers. Some of the songs were melancholy and subdued, others had the percussive rhythms of the tarantella. The vast majority of the passengers were immigrants who, like Giuseppe, had avoided the draft and only now, after the amnesty had been announced, could return home to embrace their loved ones.

Giuseppe didn't mix with the merrymakers. He was too focused on his own thoughts and on an insistent stomachache that had begun to afflict him as soon as he'd boarded the ship. He had finally managed to sell his business and he spent the entire trip thinking about what to do with the money. He wanted to buy the property at Mazzam'pet that had once belonged to Don Francesco Falcone. His mother and father had worked there as day laborers, and he had gleaned the fields as a boy. It was a fertile piece of land, and he wanted to try planting fruit trees, because he had heard about new ways of farming besides planting wheat, which impoverishes the soil. He was impatient to meet his son.

When Giuseppe first caught sight of him, he was playing with a dead lizard on the doorstep. He stared at him without saying a word until the boy began to cry. The next day Giuseppe went to the bank and with the money he had brought from America he bought a certificate of deposit in his own name and his son's. Then he went to bed.

During the trip he had caught a viral infection. He had not given it much importance, even though at times he had felt weak, dizzy, and had suffered bouts of diarrhea. He was too excited to be home to worry. But now that everything had fallen into place, the illness was finally able to gain the upper hand. Giuseppe climbed into bed and shivered for two days. Lucrezia tended to him as they waited for the doctor, who never arrived. On the third day Giuseppe asked her to come to him and swear that she would make sure their son went to school. Lucrezia swore, and when he died, she declared war on God.

La formicuzza in un campo di lino
disse al grillo dammene un pochettino
e la rizumpalallillallero e larizumpalarillà.

The little ant in a field of flax
said to the cricket, "Gimme some of that!"
and a ricky-ticky-tick, and a ricky-ticky-tack!

Chapter Eight

The Salandra/Grottole train station was located about eight kilometers outside of Grottole, beyond the bridge that connects the town to the railroad track, and about fifteen kilometers from Salandra, in an area of steep calanques. In the late nineteenth century it had fallen into disuse, but in the thirties it was revived and became a stop on the Potenza–Metaponto line.

THE TRIP IN THIRD CLASS felt as long as a transatlantic crossing. Between Zagarolo and Grottole, Cicia, the new midwife from Ciociaria, south of Rome, had been forced to switch trains seven times, and her stomach felt like it was coming out of her eyes. If she hadn't thrown up, it was only because she was used to stoically putting up with all the hardships in life, otherwise she would never have become a midwife, and she would not have found herself on that train, nor would she probably have survived the meager rations her grandmother had fed her as a child.

As she stiffly descended the steps of the wooden railway car and tugged at the light suitcase containing all her earthly belongings, she tripped on the final step. She looked around. The bare valley of the Basento shimmered in the sun. The station was empty. All she could hear was the crackling of crickets. Cicia had made a mistake.

She watched the train roll away slowly, puffing along, and looked around desolately. She regretted not having stayed in Rome, even as a servant to her mother and her common-law husband, Signor Lorenzetti. At least she would have been among civilized people. Now, as she stood there, she almost expected to see Indians ride over the hill at any moment as in the Western she had seen the day before she left. They would encircle her, yelping savagely with their hands over their mouths, and then they would string her up like a *salame* on a pole. They would skin her, and who knows, they might even eat her. She thought she saw a condor fly across the endless azure sky.

Geography had never been her strong suit. At the age of ten she did not even know how to read or write. At fourteen, thanks to a bout of ringworm and to Signor Lorenzetti, her mother's latest boyfriend, who had unexpectedly turned out to be a lovely man, she had been able to take the entrance exams as a private student, and at seventeen she had obtained the midwife's diploma. At eighteen, after doing well on the nationwide competitive examination, she had found herself staring at an alphabetical list of towns, and had chosen Grottole, convinced that it was located somewhere in Lazio, near Grottarossa, the town where Rosina, a seamstress and her only friend, lived.

When she realized that Grottole was in fact located in a god-forsaken place called Lucania, or Basilicata, down near the heel of the boot, that spot in the foot where blood stagnates and has trouble flowing back up the leg, it was too late. She barely had time to alter one of her mother's old coats; she had been told that in those parts it was cold as hell in winter and unbearably hot in summer, and that there were wolves. Rosina sewed her a fancy outfit to wear to lunch at the house of the local *podestà*, she said good-bye to her mother with feigned affection and to Signor Lorenzetti with feigned indifference, swallowed her tears (something she had learned to do before even learning how to speak), put two vials of quinine—in case of malaria—in her bag, and departed, to her mother's great relief. She was not happy to have her daughter, a young woman in full bloom, in the house just as she herself was beginning to fade.

Cicia heard someone speak, and jumped. It was Ciola Ciola with the *podestà*. They had come to collect her in a cart dragged by a mule who had dug in its heels along the way, making them late. Cicia accepted their apologies with the grace of a queen and climbed into the cart like Marie Antoinette on her way to the guillotine, making sure not to get her skirt dirty. She pulled down a white veil from her straw hat, to keep away the deadly mosquitoes and other dangerous insects.

That was how they arrived in town, and how Candida saw them from the veranda of her house when they reached the piazza where the fountain stood. They were followed by a long train of barefoot, crooked-eyed, big-eared children whom Cicia watched with a combination of pity and repulsion. Candida was fascinated by Cicia's hat and its little veil, her low chignon, and her dark-blue traveling suit. Cicia looked as if she had walked out of one of those silly novels that Candida no longer had time to read, and Candida wanted more than anything to become her friend.

They soon had the opportunity to meet. Later the same day, when the usual lunchtime battle was raging and the boys were shooting bread crumbs at each other and playing practical jokes on Uncle Oreste, receiving warnings and slaps in response, and people were being pinched, and there was crying, screaming, and the inevitable retaliation, someone knocked on the door. Ciola Ciola invited Cicia to go in and the ruckus immediately stopped.

Cicia was the first official state midwife to arrive in Grottole, and she needed to be lodged with an honorable, clean family.

Oreste, who for once had the backing of Albina and Concetta, was completely opposed to having a stranger in the house, but there was nothing they could do. The days when Candida had calmly accepted her fate were a distant memory. After consulting with her husband, pro forma, she let Oreste stew in his juice and agreed, with ill-concealed enthusiasm, to take the foreigner as a boarder in her house.

At first Cicia kept to herself; she didn't want to mix with these dirty, primitive, wretched people. Then, one day, she realized that for the first time in her life, she felt at home.

CANDIDA HAD SIX SONS: Mimmo, Vincenzo, Emilio, Michele (known as Lillino), Cataldo (known as Dino), and Francesco (known as Ciccio). They buzzed around her all day long. Since her wedding, between the miscarriages, complicated pregnancies, breast-feeding, and illnesses, she had barely left the big double bed that Colino had brought for her from Bari. Despite her anemia and exhaustion, at night she gave herself blissfully to her marital duties. During the day she managed the house from the bedroom, which had become the most important room in the house. Albina and Concetta spent their days there as well, sitting by the windows in mourning, one with a belly as full as the hull of a boat and the other dried up like a leftover scrap of bread. Both now lived as guests in the house that had once been theirs. They prayed for the dear departed, sighing discreetly, secretly reassured by the fact that Don Francesco was highly unlikely to return, wherever he now resided.

Concetta mumbled prayers for the dead from morning to night. Albina crocheted bedspreads, using ever finer thread as the years passed, as if in a vain attempt to weave a spiderweb in which to capture the hours of her past life. Every so often mother and daughter would interrupt their confabulations with eternity and return brusquely to the present to comment listlessly on something they had seized with their sharp gazes from behind the curtains.

There were always a handful of townswomen in the room. They sat in a circle next to the windows, endlessly discussing the same topics, adding slight variations to stave off boredom, and pronouncing theories that carried the weight of truths. In addition to gossip, the local bon ton mandated that they should only speak of misfortunes, illnesses, accidents, and deaths. Whenever an outsider visited, Albina would quickly hide the lace she was working on. She was convinced that her sister Costanza sent spies to copy the designs she invented as if in a trance. They were so delicate and complex that they could only have been inspired by a long life full of misadventures.

She had heard that Costanza made marvelous bedspreads, and thus her envy lived on even in old age, as she remembered all the undeserved gifts that wretched woman had received, without ever a word of thanks. Even now, Albina asked herself how the Lord could favor someone who had seduced a man who had dedicated his life to Him. She couldn't help feeling a certain antipathy toward the Almighty for his spineless acceptance. She pursed her lips and said nothing when the women of the town expressed their appreciation for her sister's bedspreads. Instead, she would select an even finer cotton thread and start making yet another bedspread with a fantastical design that told a story in code, interwoven with words of hatred and wasted love and the desire for vengeance, which she transmitted to future generations like messages in a bottle. But there were no granddaughters to inherit these bedspreads. They simply piled up in the dowry trunk, as plentiful and intangible as thoughts.

THE BOYS WERE like an earthquake. They climbed over everything, spreading across the town like an oil spill, losing their shoes and getting lost themselves; when it was lunchtime they had to be counted and there was always one missing or three or four extra. The absent ones would return at night, telling of improbable adventures and preposterous encounters, and hiding behind the furniture to avoid the blows. Mammalina spent her days running after them, tending to their wounds and curing their bruises with slices of potato or bronze coins, pulling them apart when they fought, cleaning up their messes, and picking up the pieces of everything they broke. The only time they calmed down was in the early afternoon, when Candida told her stories, stories that reduced little Ciccio to a flood of tears, while Vincenzo, who had always been the sly one, dismissed everything with a shrug of the shoulders.

They adored their mother, and Candida returned their love lightly, confounding them with her long-winded stories, and sometimes slept with all six of them in her bed—where they clumped together and kicked at one another—and sang songs in a funny language that she claimed was either French or English from America.

Mimmo, the craziest of the bunch, bore the weight of Candida's promise to the marble Christ in the church. "If you let me marry the son of Minguccio the Merchant, our first child will be yours," she had said. After Mimmo was born, she dressed him in monk's clothes for the first three years, and then tried everything she could to inspire in him a religious fervor to which he seemed completely resistant. At five he became an altar boy, but he sang the hymns off-key. At six he drank the communion wine and was drunk the rest of the afternoon. At seven he sold the consecrated Host to his schoolmates in exchange for a shell inside of which one could hear the sound of the sea.

Candida did not lose hope. She was convinced that, as in the lives of the saints, when the time came his vocation would manifest itself, unequivocal and clear, however turbulent his adolescence, and she began to make inquiries about seminaries nearby.

Meanwhile, she and Cicia had become inseparable. Even as a little girl, Candida had been irresistibly attracted to new things; this tendency remained with her even into old age, when she was able to use devices that her daughter was afraid to even touch. Cicia, a foreigner, became an inexhaustible source of information about a world whose actual existence Candida sometimes doubted, and for this reason Cicia never ceased to fascinate her.

On summer evenings, when the children peeked out of basement windows to see the farmers taking off their clothes, the two women would sit outside and Candida would pepper Cicia with questions about her experiences when she worked as an extra on a movie set.

Assuming the dreamy air of a diva in hiding, Cicia would describe the flurry of stagehands, the realistic-looking sets made out of wood and plywood, the ancient Romans draped in togas. She did not bother to mention the endless waiting, the heavy winter clothes worn in summer and the summer clothes worn in winter, the insults, the vulgarity, and the man who directed the extras with a stick.

"Last night I had a dream . . . ," Candida said one day while she and Colino were drinking their morning coffee. Colino looked at her perplexed, as he always did when she came up with a novelty. The following week, they traveled to Rome.

The first thing they visited was the Basilica of Saint Peter's. Candida stood, open mouthed, in the vast space of the church. She looked at her husband, disconcerted. The statues, above them, were large and threatening, like the cruel giants in a folk tale. It seemed to her that the God who lived there must be an arrogant and ill-mannered lout like the people outside in the street whom they had asked for directions. Rome did not resemble Cicia's stories or the image Candida had formed in her mind as she listened to them, and so Saint Peter's was also the last thing they saw in Rome. Candida decided to return to Grottole to venerate her more familiar, less grandiose Christ, and imagine the glories of the capital as she would have liked them to be.

In Candida's company, Cicia quickly forgot her unhappy childhood, shuttled between a grandmother and an aunt, barely tolerated, and exploited. By telling a new version of her life, revised and improved, filled with invented details that slowly became part of her memories, she constructed a happy past for herself that consequently propelled her toward a joyous and prosperous future. Her hair became more lustrous and her eyes sparkled, and soon she married a corporal with a few firmly upheld convictions, who was able to provide her with the order and rigor she craved. He took her to live in Vercelli where he had been transferred, and she adapted quickly, even to the fog, and painlessly left behind the town that had so lovingly welcomed her, as well as Candida.

They corresponded for the rest of their lives. Later, when little Clelia hid in her skirts, Candida protected her lovingly in memory of the stories her mother had told her, her low chignon and the blue dress she wore the first time Candida laid eyes on her.

. . .

CICIA BROUGHT ALBA into the world, at seven months.

As long as her fertility lasted, Candida was always pregnant. She would give birth and start over. Abort and start over. "It's not possible," Colino said every time, but every time, it was so.

Her water broke earlier than expected one night as Cicia was telling her about a movie she had seen while a full orchestra played, underscoring the dramatic moments. The movie told the exciting and terrifying story of an unfortunate girl by the name of Cabiria. Candida began to feel tremendous pains and it was only due to Cicia's skill that both mother and child were saved. Cicia managed to control the hemorrhaging and kept Candida alive until they made it to the hospital in Matera, where they removed her uterus. And that was how Candida's fertility came to an end.

Alba was as tiny as a kitten, but otherwise perfect. When her mother returned from the hospital and tried to breast-feed, the baby was completely uninterested in attaching herself to the breast, and Candida didn't insist because that child had destroyed her, and she preferred to keep her distance. Without Mammalina, Alba would not have survived.

Mammalina kept her warm with her generous body while the doctors operated on her mother in Matera. She couldn't breast-feed because her children were already grown, but she kept Alba alive with wheatmeal and found her a wet nurse. It took some time, but eventually she found the perfect nurse, a young donkey with light-colored fur and the elongated, soft eyes of an Ethiopian princess. Alba did not seem to mind, and she didn't die. She was nourished by milk from Filomena, the donkey, and by Mammalina's affection; she would calm down only in Mammalina's arms. As she grew, she resembled neither her mother nor her father, but rather the donkey who had fed her.

She had Filomena's eyes, her elegant movements, and sometimes even her stubbornness.

As soon as her mother took her in her arms, she would begin to cry. To calm her, Mammalina used her arsenal of tricks, making dolls out of paper and Chinese shadows on the wall, the same tricks that would one day distract Gioia when she had one of her tantrums.

LUCREZIA WAS FURIOUS. When she had gone to the post office to withdraw the money her husband had left in an account, the clerk told her that she could not touch the funds until her son was of age. In seventeen years. Lucrezia could not understand. Her husband had left her this money. What the hell was a "certificate of deposit" anyway? She lost her temper, cried, begged, screamed. This was her money! Her husband had given his blood. He had gone all the way to 'Merica, may his soul rest in peace. Nothing. There was nothing they could do. She couldn't read the documents, but it was all written there. What had he been thinking? Rocco had to go to school. May you rot in hell! *Ca t voln accid!* May Christ strike you down! May you spit blood! And your children, and your wife too! She had to be dragged out. She grabbed chairs and doorways, scratched, spit, banged her face until it was black and blue, and pulled out her hair. But there was nothing to be done.

Lucrezia was forced to go work in the fields. She either left the boy with someone or took him with her as she had when he was still in swaddling clothes, when she would leave him in the shade of a tree and pray that a wolf or marten didn't carry him off.

She got up at three in the morning and walked to Ai Mar, Mazzam'pet, or San Lazzaro to be ready to begin work at dawn.

She followed the plow, planting seeds in the furrows; she pulled weeds, cleaned fava beans, tended vines, and when it was harvest time she made bundles of grain with the men. When it was threshing time, she put the grain out to dry. In the fall she picked grapes, then olives. When it was neither the grape harvest nor threshing time nor olive-picking time, she dug for *lampascioni* to cook, or gathered wild chicory, oregano, and chamomile flowers.

She was paid half a lira for a day's work. She made the most of it, and sometimes she even had a bit left over. She spent money only on Rocco, so he would have a fresh egg every morning, and bread soup in the evening. She herself ate whatever she could find. Wild chicory, snails, even grass when there was nothing else. Her skin was the color of earth and crisscrossed with deep wrinkles etched into her still-young flesh, like the cracks in the earth at Ai Mar when there was a drought.

She hid the money she was able to save in a hole next to the fireplace. Nothing in the world, not even the fear of death, would have convinced her to deposit it in an account at the post office.

But she still went from time to time to inquire about the money her husband had deposited, and did everything she could to convince the clerk to give it to her. Each time, she left murmuring insults and curses under her breath, wishing for a thunderbolt to strike him down, because he had her money and would not give it to her. Money with which she could have bought and farmed a piece of land. With which she could have sent her boy to school. But still, she was determined that he would study, because she had made a promise, and also out of spite. She would keep him at home until he learned how to read and write, even if it killed her.

At night she wove baskets out of leftover straw from the threshing floor, repaired sacks, stuffed chairs. After a while she was able to buy a hen, which she kept under the bed. Every day she fed her son a fresh egg and in the spring she set the hen. She killed one of the cockerels and fed it to her son on the Feast of San Rocco. She sold the rest. With the money she set aside, she bought a piglet at the farm fair, a chubby, grunting little female with a curly tail.

ROCCO WAS A LONELY CHILD. The long hours he had spent as an unweaned baby wrapped in swaddling clothes under a tree, staring out at the threatening world around him—tree branches swinging in the breeze, shrieking birds, the burning sun and the arid wind—stewing in his own excrement while his mother worked and could not come to ease his discomfort and hunger, had marked him forever. He was alone his whole life, even later when he was surrounded by Communist comrades, by fellow protesters, by the farmers whom he taught to read and write, by his wife's colorful and plentiful family, and by his own daughter.

His mother's ferocious love did not keep him warm, in fact it dismayed him, but there was nothing he could do; it is easier to fend off hatred than love. He bore it stoically. Lucrezia did everything she could to separate him from the rest of the world. She did not send him into the fields, as was commonly done when children were four or five years old to familiarize them with hard work. She raised him to be a gentleman, with clean hands and a melancholy gaze, always ill at ease, shy, but loved by all.

Even as a boy he had been serious and reticent. It was difficult for him to recognize humor, but when he laughed, he lost all sense of proportion. He felt awkward in groups because he did not know how to behave; he was neither a gentleman nor a farmer.

Whenever Lucrezia saw one of the farmers' lice-and-tick-ridden children approaching, she would drive him away with her broom. If he came back, she threw rocks. She was especially ruthless with the Della Rabbias, her own blood. She threatened to kill them if she ever saw one of them come near her son. She was afraid they would steal his food or taint him with their poverty. She dragged him away and told him not to answer if they spoke to him. He wasn't like them. She reminded him of the money waiting for him at the post office, and made him swear that he would never trust anyone. Rocco sacrificed himself to his mother's love, and repaid it with a feeling he could not name. His childhood was illuminated by a single bond of affection, his love for his pet pig.

Chapter Nine

When Fascism arrived in the town, all the dons immediately joined the party. Don Gabriele, Don Raffaele, and Don Valentino hired only day laborers who carried a party card. They sat for hours on the sidewalk in front of the landowners' club in the piazza expecting everyone who passed to pay his respects. Groups of children, back from the "heliotherapy camps" where they were conditioned to employ violence at the slightest suggestion of dissent, which could include as little as a disrespectful salute or an insolent glance, saluted them and stood at attention. They showed no mercy, even for their elders.

The farmers became even more taciturn than they already were, and bowed their heads—after all, they were used to it—but they weren't particularly enthusiastic supporters. They got used to allowing their children a day off from the fields so they could participate in Fascist activities on Saturdays.

The parades, the uniform consisting of breeches, black shirt, and fez, Mussolini's thunderous speeches . . . People looked upon these things with the diffidence and irony they reserved for anything unusual. The children chanted, *"Duce, Duce, portaci la luce!"* ("Duce, Duce, bring us light!"), but their parents shook their heads. They had never expected anything from anyone, and if someone gave them something, they were convinced it was a trap.

Along the Via Nuova, the bushes and wild grasses were pruned, creating perfectly squared edges from which nary a leaf dared to protrude, perhaps as an illustration of what would happen to anyone who dared to deviate from the accepted path. The townsfolk looked upon such precision as a kind of miracle, while asking themselves what purpose it could possibly serve.

The most enthusiastic adherents to the party line were the idlers, most especially Oreste Falcone, Don Francesco's much anticipated son. Before, he had wielded power only over children, Candida's children in particular, whom he tyrannized at every opportunity. The opportunities were not many, however, because his sly niece kept a wary eye on him at all times.

At the age of sixty-something, Oreste became inflamed by the ideas of Mussolini. What attracted him the most was the promise that Italy would become an empire, that it would conquer its place in the sun. For him, Ethiopia became the embodiment of the kingdom that destiny had stolen from him.

He walked around town proudly, whistling student songs under his breath. Since the party encouraged volunteers, he was given small tasks to perform, and he spent his days at party headquarters, gathering information about the activities of the Italian army in Ethiopia and announcing them to the town in the warlike terms he had quickly adopted.

People saluted him deferentially, and then snickered behind his back with a mixture of fear, amusement, and pity, as they always had. But Oreste was no longer willing to ignore such slights; he felt his moment had finally come. When his comrades treated him with derision and laughed behind his back, he had no choice but to suffer in silence, but beneath the surface his vicious nature rebelled and he cultivated a secret desire for revenge.

He began to test his power over the townsfolk. If someone was bold enough to make a joke about Mussolini, he could count on being called into the party offices the following day. The slightest complaint came to the attention of the "authorities," and appropriate sanctions were applied: beatings, exile, the revocation of licenses. Little by little people began to trace these punishments back to Oreste, who was quite capable of inventing transgressions in order to get revenge for ancient affronts. And there was no shortage of people he wanted to punish, because over the years he had accumulated a massive dose of resentment.

But his greatest enemies were in his own home, in his family, who had always tolerated him, seldom feared him, and never loved him. His principal target was the placid Colino, who stood at the very heart of the family, strong and silent as an oak tree, never needing to impose his will in order to make his authority felt.

Oreste considered him a traitor because at first he had not even bothered to obtain a party card. Not that he was heroic or intended to resist the regime, but he had a few simple principles that he always followed, the first of which was: Stay away from politics. He had inherited this belief from his father, Minguccio the Merchant, who, in turn, had inherited it from his grandfather and a long line of merchants. All attempts to convince Colino of the advantages of joining had proved fruitless. He would close in on himself, as he did when Candida wanted to force him to try a new dish. But when he was thrown out of the merchants' association, he had to accept that times had changed. He could no longer follow the advice of his father and grandfather. Even if he did not approve of Fascism—just as, for the same reasons, he would never have approved of Communism—he forked over the five lire for the party card.

But he continued to buy and sell on the black market. He would buy whatever portion of the harvest the farmers were able to hide from the officials under the table and at free-market prices. Then he would quietly resell it to the mills in the area, who were obligated by law to buy from farm consortia in quantities that were always insufficient. The officials turned a blind eye to these activities, except when they received a tip-off.

Shortly after the harvest, when Colino's storerooms held a large quantity of illicit grain, he might have ended up in jail if Ida Miranda, the wife of the police chief—who, as everyone knew, nurtured a platonic passion for Colino—had not rushed over to warn him just as the family was sitting down to dinner.

Colino and his older sons spent the entire night in the storeroom, concealing bags of grain behind the mess he kept in there. Candida stayed at home with the little ones, her stomach filled with venom.

At dawn the inspectors came. They turned the place upside down, but came up empty-handed and eventually gave up, warning Colino to play by the rules.

It was never known who had set things in motion. But one morning in the piazza, on the wall where advertisements and proclamations were usually hung, someone pinned up photographs of Oreste dressed in women's clothes, wearing eye shadow and lipstick. They all tried to keep the news from Concetta, but she was the first to mention it at the table, during one of her rare moments of lucidity. Obviously, she had always known. "Thank God," she said placidly, "my dear departed husband was killed by the bandits." Albina swore she was so ashamed that she would never leave the house again, but the truth was she hadn't gone out in years. Candida said nothing.

Everyone else laughed about it for months and made insinu-
ating remarks, even after Oreste had been missing for a while.
That day when he went out in the street he noticed that everyone
was staring at him and smiling; when he reached the piazza he
discovered the reason for their hilarity.

People watched as he walked around to the other side of the
wall, his back as erect as his age allowed, breeches swishing like
sails, fez sitting proudly on his head. He was never heard from
again. The tomb that his father had prepared for him, with a
photograph and his date of birth, remained empty. In the space
for his date of death was a question mark.

Nic non vol le maccarun ca so pic.

No one wants the macaroni,
'cause there's not enough anyway.

Chapter Ten

ere, piggy, piggy, piggy. Here, piggy, piggy," was heard all over town. A moment later, Rocco would appear, followed by the pig, or the pig followed by Rocco. They spent their days together grazing in empty lots amid garbage, digging holes in the ground, rolling down hills, chasing after each other, or playing hide-and-seek, and staring up at the sky. They were friends, siblings, mother and son, father and daughter, and every other relationship that can unite two living beings.

At first Rocco paid no attention to the pig, just as he paid little attention to anything having to do with the countryside and animals. But one day there was a storm.

Even though it was still dark, Lucrezia had already left for work. Rocco was in bed when he heard the first thunderbolts crashing like metal. A deep silence froze everything in its place for a few moments, and then he heard a rumbling sound. Hail began to beat down against the windows and water poured from the sky, as if to flood the town.

Rocco was suddenly seized by an overwhelming, monstrous wave of terror, as if he were a ship in a storm, or as if it were the end of days. It was an ancient fear, older than he, and so overpowering that he felt himself drowning in it. He began to sob, knowing that no one would come to console him.

Something moist and warm touched his leg. It was the piglet's snout, as she looked up with her beady blue eyes and began to tenderly lick his leg. Rocco pulled away; he wasn't used to being touched, and it frightened him. But again the pig licked his leg. Hesitantly, Rocco reached out and touched the pig. Then he pulled her toward him. The animal grunted with pleasure. They waited together, in each other's arms, until the storm ended, and from that day on they became inseparable.

Rocco could not fall asleep without holding the pig in his arms. During the cold winter nights she kept him warm, and a few times she probably saved him from freezing to death. With her, he was able to experience the full range of affection. When he first noticed her, she was small, plump, and pink as a newborn; he watched her grow, as spirited as a young boy, until she was as big as and then bigger than he was—he had the dimensions of an underfed child—and eventually became enormous. He abandoned himself to her consoling embrace, drowning in her warm flesh and sweet fragrance.

Even Lucrezia loved the pig, in her own way. When she came back from the fields she prepared its mush with great care, almost as much as she applied to making her son's soup. She herself ate almost nothing. She was content to look at the pig and caress it with her eyes.

In February, when pigs are slaughtered, Lucrezia went to talk to Luigino the butcher, and they made an appointment for the following day. But at dawn when she got up she found neither her son in his bed nor the pig beneath it. She searched in vain the entire day. She begged for help from everyone in the town, and even went to the police, crying and pleading for help; she crisscrossed the bare fields calling out for her son at the top of her lungs. No one could keep up with her, not even the dogs. The night passed, and still she hadn't found him. People whispered about bandits, devils, and Gypsies, but Lucrezia did not lose hope. The following day at dawn, Giovanni Mastrandrea and Ciccillo Sarchiella, two generous souls, joined her search.

The weather was uncertain, with puffy gray clouds covering the sky. It looked like it might rain. She found Rocco at the edge of the forest of Salandra, under an oak tree, hugging the pig in his arms, half dead from cold and fear. When Lucrezia saw him she slapped him so hard it practically knocked his teeth out, and then she began to kiss him over and over, as if she would never stop.

The pig was spared. They kept her so she would produce a litter.

The following year Rocco started elementary school. He needed a pinafore, notebooks, and some presents to butter up the teacher. At Christmas, she explained the advantages of joining a Fascist youth group, becoming first a *Figlio della Lupa*, and later a *Balilla*. He would have access to the mutual aid society, summer camp, gymnastics, and the tuberculosis clinic should he need it. But he would have to buy a uniform. And Lucrezia did not have money to buy a uniform.

On a cold, windy day in February, Lucrezia asked Rocco to fetch the pig. She told him that she had made a bet with her friend from Trivigno, who refused to believe how big the pig had grown, and so they needed to weigh her. Rocco believed his mother. But the pig knew.

It took four people to tie her up in Colino's yard, and still it was no easy task. She struggled with all her might, as if she had a presentiment of what was about to happen, and bit Rocco's arm. The small, pale mark never disappeared, and would swell up slightly on humid days. She weighed almost four hundred pounds, Rocco told his mother proudly.

The following day when he went to fetch her, she refused to follow him. Rocco had to use all of his tricks to convince her. He scratched her neck for a long time, and then kissed her ear, and she trembled. Finally won over, the pig complied.

When they reached Luigino's house, he was sharpening his knives. Felice and Chinuccio swooped down on the animal. The pig struggled, letting out screams that could be heard from the Via Nuova. It sounded like a person calling for help. Rocco watched the scene in stunned silence, unable to react. The men picked her up and placed her on a wooden table with raised sides, like a coffin. On one end there was a hole, through which they stuck the pig's head. Meanwhile, they bound her legs. Rocco stood in a corner, silent and pale. The pig watched him, pleading for help, but he could do nothing. Luigino plunged the knife into the pig's neck, and she let out an excruciating scream. Luigino turned the knife, taking care not to kill the pig right away. It took half an hour for the blood to flow out and for the animal to quiet down. Lucrezia held a basin under the gushing fluid. *"Ca pozz scttà un sagn d'angann!"* ("May you vomit blood!") She collected the blood and stirred it. Then she added raisins, dried figs, almonds, milk, and sugar. She placed the mixture over the fire and stirred it as big, flaccid bubbles formed on the surface.

Meanwhile Luigino, Felice, and Chinuccio picked up a cauldron of boiling water and poured it over the pig. The air was filled with vapor and the nauseating smell of cooked bristle. Her eyes by now veiled, the animal gave Rocco a final look that he did not forget for the rest of his days. Luigino and Chinuccio scraped off the bristle with their knives. Rocco's mother asked him, "Come on, why don't you help them?" Rocco did not move. The knives traveled quickly back and forth across the pig's body. Soon she turned the tender pink color of a naked woman.

They straightened her body in the coffin. When every centime-
ter had turned a pale pink, they picked her up and hung her, upside down, from the doorframe. With a single stroke of the knife,
Luigino sliced the pig open from top to bottom. He worked his
way quickly inside, extracting the liver, lungs, and heart. He un-
wound the intestines with the agility of a juggler. Lucrezia emptied them, washed them, and left them to soak in water mixed
with orange peels.

Meanwhile, the blood sausage had cooked, cooled down, and
congealed. Lucrezia served some on a plate. She gave it to Luigino, Felice, and Chinuccio to taste. "What about you, would
you like some?" Rocco didn't move. "Have some blood sausage,
come on. Why don't you say anything?" Lucrezia took a big
spoonful and stuck it in Rocco's mouth. Rocco felt the grainy,
soft substance beneath his palate and tasted the sickly sweet flavor, with its faint bloody aftertaste. It slid down his throat, and he
managed to swallow. The sickening taste invaded his body. His
stomach rose up and out of his ears. He threw up over and over
again. He threw up everything, even his soul.

Chapter Eleven

ho put a spell on you? The evil eye, dark thoughts, and envy. Who will release you? The Father, the Son, and the Holy Ghost. Who put a spell on you? The evil eye, dark thoughts, and envy. Who will release you? The Father, the Son, and the Holy Ghost. Who put a spell on you?"

"I believe in God, the Father Almighty, Creator of Heaven and earth. And in Jesus Christ, His only Son . . ."

"Our Father, Who art in Heaven, hallowed be Thy Name. Thy kingdom come. Thy will be done . . ."

"Hail, Mary, mother of mercy; our life, our sweetness, and our hope . . ."

Yawning and with tears running down her face, the witch doctor went to the dispensary to fetch more salt and three smoldering pieces of wood she had lit on the hearth. She dropped them in a basin of water, dipped her left hand in the liquid, and made the sign of the cross on Rocco's forehead.

When it was all over, Lucrezia gave the witch a feisty cockerel she had brought along as payment, took Rocco's hand, and departed. For two years, they had visited all the witch doctors in Salandra, Tricarico, Valsinni, and the town that cannot be named. To no avail. No one had been able to undo the evil eye, but they all agreed that it was a spell. A spell so strong it could not be undone. Who had cast this spell? One witch doctor said it had to be a man, because she yawned when she said Pater; another said it was a woman, because she had reached the Ave Maria; and a soothsayer in Genzano hazarded to say that it had been a priest, because she had gotten to the Gloria. Lucrezia treated everyone with suspicion, man, woman, priest, or nun, convincing herself in turn that this or that person was responsible, and cursing him in her heart.

For two years, Rocco had not spoken. She sent him to school and he learned to read and write, but he did not utter a word. He understood everything and did all his schoolwork: he drew lines on the page, then letters, and finally words. He placed the accent marks in the appropriate spots, employed commas correctly, but his mouth refused to form even a single syllable. Lucrezia had tried everything, even startling him in the middle of the night. But still, he did not speak. What little Lucrezia owned, she gave to the witch doctors. Her young rooster. A basket of snails. Wild berries. She handed it all over to them. In return, they rubbed Rocco's forehead, intoned spells, and absorbed the evil eye until they fell asleep. And still, nothing. This spell was so powerful that it refused to go away. It was a trap set by misfortune. "May they vomit blood! All I had was my son, and look what they've done to him . . ."

The only witch she hadn't visited was Zí Giuseppe in Albano. Lucrezia hadn't gone there yet because it was far and difficult to reach. She took her son's hand one August afternoon; they hitched a ride on a truck to Tricarico and then walked from there. They walked down toward the valley of the Basento, among eagle and vulture nests. By the time they crossed the bridge they were dusty, their lips were parched, and their feet were covered with sores. In an open area above the cliff there was an ancient house that looked as if it might crumble at any moment. It was dark inside.

Lucrezia could hardly distinguish the man who stood there, but as her eyes grew accustomed to the darkness, his features appeared increasingly monstrous. His large nose was covered with warts. His eyes were small, blue, shiny, and clear. His ears were enormous, with tufts of hair sticking out. But his lips were full and shapely, like those of a beautiful girl. He turned to Rocco, placed his hand on the boy's head, and stared at Lucrezia inquisitively. She shuddered at the thought that he had immediately understood what was wrong. She remembered that someone had told her that Zí Giuseppe was born before Jesus Christ. Then, little by little, the beating of her heart quieted down, as she remembered that he was a friend to the poor and would not ask her for money. Each gave what he could afford.

Giuseppe picked a card out of the deck, placed it on his chest, then held it out and stared at it for a long time. Lucrezia waited in silence. Giuseppe placed the card back in the deck. He shuffled the deck and asked Lucrezia to cut it. The cards were unlike any she had seen. One had an illustration of a dog, another a blaze of fire, another, three hearts. "It's not the evil eye, it's witchcraft." He made the sign of the cross on Rocco's forehead, opened his mouth, and made the sign of the cross on his tongue as well. Then he put a finger in his own ear and stood there for a long time, listening. He told Rocco to go outside and wait.

"The son and the mother are linked," he said to Lucrezia.

He took a piece of yarn, wound it around his index fingers, and asked Lucrezia to cut it with her teeth. He held out a mirror and asked her to show herself to it. Lucrezia was mortified, but she forced herself to comply for her son's sake. Rocco watched all this through a crack in the door. He saw his mother open her dress and the reflection of her pale, youthful, fresh breast, in contrast with her face, which was old and shriveled. He saw Zí

Giuseppe place his hands on his mother's skin as he pushed her dress aside, exposing her white, firm body, the round behind that had once charmed Rocco's father, her belly, her finely drawn navel, and her wrinkled hands and face. Rocco was amazed.

He opened the door impetuously and peered inside. The contrast between the darkness inside and the brightness outside blinded him. He threw himself on Giuseppe, punching him with his small fists. *"Basta! Basta!"* Then he turned to his mother. *"Andiamo via,"* he said, in perfect Italian, "let's get out of here." Lucrezia pulled her dress back on and fell to her knees, kissing Giuseppe's feet, bathing them with her tears, as Mary Magdalen had kissed the feet of Christ. "My child!" she cried out as she fell into Rocco's arms and pinched his cheeks with her calloused hands, covering him with voracious kisses. Rocco and Zí Giuseppe exchanged a tense look, full of rivalry. Even though Rocco was only a child, he had adult eyes, tired and serious, while those of Zí Giuseppe sparkled with childish malice and adolescent vigor.

In payment, Lucrezia gave Zí Giuseppe the most precious thing she owned, the braid she had cut off at the age of sixteen, the day she was married. The hair in the braid was black and thick as twine, and the filaments that escaped from it pricked her fingers. Zí Giuseppe caressed the heavy braid in the palm of his hand; it looked like a mouse. Then they left.

On the way back, they took the reverse route, but no one gave them a ride. They walked for two days and two nights before reaching their home. They stopped to drink from the Basento river, to rest beneath the oak trees, and they ate berries, acacia flowers, and cardoons. Lucrezia held Rocco's hand with an iron grip. From time to time, she would kiss his blessed lips. *"Oh figgh mí, ce aggh patut, t'avevan nvidiat, t'avevan affatturat, ca pozzn sctt vlen, figgh mí, famm sent com parl bell."* ("My boy! You can talk!

They put a spell on you, may they vomit poison, my boy, let me hear you speak!") "Yes, mamma, I can speak now." And he recited the Giovanni Pascoli poem: "Oh Valentino, with your new clothes, / like the spines on the hawthorn! / On your tiny feet, marked by the briar bush, / you wear the shoes your mother made you." "What are you saying, child? I can't understand you!" And he began again, "I love you, oh sweet, beloved Italy, glorious and beloved motherland; the soul, with a new joy, has learned to love you better . . ." "How well you speak, my boy, but what are you saying?" And they went on like this, with her speaking in dialect, and him in classroom Italian, which his Fascist schoolteacher had taught him with the aid of raps on the fingers. "What are you saying, child? What did you say?"

Part

II

The remains of Cro-Magnon man had not yet decomposed in their semi-circular tombs on the Murge plateau in an area of Basilicata about one hundred kilometers from the Puglia coast when the first human settlements were being established in the caves above the Gravina. A few centuries later, the Sassi in Matera were the troglodyte capital of the peasant world.

These homes dug out of limestone were occupied at various times in history by the Italiots and the dispossessed of all races: Albanian refugees, Greek monks, heretics, Jews fleeing oppression. Once they settled into the rocky abodes that resembled cavities, these peoples quickly forgot their places of origin and the reasons for their departure. They had one thing in common: hunger. Matera presided over the hunger of the surrounding lands; it was at the heart of a vicious cycle of exhausted laborers who went from farm to farm, feeding a dysfunctional system. And all around it, the towns of Grassano, Miglionico, Ferrandina, Montescaglioso, and Grottole perched on the crumbling cliffs. They had no history, only hunger.

Chapter Twelve

When Albina turned eighty-nine and Costanza ninety, Costanza asked if they could meet. They had not spoken since the day Costanza had run off with the local priest, even though they lived in a town of no more than three thousand people. The few times Albina had caught a glimpse of her, she had quickly crossed the street or hidden in a doorway. But those were rare occasions, because Costanza, served and revered by her sons and daughters-in-law, seldom had cause to leave the house. But on this occasion, despite the fact that she was the elder of the two, she made the effort to go to her sister's house.

She had become very fat but still moved with self-assurance. Her full-moon face exuded an air of well-being and she had the same boat-shaped belly as her sister.

Albina received her in Candida's bedroom. They did not make the slightest reference to the reason they had not seen each other in almost a century. With an Olympian composure, Costanza asked her sister about children and grandchildren and told her about her own, and about the bedspreads she had made for their trousseaux. Before leaving, Costanza said that she was happy to see Albina looking so well.

No sooner had she gone downstairs than Albina began to complain of a terrible headache, strange pains, light-headedness. She was convinced that she was about to die. Envy. Her sister. Her sister had given her the evil eye. Did you hear what she said? How well you look. Mmmmmm. Did you see how she looked at me? Mmmmmm. Candida had to put her foot down to keep Albina from going to the hospital in Matera, where she was convinced she would expire.

Instead, it was Concetta who died, a few days later, on a spring morning.

She got up earlier than usual, without a sound, as if she were afraid that someone might stop her. In the unusually quiet house, one could hear little more than a grumbling here, a sigh there, and the heavy breathing of many sleeping bodies. Concetta dragged her feet over to the chest in the storage room. With trembling hands, she pulled out a needlepoint bedspread and then the cretonne bedspread beneath it. It smelled of dust. Who knows how she managed to open the chest; she was so old that it was difficult for her even to raise a spoon to her mouth. She pulled out a length of immaculate linen. Beneath it lay a dress she had placed there many years earlier, and which she checked from time to time. It was black, made from fine cloth.

Concetta put it on with the same agitation she would have felt if she had been dressing for her wedding. All those years since the wedding with Don Francesco had failed to materialize, her wedding gown had hung in a closet.

That morning she felt well, better than she had for years.

Little by little, she had lost interest. In money, in her children, in her grandchildren and her great-grandchildren. She confused their names and forgot their birthdays. There were too many names, too many things to keep track of. She dreamed of the pink and black marble vault in the family tomb that was going to waste. She dreamed of Don Francesco, who awaited her in the afterlife and had surely grown impatient.

She lay down on her bed with her hands crossed over her stomach, wearing the jewelry she had refused to take off since the day the barrels had been found. They buried her like that, like the statue of the Immaculate Virgin on her feast day, the hunger of her childhood long forgotten. They cried sweet tears for her, as soft as the March showers that soaked the earth on the day of her funeral.

MIMMO, HER FAVORITE GREAT-GRANDCHILD, did not hear about her death until one week later, when his mother came to visit. He had been gone a few years. He was studying in Matera, where he rented a room in the home of Marietta the widow. Rocco also had a room there. The widow's house was built out of volcanic rock, and overlooked the Sassi district.

From its narrow windows they could watch the lives of their neighbors, and observe them cohabiting with their animals, squatting to shit behind containers, and sometimes coupling there as well.

Once, just after his arrival, Rocco had lost his way among the houses of the Sassi neighborhood. He wandered around, climbing up and down steps, too shy to ask for help, until he spotted the castle and was able to orient himself. Since then neither he nor Mimmo ever went to the Sassi, and they looked away whenever they passed by, as if it were a breeding ground for infection. They had learned to lie whenever someone asked where they lived, because the Sassi was a source of shame, something to be kept at arm's length.

Rocco and Mimmo were better off than most of the students because of the packages Mimmo received from his mother, which he shared with his friend. Rocco also received provisions from home. Once every two weeks Lucrezia would walk from Grottole to Matera with an egg, a snail and oregano pie, roasted sparrows, and the fruit left on the trees after the harvest.

She would tell him to hide the food and eat it by himself, not to share it with anyone. She would stress the word "anyone," staring at Mimmo.

Lucrezia went on and on about how difficult it had been to bring these things, how she had walked the entire distance from the fields under sun and rain. She mentioned all the times she had stumbled as she crossed a river, and the voices she had heard in the dark as she walked through the fields at night; she swore on her grave that someone—someone from beyond the grave—had tugged at her skirt . . . And she would tell him of her masters' unexpected acts of generosity. They respected her because she never shrank from work, no matter how difficult, and she was paid less than the others, and so was like part of the family. Lucrezia had perfected the art of lying, and the more she invented these things she had seen or felt, the less she was able to distinguish reality from fiction. She spent her final years in a state of constant hallucination, in the company of her many ghosts at the Villa Clara, the immaculate rest home where Rocco took her to live, hoping she would finally be able to find peace.

As soon as Lucrezia departed, Rocco was faced with a dilemma. He and Mimmo shared everything, but if he shared his food he would be disobeying his mother. Either way, he would be betraying someone. In the end he shared his food with Mimmo, who accepted only in order to avoid offending him. Later, he secretly threw the gifts away. Meanwhile Rocco suffered from a tortured conscience.

Rocco and Mimmo had discovered each other at the seminary after spending their childhood in the same alleyways. They had become inseparable.

Mimmo had come to Matera when he was eleven, in accordance with the vow Candida had made before he was born. A thought tormented him: he did not want to become a priest. Every night he reflected on his dilemma and was overcome by a deep sense of guilt, an emotion which the priests had had ample time to acquaint him with. He basked in the indignity and mortification of his betrayal, invoking a God he did not believe in for salvation.

Despite knowing what the future had in store for him, before he left for Matera he had not worried much about it. Candida had great trust in him; her plans for her children, which were extremely precise, included one priest, one teacher, and one doctor, and she never imagined for an instant that she might be disappointed.

The fact that Mimmo was an unmanageable child did not worry her in the least. From the moment he learned to walk, her eldest son had spent his days wandering around town, tearing his trousers when he climbed trees, and getting his shoes stolen when he removed them in order to wade in a stream or for the simple pleasure of going barefoot. He and Rocco had sometimes played together, for example pushing a bicycle wheel down the street with a stick, but they weren't exactly friends. They were both members of a band of boys that laid waste to kitchen gardens, stole fruit from other people's orchards, and braided horses' tails, always laying the blame for their mischief on Monachicchio, the ghost of children who perished before being baptized. Candida invoked the help of God the Father, because Mimmo's vocation had still not manifested itself. Later on, she asked for Don Arcangelo's help, and that was how Mimmo ended up at the seminary.

Before that day, Mimmo had never really reflected on the word "seminary," which he had heard as long as he could remember, or on what that word actually meant. Now, suddenly, he knew its meaning, because he was there. The waxen cheeks of the priests. Their liquid, dull eyes. Their trembling hands and voices.

In the stagnant air beneath the arches of the seminary, he guarded his dark secret. He was convinced that terrible things would happen if he shared his secret with anyone. Demons would come in the night and take him away, prick him, poke him, and roast him alive. He dared not even imagine how awful Hell must be. He kept his mouth shut and did not reveal his secret to anyone, especially not to his mother, who came to visit him once a month. But he knew that this terrible sin, the worst of all sins, was imprinted in his soul, where God could certainly see it. He did not believe.

"Father, I don't believe in God. I don't believe in God, the Father Almighty, Creator of Heaven and earth. God's will seems like a stupid children's game. Ten Our Fathers, fifty Hail Marys, repeat the Act of Contrition a hundred times until it works its way into your mind and heart. God forgive me, I don't believe in you, I have doubts, my heart is full of questions. Punish me, strike me down, but don't let me lose my way."

By the end of his third year he had had his fill of deacons lurking behind the curtains, of not being allowed to laugh during Lent, and of seeing how the workmen grabbed their crotches in order to fend off bad luck whenever the seminary students walked by, so young and dressed all in black.

One Sunday morning when he was assisting at Mass, he began to curse the Virgin and all the saints, softly at first, then louder and louder, until his voice rang out clear and true in the church. He drew from the fine repertory of insults his grandfather Vincenzo had taught his mother when she was a little girl, emphasizing each new epithet with a swing of the censer: God the dog, God the pig, Madonna the cow, the shameless whore. A boy sitting in the first row wilted and fainted to the floor; it was unclear whether in response to the blasphemy or to the suffocating waves of incense so early in the morning, and on an empty stomach.

When they sent for Candida to inform her of what had happened, she was speechless for a moment, as if struck by some sort of facial paralysis. She sat in the frowning presence of Father Virgilio and Father Mario, who at first took her silence for contrition and were prepared to forgive the sacrilege after a serious show of penance. Then she let out a quiet groan, almost a whisper, like a ball beginning to inflate, and in front of the two horrified priests who knew nothing of her life or the trials she had suffered as a child, she began to laugh uncontrollably.

Mimmo heard nothing of this episode. He was kicked out of the seminary and bore the burden of his remorse for the rest of his life.

ROCCO WENT TO THE SEMINARY because it was the only way for him to receive an education. The priests were willing to cover the tuition for children who had a vocation, and so, on his mother's instructions, he feigned a calling. But the irony was that he truly had the vocation.

It had come accidentally.

Lucrezia had never paid much attention to religion. Except for the procession on Holy Friday, which she always took part in, her feet bare and hair loose, in an attempt to expiate a year's worth of sins, her most frequent communication with God was in the form of insults related to the old debt he still owed her.

She worked even on Sundays and had no money to spare for

charity. Rocco did not go to catechism, nor did he say his prayers before going to bed. But after the third grade, when he was preparing for his entrance examinations, his mother sent him to Father Giuseppe in Grassano for tutoring.

He went three times a week to study Latin. In return, he washed the priest's feet and did a few errands. Lucrezia paid what she could.

Like Candida, Lucrezia had very precise notions about her son's future, but they were the opposite of Candida's. Rocco would get his diploma and become a teacher. And get married. When he reached the legal age, he could use the money the dear departed had left him to buy a piece of land and there she would build a house for him and his children, who she hoped would all be boys.

As he cultivated his secret vocation, Rocco developed the habit of taking refuge in a hidden corner of his mind where the inexplicable mysteries of the world—his mother's voracious love, the lies he was forced to tell, and the expectations of others—could not reach him. He revealed his thoughts to no one. Mimmo was his only friend. Brought together by their need to betray either themselves or the people they loved most, condemned to futures they would have preferred to exchange, they found comfort in their shared doubts.

On one of their free days off, by chance, they went into a used bookstore. Neither of them had a particular interest in literature, but a book caught their attention because of the title on its worn cover. It sounded like an exciting story, full of crimes and adventures. When they went to pay, the owner of the shop looked at them with a mischievous grin. The author of the book was Dostoevski. The book was *Crime and Punishment*.

Thereafter, they returned to the shop every week. They sold one book to buy the next. To cover the difference, Rocco would sell the eggs his mother brought him.

They discovered a world they had never even imagined, often as filled with suffering as their own, but where there was always hope, or meaning, or a possibility of change. It was a completely new concept for them, one that opened infinite possibilities and at the same time eliminated all certainties. They careened toward adolescence like two derailed trains, digging a trench around themselves that separated them from the rest of the world, or at least from their world.

They discovered England, full of thieves and beggars; the titanic struggle against nature in the New World; Paris, the destination of tormented Russian nobles and setting of titillating novels that initiated them into the mysteries of sex. They made a pact that one day they, too, would go there.

One pallid gray morning at seven o'clock, Gioia arrived at the Gare de Lyon. It was the first time she had seen Paris. The traffic along the quays, the Seine, the Pont Neuf, the boulevards with their gray light and soothing sounds, the fragrance of butter croissants, the colorful wooden signs of the shops—all this captured her imagination as if it were the realization of a dream that had been waiting for her since the beginning of time.

ROCCO STAYED AT THE SEMINARY longer than Mimmo. Every year Mimmo was sent back, because even though Don Giuseppe had taught him to love the Good Lord, he had neglected to inculcate in him the most basic rules of grammar. He was so taciturn by nature that he found it difficult to speak when the teacher asked him a question. His only advantage was his obstinacy. He failed the first year, then he completed two years at once and failed again, and then three years at once, and again failed. In the final year, when his mother suggested that he leave the seminary, he gathered all his courage and said no. Then he fell ill with tuberculosis. He spent several months in a sanatorium, but he survived. When he was well again he could no longer return to the gelid walls of the seminary, and so, finally, he gave up, said his good-byes to the priests and to Jesus Christ, and joined Mimmo at the widow's house before attempting the impossible—four years of school in one.

In the end, despite all the lost battles, like Napoleon—with whom he shared both his diminutive stature and his incisiveness—he won the war. He and Mimmo graduated on the same day.

Candida took them out to dinner at a trattoria and did not say a word to her son about the promise she had failed to keep. She consoled herself with the thought that at least there would not be another defrocked priest in the family. She was already developing a new plan for her son, unbeknownst to him. He was consumed by the secret fear that one day the Almighty would pay him back for his betrayal by punishing him or his loved ones. He was saved from this torment only later on, by his discovery of historical materialism.

After graduation, Rocco took the competitive exams for a teaching position. He applied for a spot in the province of Reggio Emilia, because he had heard that there was less competition. He was offered a job, swore loyalty to the National Fascist Party, and was given a party card. Then he left.

Chapter Thirteen

Cleanliness. This was what Alba desired more than anything. Animal excrement on the roadside turned her stomach inside out, as did the yellowish, thick fingernails of farm laborers, framed in black like funerary announcements, and the sweetish stable smell of the women in the town, bare-bummed babies with snotty noses, scabby dogs, the pigs that trotted around with their placid, bouncing flesh, chickens under the bed, the herds of goats that returned in the evening from the fields trailing their pungent odor, and the clouds of flies that hovered over figs laid out to dry. Alba was disgusted by the heavy exhalations of women who breathed in her face, and by food, which rots inside of you and becomes shit.

Ever since she was a little girl, she had shrunk in horror whenever someone tried to touch her, caress her, or worst of all, kiss her. She would hide in a corner like a hunted animal, and when there was no other solution, she would bite. She would leave a clock-shaped wound on the offender's arm, each indentation left by her small, tapered teeth sprouting a tiny drop of blood. Such was her reluctance to be touched that her mother had never been able to cut her hair or braid it like the other girls'. Her hair hung down to her ankles, like a long, black, undulating cape in which she could conceal herself. All one could see were her enormous black eyes in the middle of a tiny face. She was very thin. Not only did she not want to be touched, but she refused to eat.

Not completely. She ingested just enough food to ensure her survival. Three grapes, a wedge of orange, two chickpeas. She ate elegantly, without pleasure, after a lengthy inspection of the morsel she was about to place in her mouth. Only when the inspection was complete would she accept to introduce the foreign object into her oral cavity. Once there, she moved it lazily around with her tongue as her eyes assumed an indifferent expression and she waited for the salivary fluids to begin the corrosive process. She shifted the morsel left and right, like a crocodile waiting for its gastric fluids to do their work after swallowing its prey whole. It was as if, instead of a grape, her mouth contained an entire steer, horns included. Only after that would she decide to sink her teeth into it, with a clean slice of the incisors, dividing the object in half. Then she paused again, after which she once again divided the morsel with another slice of the incisors. She hated to use her molars; the idea of reducing food to mush disgusted her.

Her manners had created an atmosphere of admiration around her like a glass bubble. Protected from the outside world by her immaculate clothing and pallid skin, Alba spent her days in a dreamy solitude, barely deigning to touch the ground with the soles of her shoes, carefully avoiding friendship and affection.

She had a habit of counting things. The number of steps she had to climb to reach her house. The number of paces between the piazza and the Via Nuova, the number of stars in the spring sky. She counted the days since she had been born, and added up the days, minutes, and seconds her father, mother, and all her brothers had been alive. She felt comfortable in this highly synchronized world. Her relationships were clean, without waste or imperfections.

When she went to her father's shop, everyone was amazed. While her brothers played with blue copper sulphate crystals and rolled around in the barrels of beans, she performed complicated calculations in her head. Everyone considered her a superior being with almost magical attributes.

She had no friends, nor did she want any. She didn't play with apricot pits, spitting on them and rubbing them against a rock until they broke apart. She didn't dig in the yard for shiny stones. She didn't listen to her mother's stories, which fascinated her brothers. She felt affection only for Filomena the donkey. She would visit her every day and stay half an hour; on her return, she was happy and serene. Whenever someone questioned anything she said, she claimed that Filomena had told her it was so.

At first Candida did not pay much attention to these peculiarities, busy as she was with her sons, her beloved husband, and her next-to-last child, a delicious boy who was all dimples and smiles. Candida dressed him in frills until well past his third birthday. At times, she felt that Alba was not her child. It was as if she had simply loaned her body so that this child could come into the world, like the farm wives who bore children for rich ladies unable to conceive their own. Only later did she begin to suspect that none of her children truly belonged to her and that she had raised a small colony of strangers, people with whom she had only a passing resemblance.

On foggy days, as she recovered from a headache, Candida reflected on her family's sins—her aunt, the priest, the broken vows—and, not knowing what else to do, she would double her offering to the statue of Our Lady of Sorrows, the one with the knife through her heart that was carried from house to house.

But then the sun would shine again. As she hung the laundry out to dry, Candida would respond to the greetings of passersby, and Don Francesco's dream once again glistened in the distance like a landscape after the rain. It was a meticulous and magnificent vision of the future, in which, whether or not they desired it, his children, grandchildren, and great-grandchildren were the protagonists.

Unbeknownst to all, Candida had inherited Don Francesco's dream, along with a mole on her back, the barrels of rusty coins, and three pieces of wax fruit, which she kept on a side table; she dedicated herself to its realization with the stubbornness and facility she applied to everything. Staring out threateningly from the daguerreotype in the parlor, above the couch, Don Francesco Falcone encouraged her efforts, or so it seemed to her.

One day, toward the end of adolescence, as she mulled over her parents' dreams in search of an escape, Gioia had begun to understand that their dreams formed only a small part of the dreams of others, far grander and more ancient than their own. She felt them all around her, as if she were sailing toward an improbable New World over a never-ending ocean.

AS FOR MIMMO, now that he was free of his religious duties Candida decided that he should nevertheless continue his studies. If he wasn't going to be a priest, he should at least get a diploma. Even when their storerooms were broken into just before the start of the town fair, full of merchandise that still had to be paid for, she was not discouraged.

Following this calamity, the thing that they feared the most—after politics—came true: they were submerged in debts. Fortunately, Colino never knew.

It was not the only thing he didn't know.

After they were married, Candida had arrived at certain conclusions, one of which was that love is built from lies. She lied to

Colino about many details of their daily life, to herself about certain emotions, and to her children about everything, because children should see things not as they are but as they should be, since they will inevitably find out on their own soon enough how they really are.

Candida told her husband that she had set aside money for Mimmo's education, money that she would use only for that one purpose. After Candida had yelled the words "For university!" a few times, Colino agreed.

When it came to their children, they had always held differing views. In her calculations, Candida ignored a detail that seemed unessential to her, one that she had been lucky enough to experience in her own life: happiness. There were more important things. Such as bettering oneself and distinguishing oneself in life, always and in all circumstances.

Colino held the opposite view. Better to remain lost in the crowd, he thought, because protruding heads are the first to fall. He could not understand who had put these notions in his wife's head, or why the boys should not do the one thing that seemed to him the most logical: help out in the store. There was enough work for everyone. They could load and unload fertilizer, beans, grain. They could go and pick up the disinfectants, or gather eggs from people around town. He tried to get them to work with him until one day Mimmo caught an infection while unloading beans and had to take his first university exam covered in blisters.

Candida was livid. "Don't you have any feelings for the boy?" she yelled. "Your son is practically a professor! Forget about the beans!" It was the only time they had ever argued. From then on Colino let Candida have her way when it came to the education of their children. He limited himself to receiving a kiss from each of them in the evening in order of seniority, polishing their shoes until they gleamed on Sundays, and measuring them once a month to see how much they had grown.

Rather than weakening their marriage, their disagreements and the subterfuges they employed to overcome them nourished it and made it stronger.

The truth was that Candida had not set aside a single cent for Mimmo's studies.

How could she have? Colino had no idea how much it cost to keep the family afloat. He seemed to think they never needed to buy anything.

His wife always found a solution.

Once, when they were newly married, Colino bought some expensive cloth that he had been unable to sell. She used it to make a shirt for him, and another when that one was worn through. He did not even notice. She used it again years later, and then one more time. They were past middle age when one morning, before going to work, Colino suddenly exclaimed, "Damn, that cloth was expensive, but what quality! Look at this shirt! I've had it forever and it still looks as if it were made yesterday!"

To pay for Mimmo's studies, Candida began doing embroidery, something she hadn't done since childhood. After her mother took her out of school, it had become one of her passions, but she hadn't picked up a needle since her wedding.

There were many things she hadn't done since then, so many in fact she could no longer remember. The few times she was reminded of this fact it was only because the child for whom she had sacrificed herself was standing before her, hair a mess, knees scraped, completely indifferent to what she had done for him, and then she told herself that her old desires had grown legs and were walking off wherever they pleased.

. . .

MAMMALINA KNEW there was a lady in Grassano who wanted fancy linens for her daughters' trousseaux, and she took the order without revealing the name of the embroiderer. Candida spent her nights working on linens and towels, covering them with infinitely delicate designs, in different overlapping shades, creating imaginary animals in cross-stitch: deer with eight legs, butterfly fish, and other figments of her imagination. Meanwhile, in the next room, Colino grew impatient. He never suspected that his wife was doing embroidery for money. In his house, love and lies reigned.

Mammalina pilfered right and left from the houses where she cleaned, picking up whatever superfluous object happened to catch her eye. Linens, flour, patterns for lace, plant cuttings. She brought everything to Candida's house, where these objects would miraculously appear on the credenzas.

Candida did not ask questions at the time, nor did she ask them later, when their financial problems had been resolved and Mammalina began stealing from them, taking the same things she had once brought to their house: linen, flour, cuttings. Mammalina gave the loot to two or three impoverished families she had taken under her wing.

Candida worked secretly until she was able to pay back their debts. Every so often, she fainted during the day as a result of the sleepless nights and her anemia. Colino worried; he feared nothing more than the possibility that his wife might die before him. She, on the other hand, was consoled by the idea that she would die first, because nothing terrified her like the possibility of having to live without him. But in the end neither of them died and Mimmo got his degree in literature from the University of Bari.

Alzatevi la camicia donna Calandra,
che ora ci appoggio il mio strumento . . .

Pull up your shirt, Donna Calandra,
I'm going to place my instrument there . . .

Chapter Fourteen

*R*occo's departure for Reggio Emilia was as heartbreaking as a funeral. "Why didn't I raise him to be a cobbler!" Lucrezia complained to her neighbors, pulling her hair and punching her chest with grief. She had wanted him to study so that he would never have to leave. She mourned for him as if he were dead.

Rocco had tried to explain to her many times that the chances of getting a teaching position in northern Italy were much greater. He had tried to explain what a competitive entrance examination was. And a thousand other things. They couldn't understand each other. Neither the words nor their context. Rocco was trying to describe a world that was completely alien to her. The only thing she understood was the pain of losing him. If she hadn't encouraged him to study, they would have spoken the same language. She took it out on the dear departed on the rare occasions when she went to the cemetery. As she knelt on the stone slab, she cursed Giuseppe.

It was sunny when Rocco left for Reggio Emilia. As the train advanced, the sky grew grayer and grayer. By the time he arrived, the sky was dark as lead, and he had to put on his overcoat. This made him happy. He had not opened his mouth once during the entire trip. He was grateful for that town and its dark sky that embraced him, and to the fields, with their stench of pig excrement.

For a month, he was forced to communicate with hand gestures and head movements in order to facilitate the process of finding a room to let, buying food, and hiring someone to wash and iron his laundry. He spoke only in the classroom, where, with the help of a dictionary he had purchased on the day of his arrival, he carefully selected the most appropriate words with which to express each thought. The students made fun of his accent. They could barely understand him, because he did not speak their dialect, and they did not speak standard Italian.

That teacher from the south sure was strange! He did not seem to favor the class pets, the sons of the mayor or the doctor or the pharmacist, but rather the slow kids, the flunkies, the ones that other teachers educated with raps of the cane, the ones who were usually relegated to the back of the class so the teacher wouldn't have to see them. Rocco only had eyes for the lice-ridden louts with calloused hands who could not hold a pen without breaking the nib.

When he noticed a student sleeping with his head on the desk, he did not sneak over and pull his ear until he screamed, as his colleagues did. He stood there looking at him, shaking his head, and walked away quietly so as not to wake him.

If one of the kids skipped school every other day or was absent for months, he did not give up on him or suspend him or threaten to have him thrown out of school. Instead, as soon as he had some time, he showed up at the student's house and began to bargain with the parents as if he were at the market. If they sent their boy to school, he argued, he would be able to stand up to the landowners, who always did the accounts in a way that made it appear that they were owed more, and gave less in return.

They listened with amused courtesy and answered him in a dialect that he barely understood, and always offered him a glass of wine no matter what time of day it was. *"L'è sangiovese, l'è bon, la fa bon sang."* ("It's Sangiovese, it's good for you, good for the blood.") They would let the boy go to school for a week or two, and then as soon as they needed an extra hand in the fields they reverted to their old ways. So Rocco would begin his campaign all over again, and on it went until the end of the year.

Saving the fifty boys in his class from illiteracy was his own personal colonial war, fought not in the name of Fascism, as the school program prescribed, but rather in the name of certain memories that not even he was aware of.

"Superstition, superstition, superstition!" Rocco would inveigh against the old wives' tales, myths, and phantoms that inhabited the regions between the dead and the living. He detested the shadowy culture of country life. Baby mice fed to children who wet their beds, hearts torn from the breasts of swallows to be gulped down seven days in a row for good fortune. Sometimes he even hated himself.

At night he found solace in books, and the following day he would try desperately to transmit his love of literature to his students. But the miracles were few and far between. For every boy who began to show an interest there were ten, twenty, thirty who pinched and shoved one another under their desks, slowly building the cage that would trap them just after they crossed the threshold of adulthood.

Some days, Rocco felt a wave of heat rising in him, despite the malfunctioning heater in the classroom that worked only intermittently. It was rage.

One morning just before the bell, as he was trying unsuccessfully to communicate the qualities of a poem by Pascoli, he caught sight of Ceccagli laughing stupidly and rocking back and forth in an odd fashion behind his desk. Ceccagli was one of his oldest students; he had been sent back three times and already a fine beard covered his cheeks. The week before, Rocco had had to fight to keep him from being expelled after he broke a window in the hallway. For the first time, Rocco felt that he was seeing Ceccagli for what he was: a hopeless case.

In an instant, Rocco, who had never raised his hand in anger, was on top of him, punching him with a strength he did not know he had, blindly, his neck swollen with rage, his veins pulsing, while, despite being taller, the boy struggled to defend himself from the blows. Rocco picked him up by the hair and began to bang his head against the wall, once, twice, three times, four times, harder and harder. If the custodian hadn't arrived at that moment and pulled the boy out from under him, he might even have killed him.

The following day, Rocco had a high fever. From the tiny bed in the boardinghouse where he lay trembling and covered in sweat, he reached toward the night table and picked up the jagged-edged fragment of mirror he used when he shaved. He saw his overheated face, framed by flecks of dried soap, searching for someone or something in the depths of his mild brown eyes, which were lit up with fever, but then he felt exhausted and fell back asleep. Only many years later, when he was struggling with his daughter, did he remember this stranger hidden away inside of him. One day, who knows, he might resurface.

ONE MORNING A COLLEAGUE, a slight, silky-haired blonde, stopped him in the hall. Her name was Mara, not Maria—that's right: Mara. The name came from the word "*amara*," or "bitter," but to him she seemed sweet, with the soft curve of her breast and her soft *s*'s that seemed to melt between her lips. She invited him to join her that evening. He accepted, perplexed. He would never have imagined that a woman could take such initiative. That evening, she brought him to a bar full of smoke and people who came over to talk to her. He followed her around, quietly, now and then attempting to make a joke, none of which made her laugh. Mara wore her hair uncovered, did not lower her eyes when a man looked at her, and said what she thought without mincing words.

Not knowing how to behave, Rocco did nothing and simply let her take the initiative and lead him by the arm. She said strange things. She told him she had been watching him these past few months. Rocco couldn't understand what she meant, or what she was getting at. He got a better idea a few days later when they went back to the bar.

There was a certain electricity in the air that night. Little by little the people at the bar began to disappear. He realized that they were going to the back. After a while Mara indicated that they should follow. A group of people, almost all of them young, some sitting on the few chairs in the room, others standing, were listening to a fuzzy radio broadcast that kept fading in and out. A young man with a mustache slammed the radio with his hand and the voice became clearer. It was Radio Milano, reporting on the situation in Spain, which was heating up. Rocco was mortified.

All he knew about Communism came from the priests and from Fascist propaganda, in other words that it was worse than cholera, and that it was a mortal sin even to name it. He could lose his job at the school. At the very least. He thought of his mother. He looked around. Mara looked back at him, calmly. He looked at the people there, people his age, wondering what terrible crimes they had committed. But nothing came to mind.

Just as he was trying to plot a way to leave without being noticed, Mara smiled at him. He had noticed before that when she smiled, her eyes radiated light. But that was not why he stayed.

Rocco was won over by the idea of a utopian society, just as others believed in the promised land, whether it was Eden, America, Tripolitania, or Abyssinia. This was his third and final conversion, and it completely replaced the previous two. It was the last time he would believe in something with his entire being.

He packed the beloved novels of his adolescence in dusty boxes, where his daughter would one day find them. Instead, he read obscure pages of Trotsky and Marx's *Kapital*, without understanding a word at first, but gradually, with his usual stubbornness, he was able to fully come into possession of these abstruse concepts, and new perspectives opened up before him. The revolution would rid the world of injustice, give voice to rage, and imbue unhappiness with dignity.

When Mara asked him if he wanted to help out with their activities, Rocco remained silent, but only for a moment, long enough to push a painful thought into a hidden corner in his brain. Then he said yes.

They became inseparable. They would spend entire afternoons after school performing tasks for the party, talking, and making plans. Mara did most of the talking, skipping from one subject to the next in her rotund accent, unconcerned if Rocco answered in monosyllables. She seemed to intuit exactly what was going through his mind, and relieved him of the need to put it into words, which he appreciated. He began to experience an unknown feeling.

One winter morning, as the fog lifted, the inhabitants of Reggio Emilia awoke to find red graffiti scrawled all over town, on the walls under a portico, in a latrine, and on the metal shutter of a store: PANE AI BAMBINI O LA TESTA DI MUSSOLINI.

("The children need bread, or off with the Duce's head!") and VIA IL DUCE CHE ALLA FAME CI CONDUCE ("Out with the Duce, who's leading us to hunger!") or CANCRO AI FASCISTI, EVVIVA LA RUSSIA DEI SOVIET ("Cancer to the Fascists, long live the Russian Soviets!"). Written in giant red letters on the wall of the steel mill, for all the factory workers to see on their way to their morning shifts, were the words: I AM HAPPY. Many of them turned back to look more than once.

In a corner of his mind, Rocco had the thought that all this would come to an end one day, but he just kept going, like a mule with blinders, refusing to see the danger and hoping without hope it would somehow disappear.

One dull afternoon, digging among the scraps of paper and knickknacks in a drawer of Rocco's desk, Gioia found pictures from his time in Reggio Emilia, wrapped in tissue paper. She stared for a long time at the chubby-cheeked youth in those black-and-white images, wondering what he was looking at with that expression she had never seen before.

MARA APPLIED THE SAME ENERGY to politics as she did to digging in the garden, kneading bread, and pedaling on her bicycle, unintentionally leaving Rocco far behind. When he was with her, Rocco felt a sense of danger, but not the danger of being arrested or of falling off his bicycle in the futile attempt to catch up.

Because of her he began to change. He realized it one night, when they were dancing in the back room of the bar to the music of the Lescano Trio. Mara was teaching him how to waltz, so that they could pass messages without calling attention. Rocco applied himself diligently, just as he applied himself to deciphering the secret messages from their leaders. One two three, one two three. He was stiff, clumsy. He trembled as he held her soft body close. His face was red, but not because of the temperature in the room. One two three. He tripped and fell, pulling her down with him. When they were on the floor, Mara looked into his eyes. He looked at her, and was filled with terror as he felt his body taking embarrassing initiatives. Suddenly he started to laugh. At first a timid, guilty laugh, in hiccups, then bold and deep. Mara stared at him in disbelief. "Is this the first time you've seen such a terrible dancer?" he asked. "It's the first time I've heard you laugh."

Rocco's loneliness stuck to him like glue. No matter what he did to rid himself of it, it never went away, like the farmers back home who always gave off the smell of their animals. On Sundays, they filled the church with their smell; it seeped through the seams of their Sunday best despite a vigorous morning rubdown with baking soda soap.

Rocco met Mara's family, made up of farmers and factory workers, with an unbelievable number of brothers and sisters, none of whom were named after saints of the Catholic Church. Mara was the only one who had finished her studies. They lived in a farmhouse on the land they cultivated, so they did not have to get up before dawn and walk for miles to reach the fields, as his mother had always done. But the thing that amazed him the most was that they were organized in cooperatives. They shared tools and pooled their harvests when they went to market. Back home, where the farmers were convinced that a sidelong glance could destroy everything and envy was considered more dangerous even than drought, it would have been impossible.

Shaken from his usual muteness, Rocco would pepper Mara's father, Libero, with questions, which Libero did his best to answer, but sometimes in the middle of a sentence he would stop, fix Rocco with his cobalt blue eyes, and smack him on the back. "You're a real southerner, aren't you," he would say, and start to laugh. He never lost his temper, not even three years earlier when the Fascists destroyed the harvest and the family managed to survive only thanks to the party's assistance.

At lunches and dinners where everyone talked loudly and pinched and hit one another at the table, Rocco retreated into his own mysterious world, returning to reality only when politics were being discussed. Then he would become surprisingly eloquent, inflaming everyone with his oratory.

For a moment, Mara could see that this young, irascible teacher from the south would surely one day become a leader of multitudes.

They had been together for months before they made love for the first time. Rocco would never have allowed himself to treat her with disrespect, but in his dreams he experienced things that he could only try to forget in the daytime.

The only woman he had ever touched was a prostitute. He had gone to see her the day he turned twenty one.

That morning, his mother had told him to put on his good suit. She was also wearing her best. Lucrezia had waited seventeen years for this day to arrive. Walking single file, with him in front and her behind, they went to the bank to withdraw the money the dear departed had deposited there. Rocco signed the papers. He wrote his first and last name next to the X's his father had marked seventeen years earlier. Then the post office clerk counted out the bills and, finally, handed them over to Rocco.

Back when his father had made the deposit, on his return from America, it was enough money to buy three or four hectares of farmable land. But then came the stock market crash of 1929 and a devaluation of 41 percent, followed by the economic crisis. Now, the money was barely enough to wipe his ass with.

Rocco accompanied his mother back home and waited for her to fall asleep. That night he lost his virginity with a whore from Grassano. He paid her twenty lire and left her a tip she would not forget to her dying day. With the money left over, he bought a round of drinks for everyone in the piazza.

EVER SINCE SHE HAD BEEN A LITTLE GIRL—perhaps because she had lost her mother before the age of seven—when Mara wanted to do something, she did it now rather than later. And so it was with Rocco, once it became clear that he might never decide to act.

One day after school, she asked him to come with her; she said it was important. She refused to give any explanation.

She took him to her house. Rocco walked toward the door, but she stayed behind and called out to him, indicating that he should follow her to the hayloft. Rocco assumed that the pamphlets that they were going to hand out at the local factories had arrived and were hidden there. But in the hayloft there were only medicinal plants hung to dry. Rocco looked at his feet. He looked at Mara. The air was full of gnats, flying around in a beam of sunlight that came down from the skylight; he could still see them, many years later. The medicinal plants gave off a penetrating odor that tickled his nose, but Rocco didn't notice. His legs felt limp, and he had a sense of vertigo. He only realized this afterward, as if the sensation had etched itself in his brain, and in fact, from that day on, whenever he smelled the odor of medicinal herbs he felt a wave of nostalgia. Afterward, she gently touched the small, round, pale scar on his arm. "What is it from?" she asked. "It's nothing," he said.

WHEN HE WENT TO VISIT his mother in Grottole, Rocco felt swallowed up by a hole in time, a void that engulfed him and de-

stroyed his willpower. Things that were happening elsewhere arrived there only as a pale echo, so ephemeral that he began to
doubt their reality. It was as if Reggio Emilia were only a dream;
even the Revolution seemed like a dream that he had foolishly
bought into, and the only things that really existed and would
ever exist were the rituals that had marked the passage of time
from the day he was born: the church bells, conversations about
the weather, people's comments on the priest's sermon at Mass,
gossip, the procession of farm laborers returning home on their
mules at sundown, always the same, like a stream of ghosts that
made sure that nothing would ever change. He would be overcome by a sense of powerlessness that grew more and more powerful until it was time for him to leave.

He did not see old friends, not even Mimmo. He spent the
days sitting there with his mother, in silence, looking out
through the glass-paned door, in suspended time, as if somewhere, someone could not decide to change the seasons or turn
day into night. Once in a while Lucrezia would break the silence
to tell him that one of his old friends had gotten married. Eventually, he would break down and swear to request a transfer and
come home by the end of the year. When he left, he still believed
it. Then he went back north and felt himself returning to life in
Mara's arms.

When the Spanish Civil War erupted, Mara wanted to go to
Spain with the Garibaldi Brigade as a volunteer. Each time she
brought it up, Rocco changed the subject. In the end, to his relief, the party decided that they were more valuable where they
were, and so they stayed in Reggio Emilia. They often discussed
the future. They had already picked the name of their first
daughter: Pravda, like the newspaper of the Soviet Communist
Party.

The war broke out on June 10, 1940.

Rocco was able to avoid active duty because of his bout with tuberculosis at the seminary. But he was called to serve in the reserves at the military headquarters in Pescara. They gave him clerical work because there were not many people there who knew how to read and write. He and Mara wrote to each other every day. Love letters, with a few clues slipped between the lines about what was happening and the decisions that needed to be made.

On September 12, 1943, Mara showed up at the barracks. She had not told him she was coming. The night before, Rocco had had strange dreams, and when he woke up his feeling of confusion increased. In the midst of the general atmosphere of uncertainty, he was called to the atrium, and there she was. She had traveled by train, bus, and foot from Reggio Emilia to Pescara, despite all the roadblocks.

Now that he saw her standing there in front of him, Rocco realized how much he had missed her those three years. She was a bit thinner, but she still had that same resolute air and her eyes sparkled even more brightly. She had traveled all that distance so that they could talk without being overheard. She told him excitedly that the king had fled. Apparently he was right there, in Pescara. She and her brothers, and others from the group, were making plans to leave the farmhouse that very night. They were going to spread out over the hills near Civago. Many young people who had received the call were joining them. It had been difficult for her to come to Pescara to see him. Her comrades were opposed to her taking the trip; they said it was dangerous and there was no time to waste. Her older brother Lupo had left for the Veneto the day before to join another group that was forming there. "And you? What are you waiting for?" She kept telling him all the details—schedules, first names, family names— talking in that way of hers, without waiting for him to answer, taking his answer for granted. But at a certain point she stopped. She gazed at him in silence. It was a look full of disappointment that reminded him of something, a distant ache buried in his childhood.

"You'll come, won't you?" Mara asked him, her voice barely a whisper. Rocco stared at her as if trying to imprint her image in his brain. Suddenly he took her in his arms and pressed her against him very tightly. She let him, and then broke free and ran away. It was the last time they saw each other.

Chapter Fifteen

Alba was ten when she left her noisy family home, her brothers' practical jokes, and the long stories her grandmother told on hot summer afternoons.

Her complicated gifts had led her parents, or rather Candida, to decide that she should get an education, despite being a girl. Because there was no middle school in Grottole, they had been forced to send her away to boarding school. Candida chose an institute run by the Sisters of the Sacred Heart in Monopoli, which she had seen once while visiting her in-laws. It was a vast structure built out of gray stone with a Moorish dome, surrounded by a garden and protected by high walls. One entered through a gate made from a dense latticework of wrought iron. To Candida it seemed like the most prestigious place she could possibly find for her daughter's studies.

ALBA DID NOT SHED a single tear. As Candida watched her drive away in Ciola Ciola's car, she had a sudden feeling of doubt, one of those misgivings that can insinuate themselves and spoil everything, like a skipped stitch in a stocking. But she was able to capture the feeling right away and bury it under the many things she had to do that day.

Alba adapted easily to the blue uniforms, and was even willing to put her hair back in two long, tightly plaited braids hanging down to her backside. She stoically withstood the gelid dormitories, the stiff mattresses filled with horsehair, and the obscenely early call to prayer. Her reward was the smell of ammonia and bleach that filled the corridors on Saturdays, and the fragrance of whitewash and lavender in the dormitories. She was no longer besieged by the obscene, human odors of the streets of Grottole. She learned how to set the table, how to peel a peach or an orange with a single swirl of the knife, how to curtsey, and how to sit with her back straight, elbows by her sides. She even made a friend.

More than a friendship, really, it was a symbiosis.

There was a rigid hierarchy among the girls at the school, easily observable by watching the groups that formed in the courtyard during recess. Because it was one of the few girls' schools in the area, it attracted students from Puglia, Basilicata, and Abruzzo.

They did not all belong to the same social class.

At the top were the elite, the crème de la crème, the aristocratic girls, along with the daughters of large landowners and the proprietors of oil mills, water mills, and kilns. Each of these girls represented a special case, because upper-crust families usually preferred private instruction to boarding school. Then there were the daughters of affluent farmers and small-business owners, who sent their girls to school in hopes of climbing the social ladder. These were the Goody Two-shoes, the girls who memorized the dictionary and meticulously applied the rules of grammar and etiquette without ever quite absorbing them. Then there were the war orphans, the girls who had lost their fathers at the front in the first phases of the conflict; as compensation, the government paid for their studies. They represented the lowest echelon of the social hierarchy. They were constantly punished, marginalized, and often forced to clean the school, according to the Sisters, in order to complement their insufficient dues.

Maria was one of these girls. She was from Letto Manoppello, a tiny village in the Abruzzo mountains. In her case, the privilege of an education came at a high price.

She was a big, robust girl, with the simple manners and rosy cheeks of a mountain girl. The thin soups provided by the Sisters did nothing but rinse her stomach. She was tormented by a blinding hunger that affected her ability to work. She was constantly punished and had quickly become the school laughing-stock. Almost every week she was forced to skip at least a couple of meals and made to spend afternoons locked in a dark closet. Her situation had become acute, and she might even have died; people whispered that it had happened before, a few years back when a girl was left all night in the dark closet wearing damp clothes.

Within a few months of her arrival at the school, her skin had begun to turn a greenish hue and she had developed the uncertain air of someone who is walking on a razor's edge. She might easily have fallen ill with tuberculosis, but one day she noticed something very interesting going on nearby.

The Sisters of the Sacred Heart served God and filled their coffers by teaching moderation in all aspects of life, both physical and moral, but in Alba's case their efforts were superfluous. Alba felt a diffident detachment from all earthly things, and nothing attracted or impassioned her immodestly, except for mathematics. She had no interest in what are known as the pleasures of the flesh. For this reason, the Sisters' scant, insipid meals never presented a problem, other than the usual one, in other words the problem of how to get rid of them without calling attention to herself.

She had developed a series of ingenious methods to conceal her lack of appetite. She would place a small amount of food in her mouth and chew it, gradually creating a ball that she would hide in her cheek. As soon as Sister Germana, who supervised their meals, allowed herself to be distracted by the food in front of her, Alba would pretend to yawn or cough, covering her mouth politely. As she did this, she quickly and efficiently removed the ball of food from her mouth, and after a series of coordinated arm movements, under the table and behind her chair, the ball would end up in the pot of a blue hydrangea, which once a month became a carnivorous plant and the rest of the time survived on potatoes and semolina, like the flowering girls whose developing curves were nourished by those same insufficient victuals.

Maria had gradually been attracted by Alba's elegant movements, her conjuring tricks, until finally she realized that in this place where many would have killed for an extra portion of sardines or mashed potatoes, there was someone who wanted only to get rid of them. As she watched the surgical manner in which Alba sliced her food, handling the silverware just as the Sisters had taught her, Maria began to realize that this strange phenomenon might save her life. But she felt such awe toward her finicky classmate that she could not find the courage to speak to her. Maria was attracted to Alba as one might be by a strange, exotic animal, the kind exhibited at the fair.

In the end, Maria's survival instinct overcame both her awkwardness and Alba's detachment, and even the vigilance of the Sisters, who were opposed to any kind of exchange. The girls made a pact during recess, and it was the beginning of a symbiosis that allowed both of them to survive those difficult years of middle school unscathed. They did not talk much, but they managed to pass food unnoticed, and on especially cold nights they defied the scrutiny of the nuns to share a single bed and keep each other warm. During recess they didn't mix with the other girls, or take part in the eternal power struggles that dominated life at the school. They did not try to undermine the others nor did they live in fear of being undermined; one was enough for the other, and they were satisfied with their uncomplicated existence. If someone bothered them, blackmailed one of them, or attempted to turn one against the other, it was Maria who defended them both, using as her only defense her considerable size and her faith in the alliance she had with Alba.

But in the first year of high school, everything changed.

ONE AFTERNOON IN NOVEMBER, after All Saints', Alba heard the notes of a piano ringing through the silent halls of the Sacred Heart, as well as a warbling voice. She had never heard anything like it. With a strange feeling of joy she walked toward the source of the sound. She opened the door a crack and stood there, listening. The girl sitting at the grand piano was Gioia.

She had just turned fourteen, but her beauty was already evident. She was from Lecce, and had the archaic air of women from those parts, a beauty lost in time, of Greek proportions. Tall and harmoniously built, she had blonde, coppery hair framing a cameo-like profile and two large green eyes. She had bright, pale skin, tapered hands, and slender ankles. It seemed as if no filth could touch her.

Alba stood by the door for a long time, as if hypnotized, but when the girl at the piano glanced toward her while turning a page of music, she scampered off like a squirrel, or at least that was Gioia's impression.

Gioia careened through the corridors of the school like a wild animal, emanating a fragrance of jasmine with each movement. She had been sent away by her mother because, as she grew, her beauty overshadowed that of her sister, who was of marriageable age. This exile had filled her with malice. She wore a frown like a goddess from Mount Olympus and tyrannized her school-mates, especially her direct underlings, four girls from good families who followed her around, obeying her orders and enforcing them in the school like the private militia of a royal princess.

Gioia decided every aspect of the girls' life outside of the prescribed school activities. During the morning service, she sat in the third seat of the second pew, a seat which for some forgotten reason had for generations been considered the most desirable spot in the church, and a source of contention, feuds, and vendettas. She decided what game would be played at recess, who would be allowed to take part, and who would not. She might also decide that on that particular day there would be no games at all.

Her orders were executed by her faithful followers. A note would announce a fall from grace or rehabilitation, ostracism or promotion. Among the various privileges Gioia reserved for herself was the honor of completing her homework. She considered studying to be an activity fit only for poor girls looking for social advancement.

The Sisters turned a blind eye, allowing the girls to manage as best they could, because there was always, would always be, and had always been a Gioia to tyrannize the others. All the girls yearned to be allowed into her entourage, but few succeeded.

The first division between the nobles and the plebes took place during meals. Among the uniformly dressed girls the best way to recognize social background was to watch them eat; freshly acquired manners could never completely disguise a voracious appetite. After her first few months at the school, when Gioia finally deigned to notice Alba, she was impressed by the elegance with which she treated her food. Gioia watched her for about a week. Then she sent a note.

When Alba received the note, her heart began to race beneath her fragile ribs like that of a frightened kitten and did not stop on the day of their meeting, when she found herself standing before Gioia during recess, in the courtyard.

They stared at each other in silence for some time. Alba's eyes were deep as a coal mine. They sparkled with fear. Gioia's were a transparent green. I'll kill her, I'll scratch her, I'll bite her. Who do you think you are? "I'd like to be your friend," Gioia said.

The impossible happened. Without ever having desired it, Alba was admitted to the complex rituals of the elite. They shared the candied fruits they received from home, which she appreciated mostly for their shape and color and kept in a paper wrapper in her assigned drawer until one day she discovered they were full of worms. She was allowed to be part of myriad little secrets. She got to play pretty statues. She leafed through issues of *Vogue* sent directly from Paris. She spent hours listening to Gioia play the piano, recognizing in the symmetries of the music the same ideal relationships that she so loved in mathematics.

Maria was forgotten. Alba continued to pass over her leftovers as a gesture of charity, but beyond that she barely deigned her a glance. Alba and Gioia had become inseparable and inhabited a world that no one else could penetrate. Maria suffered her loss in silence.

In the spring, the situation worsened.

. . .

BEYOND THE WALLS of the school the bougainvillea and *bella-di-nottes* were in bloom. The first suggestion of their disquieting fragrance began to spread at sundown. A restlessness awoke among the girls, one that did not subside as the hours passed and the night air enveloped their bodies in a sinful sweetness that the Sisters could do nothing to combat. Somewhere in the distance, sordid, sublime activities, tender and cruel hormonal epiphanies, were taking place. Beyond lay the sea. Alba caught a glimpse of it once a week, during their Sunday stroll. Its translucent outline glimmered at the end of a long road, and the sky near the horizon was a lighter shade. But its presence could also be felt within the walls of the school. A salty breeze with a tonic fragrance filled the air with all the colors of the rainbow. The colors hung there, trembling, and then dissolved like soap bubbles. Sometimes, carried by the wind, the girls could hear the call of a fishmonger, the mewing of a cat, the echoes of a quarrel, or the screaming of children. More often, their days were accompanied by the mournful singing of the nuns. But youth bloomed where it could, like the exuberant weeds that Sister Giovanna, the gardener, constantly and pointlessly pulled in the courtyard.

Gioia did not speak to Alba about love, but about its presentiments. Senseless, infinitely soft words came to her, phrases that asked only to be deciphered, and the spring felt like an invitation to discovery. Those days, love existed only to be told. It was present in the dreams and premonitions of two young girls as their hands touched and they caressed each other with their eyes, each discovering her own beauty in that of her friend, the delicacy of her skin in the other's, the roundness of one girl's forms putting in sharp relief the angular contours of the other. Their love was a game of mirrors.

Your joy is mine. Life, what we can imagine together. Our pact is indestructible.

Gioia led Alba, instructed her. She taught Alba her ways, and time became like an infinite hallway with communicating doors. They were rehearsing for something that was meant to be but in the end would not come to pass.

The velvety eyes of the milkman's assistant, the mustache of the student, and the uniform of the army recruit made them swoon, but never for more than two straight Sundays. The same boy who had set their hearts aflutter later filled them with scorn. Alba had developed a virtue born of her lack of appetite, a direct inheritance from her family (the only one): a cutting and strange sense of humor that tempered the impulses of her heart. They laughed. Suddenly, they would erupt in explosions of laughter, caused by something as insignificant as a glance or even a shared thought that did not need to be externalized. It revealed itself in a contraction of the stomach, a moan, an accumulation of pressure that finally culminated in an eruption. They experienced overwhelming attacks of giggles for which they would have been willing to risk death. Unstoppable. Exhausting. They could erupt all over again many days later, should the same thought, heavy as a storm cloud, resurface in one of their minds. Life showed both of its countenances, sacred and profane, and their ultimate resemblance. If you die, I die. Death is unjust. Life is unjust. In Giacomo Leopardi's words, "Silvia, do you remember still . . . ?"

DURING THE SCHOOLGIRLS' Sunday stroll, a line of boys would form to watch them go by, and Gioia was the most admired of all. A few weeks after she turned up at the school, marriage proposals began to arrive, to be forwarded to her parents, who paid no attention.

The time for love had not yet arrived for Gioia. Even though from one Sunday to the next the two girls conjured a world of dreams based on real and invented details, inspired by the color of a tie or the angle of a glance, in the end, the romantic image of love was obscured by Sister Giovanna's whiskers, their sighs by the laughter that brought tears to their eyes.

Gioia returned from the summer holiday after that first year transformed: she was a woman. She had developed two round breasts, large enough to hold in the palm of a hand. Her waist was thinner, her hips wider. Her lips were fuller and had turned a brighter shade of red, her hair was shinier, and her eyes glistened as if with fever. And, in a way, it was so. She had fallen in love with her sister's fiancé, and he returned the feeling.

Gioia's exile, orchestrated by her mother, had only precipitated events.

When Eugenio Capece, of the line of the Capece barons from Nardò, found himself, without preparation or warning, standing before this adolescent in full bloom and still unconscious of the devastating effects of her nascent feminine charms laid out for all to see, he had been unable to defend himself despite calculation or good sense, and had plunged into a delirium of desire that completely confounded his faculties. At first Gioia was amused, but then she felt a presentiment of love growing within her, a feeling she had been carefully preparing for all those years: an overwhelming agony, a sense of exile and homecoming that had been lying in wait for the chance to come into being. And she abandoned herself to that torment which she felt was her destiny.

They had not exchanged a single word the entire summer, only a fury of glances. Gioia had grown, reaching her full height, almost unacceptably tall for a girl those days. His breath quickened whenever she walked by.

He waited until February, a rainy, cold February, more tedious than most, to impulsively make the trip from Lecce to Monopoli and produce one of those miraculous turns of events that love is capable of when it is tinged with desperation. He appeared on the Corso Vittorio one Sunday at ten in the morning, mixed in with the usual crowd at the Gran Caffè, his heart beating hard, wild-eyed. When Gioia saw him she felt the chasm of her future open up before her and after a moment of hesitation, she threw herself in headfirst.

ALBA'S CHEST WAS still as flat as a bird's; she enjoyed intrigues and she loved to laugh. She spent long evenings with her friend, gazing at pictures of her raven-haired, clear-eyed young man, speculating about the future, hearing Gioia describe the same events for the hundredth time. In the following years he mustered the courage to write to her, and they began an inane, impassioned correspondence with the complicity of the milkman's assistant, who received their letters.

There were oases, truces, and moments of desperation. Alba had no need to fall in love, because her friend had done so. She curled up in that outsized love and took pleasure in its reflected luster. She remained cold, creating sublime equations that moved only Signorina Invernusi, her math professor.

WHEN THEY WERE in their last year of school, Gioia and her suitor quarreled. They interrupted contact for several months, and Gioia told Alba that she felt completely liberated. She invited Alba to spend the summer with her in Santa Cesarea. She showed Alba a photograph of her family's Moorish-style villa and described the gardens filled with maritime pines that descended down to the sea, mulberry trees, caper shrubs, and jasmines that the women picked and stuffed into their dresses. She told Alba about the dances, almond sweets, and her wild cousins. One of them would surely suit her! She showed her a photograph of the family, thirty people in all, the faces too small to make out their features. In the photo, she said, her cousin was only thirteen, but now he was very handsome, with liquid green eyes. He was at university, but failed every class because he was always playing the clown, driving his father to desperation.

During her free time Gioia gave Alba lessons. She taught her how to waltz and Alba did so marvelously well, with lightness and grace. She suggested certain attitudes and manners, because some of her female cousins were envious gossips and one had to watch oneself with them. She talked about their family friends, how silly they were, and about her parents and their obsessions—her mother's fixation with clothes—and about her horses, especially her favorite horse, which she had had since she was a little girl. She assured Alba they would have a marvelous time.

Over Easter break, Alba received permission from her parents to spend the summer holidays with her friend. She had the seamstress make her a dress copied out of *Vogue* with some leftover material from her father's store, a rustling, prune-colored taffeta. The seamstress did her best to re-create the complicated design and in the end she pulled it off, but the dress came out so small that even though Alba was very thin, she had to hold her breath to fit into it.

Years later, after taking out the waist, her daughter wore the same dress to her sixteenth-birthday party, where she got drunk on Fundador brandy and kissed a boy for the first time—a boy she had never seen before.

Back at school after Easter, Alba and Gioia counted the days until the end of the year, but then things took a different turn. After three months, Gioia's young man turned up again, and she instantly forgot all her good intentions, without the slightest sense of guilt.

With Alba's help, Gioia was able to slip away for a few hours, and when she returned her cheeks were red, her eyes limpid, and she had the ecstatic expression of Saint Teresa. She spoke at length and in great detail of her deflowering, sparing none of the particulars. Alba found the whole thing repulsive, but said nothing. By that evening, somehow, the Sisters had also heard all the details. Gioia was locked in the dark closet, and that night there was a great commotion. The following morning she was gone. Her belongings were removed from the dormitory without explanation. The girls were forbidden to mention her name. There was a rumor that she had died, like the girl whose ghost some of the girls swore they had seen, shivering as she wandered the hallways of the Sacred Heart.

Secretly, Maria cried for a long time, overwhelmed by the consequences of her snitching; she had not foreseen such a tragic outcome. She had simply wanted to win back the friend who had been stolen by the other girl, but in that she did not succeed. Alba continued to share her food, but did not give her the time of day.

When Alba returned from school she was a perfect lady. She sat at the table with a straight back and her elbows at her sides. She could peel an apple, peach, or orange in a single swirl, even if then she left it uneaten. She did not gurgle her soup in her oral cavity. She knew fifteen words or so of French. She felt a powerful nostalgia for Gioia's jasmine essence, as well as for her melodious voice and her silly fantasies. The walls of the school had protected her from life's filth. She brought with her memories of her friend, several issues of *Vogue*, and a sense of longing for the summer that never was. Instead, she returned to the airlessness and stench of Grottole, the peeling whitewash, the slippery paving stones, the mud, and the flies. And despite her sense of revulsion, she adapted.

Sorella mia sorella
mo si arrotano li cortella
li cortella so arrotati
e l'ora mia è arrivata.

My sister, sister of mine,
the knives are being sharpened,
the knives are sharp,
and my time has come.

Chapter Sixteen

A window rattled above the piazza in Montescaglioso. A club was beating boom, boom, boom. A horse's hooves beat a tattoo on the ground. Over and over, they beat against the earth where we planted the seeds just the other day. Go away! They're riding over the field with their horses, over the corn that's still underground, over my Francuzzo's head. I told him not to go. Go away from there, listen to Mamma, go away, they'll kill you, they don't care, they'll kill you, they'll ride their horses over your head, I can see the blood, just like it was with my brother. Go away from there, listen to Mamma, go away . . .

When Cenzina woke up, her heart was beating hard and she was covered in sweat even though the room was cold. Her husband was asleep next to her, snoring slightly. The baby was sleeping quietly in his crib. The other two, one at the head of the bed and the other at the foot of the bed, tossed and turned. Something went by outside the curtain, a cat, or perhaps a chicken. It was still dark out.

It took a while for Cenzina's heart to calm down. "Silly woman," she said to herself, "you should thank God instead of having these bad thoughts."

A few days earlier at the field at Tre Confini, when they had occupied Baron Lacava's land, the police had come. They had already plowed and sown the field. They had also taken over Count Galante's land in Dogana, and some state land at Imperatore, wherever they found fallow land. They had planted enough wheat to feed all of Montescaglioso, her husband said. A while ago, Peppino had joined the Communist Party. At first she wasn't happy about it, but then she joined too.

On the day of the protest she had been in the first row, with Nunzia Suglia and Anna Avena. It was a strange kind of procession, without saints or priests. She carried a red flag attached to a hoe. And a sign on a spade that she had been told said something about private property. That morning, the police had left them alone. They had ceded the road to the tide of children, women, and farm laborers; it was incredible. Cenzina turned over under the quilt, on the frigid sheets, and positioned herself beneath her husband, seeking some warmth. And perhaps something else too.

They usually made love at this time, just before dawn, when everyone was sleeping soundly, but not since the beginning of the land occupation. On that particular day, perhaps because of her bad dream or the relief she felt at how things had turned out, Cenzina wanted to feel his hands on her. But he did not wake up. When he came home in the evenings he was exhausted. So she fell back asleep and had another dream. She was beating the mattresses at her mother's house, tum, tum, tum, and then there was a bang, another bang, and her husband had been shot in the piazza. She awoke with a start. Someone was knocking on the door. This time Peppino woke up and sat up on the bed. They could hear people moving outside.

When Peppino opened the door the icy air swept in, as well as a cat, who hid under the bed, and the baby started to cry. The street was full of people. Tonino Andriulli said that they were arresting all the members of the union. Peppino dressed quickly. She ran after him in her nightgown, hair still uncombed, grabbing a cloak to cover herself.

The baby was crying more loudly now and her husband kept telling her to go back, but she had no intention of doing so, not after the dreams she'd had.

The town was dark. Later, she found out that the electricity had been cut. There was no moon, so she did not see the police truck at first. The crowd grew larger and larger, until finally it separated her from her husband. People were screaming for the prisoners to be set free, as she tried desperately to reach him.

Then she heard the shots. She knew. Giuseppe Novello, Peppino, her husband, was killed by a burst of machine gun fire. He was thirty-two. They said it was an accident. A police officer on a motorbike had fired his weapon to clear a path through the crowd.

WHEN ROCCO WENT HOME that day it was already morning. He collapsed on the bed, fully dressed, and did not fall asleep until around noon. His mother woke him shortly afterward; it was time to eat.

The news of Novello's death had already made the rounds of all the neighboring towns, and Lucrezia said that it could have been him. Each time he left the house, she feared for his life.

Rocco was the secretary of the Communist Party section that included Grottole, which was headquartered in San Nicola, in a basement that also housed the chamber of commerce. The secretary of the chamber of commerce, and also for a time the only other party member, was Mimmo.

When Rocco returned to Grottole after the war, the two friends were reunited. Mimmo was teaching Italian at the middle school in Matera, and Rocco requested to be transferred to the primary school in Grottole. Of the two, only Mimmo had been to the front, but they both felt like veterans of the war.

Their return had been difficult; at times the town treated them with diffidence, at others, with excessive familiarity. They made an effort to form new habits, and once again they had been brought together, as when they were boys, by their uncertainties. The days of the seminary felt like a distant memory. Little by little, Mimmo began to notice a shadow of regret in his friend's eyes that had not been there before. Rocco did not mention Mara, but as they walked back and forth across the piazza he spoke at length, and passionately, about the cooperatives of Reggio Emilia, about the ways in which the farmers were organized, their class consciousness, and the Communist Party. In his eyes a trace of his former happiness would appear.

They founded the local branch of the party and worked tirelessly to encourage its growth. They spent long hours at the headquarters, helping laborers with convoluted paperwork they could not complete on their own: requests for pension benefits, applications for subsidies from the farmers' consortium, welfare claims.

Rocco harangued farmworkers in the piazzas of small towns, taught night school, helped in the fields, and often he woke up in the middle of the night and could not fall back asleep.

After an initial wariness, many people had joined the party, especially day laborers, and all of Mimmo's brothers, one after the other. Suddenly Candida and Colino had a houseful of Communists.

At lunch, the talk was all about protests and party directives, and Marx and Engels's *Communist Manifesto* lay among the spools of thread on the sewing machine; Candida would cover it furtively as she walked by. Don Arcangelo had refused to bless the house at Easter and inveighed from the pulpit against the misdeeds of Communism until he was purple in the face, naming names and evoking apocalyptic visions of Bolshevik horses drinking from the fountains of the Vatican.

Candida blamed Rocco for leading her sons down the evil path, starting with Mimmo, who had always had a trusting nature. Her sons laughed, embraced her, and told her that they loved her.

Colino took refuge in his muffled hearing and began to distance himself from the Church because he did not like it when people spoke ill of anyone who carried his last name. Little by little Candida resigned herself and accepted her children's Communism, just as long ago she had resigned herself to their skinned knees and torn pant legs.

THE WINTER OF 1949 was cold and full of hope. The victory of the Christian Democrats in the elections of 1948 had fueled the militants' rage, and in Basilicata many fields were occupied by farmworkers. At party headquarters, the laborers would grin mischievously and say: *"Adda vení baffone."* ("Stalin's coming.") Then, during Carnival season, there was a dance at Candida and Colino's house.

It was Mimmo's idea, as a way to celebrate the positive outcome of the land occupations. Under pressure, De Gasperi's government had decided that the fallow land should be conceded to the squatters, and this was what happened the following year.

In reality, Mimmo also had two private, highly secret hopes for the ball. One was realized, the other was not.

Alba, who had returned from boarding school the previous summer, took part in the festivities. It was her first public appearance, because during the previous months she had not set foot outside the house, refusing to take walks by the wall with the other girls. She spent her days in the room beneath the storage area, which she shared with her by now benevolent and smiling grand-mother Albina and the candlelit portraits of their dead relatives. In the afternoons she leafed through the issues of *Vogue* she had brought back from school, which she knew by heart. She filled the rest of her time with trigonometry equations.

One day she joined her mother in the kitchen. As Candida kneeled in front of the hearth, shaking the pot to mix the beans, Alba abruptly told her that she did not want to get married. She wanted to go to university. To study mathematics.

Candida was caught off guard. A woman at university? Have we lost our minds? But even as the words were coming out of her mouth—that Alba should not repeat this to anyone, even in jest, that Heaven and earth could not make it happen, that she would be taken for a madwoman or a whore—the idea began to take hold, awakening in her the old passion for novelty. They would be the first family in town to send a girl to university! Alba showed her a letter signed by Professor Rosa Invernusi. It said that "Fortunato, Alba" excelled at mathematics, and recom-mended that she be encouraged to continue her studies.

What a lovely word, "excelled" . . .

Candida brought the subject up with her husband. "Univer-sity!" he exclaimed, loud enough to make himself heard, but not so very loud after all. To Colino it was just another of his wife's crazy ideas, which he had stopped worrying about long ago, and as usual he gave her carte blanche. But an unexpected obstacle came between Alba and her study of mathematics.

A few years earlier, Mimmo had eagerly read an article in *Avanguardia Proletaria,* a reprint of Togliatti's speech about the tra-ditional backwardness of women—especially in southern Italy—and the need for their emancipation. But the idea of his sister at university seemed to him like an exaggeration. As her older brother he felt that it was his duty to discourage her, for her own good. He tried to communicate to her how ridiculous she would seem if she did something so crazy. And that was how things stood on the day of the party.

The night of the dance, Alba wore the prune-colored taffeta dress that had been made for her the year before when she was to go to Gioia's villa. It was tighter than ever. She could barely breathe, but it showed off her full bosom and her tiny waist, the most slender waist anyone had ever seen in Grottole.

She sat in a corner of the room, grimly watching couples dance the tarantella. She danced only once, pro forma, with her brother Mimmo, who kept stepping on her toes, after which she refused all other invitations. She was afraid that those boys would breathe in her face with their garlicky, oniony breath as they jumped around like savages.

The party had quickly become wild, to the delight of some and the torment of others, dashing hopes and revealing surprises, quickening glances that moved more swiftly than the dancing feet and inspiring thoughts that moved even faster.

During the period when she was subsidizing her children's education, Candida had revived the practice, inaugurated with Cicia, of taking in lodgers from northern Italy. These young teachers, haughty and dejected as dethroned queens, filled the rooms of her house with their foreign accents and the fragrance of cheap perfume with which they sprayed themselves liberally. They waxed their legs and armpits, causing much discussion among the local women, who resolved, with ill-concealed envy, that this must be a habit they had learned from prostitutes.

At first, the foreign ladies would stay in their room even during meals, seeking to avoid contact with the local population as much as possible. But once they finally accepted to take part in Candida's populous meals and found themselves immersed in the rough gaiety of her seven children and surrounded by their dark, warm eyes, their robust shoulders, and by the fragrance of clean shirts—pressed with a charcoal-heated iron—they began to smile again.

In general, after a week or so, whether the lodger was ugly or pretty, tall or short, young or long in the tooth, Mimmo would fall in love with her, discovering in each of them, even if she had no great physical attractions, a sensitive soul and a delicate heart. He would describe them ardently to Rocco as they paced back and forth across the piazza with their hands behind their backs during pauses in their political activities.

It took only a few weeks for the teachers—sometimes longer, sometimes less, depending on their personality—to fall for Vincenzo, who did not write poems for them like Mimmo, and was not as handsome as Cataldo, nor as affectionate and helpful as Francesco, and perhaps precisely for these reasons was irresistible to them. He would dazzle them with one of his sidelong glances, and by the time Mimmo had decided, after much hesitation, to declare his love, Vincenzo had already taken the lady in question to bed and forgotten her.

Mimmo would become the confidant of their heartbreak. All of this irritated Candida to no end. She had had enough of the teachers, Vincenzo, and even Mimmo, and encouraged her disappointed lodgers to request a transfer, after which another one would arrive. On this particular occasion it was a girl from Pesaro, Guglielmina, with wavy hair and thick ankles, to whom Mimmo wrote poems full of blazing tenderness. Clelia, Cicia's daughter, was also staying with them; Cicia had remained in close contact with Candida, and they wrote to each other weekly, despite the fact that they had not seen each other since Cicia left town.

Clelia, however, had spent every summer at Candida's since she was a little girl, giving her mother a periodic rest. She was a little blonde with cerulean eyes and an air of insignificance, to whom no one paid any attention. She hovered by the walls and spoke only if spoken to, and even then she usually repeated something she had heard said by someone else. She wore dowdy dresses imposed by her military father, with sleeves down to her elbows and her hair done up in two braids around her head, a style that had gone out of fashion long ago. At sixteen, her chest was still flat and she had the air of a child who would never grow up.

Perhaps because of her old friendship with Cicia, and her memories of the many times they had laughed together and of the way Cicia's teeth shimmered when she laughed, Candida was crazy about the little girl. The love she had never known how to show her daughter she showered on her friend's child. She took Clelia with her wherever she went, justified all of her actions, and praised her on the slightest excuse. She showered her with affection in a manner that irritated Alba and drove her to seek revenge. Though she was forced to play with Clelia, Alba took every opportunity to tease and humiliate her, usually abandoning her somewhere. She was even willing, in so doing, to vex her mother, who would scurry off to console the poor child with kisses and sweet talk that enraged Alba all the more.

Clelia had been deeply in love with Vincenzo ever since they were children, when they played hide-and-seek in the ravines and touched each other in the dark. Between his other adventures, Vincenzo was happy to receive this unconditional love that had accompanied him through the years.

That night, Vincenzo danced a mazurka and a polka with Guglielmina, after which they disappeared together. As Mimmo

gazed at them with a heavy heart, Clelia stood by the wall without revealing her disappointment, which of course no one
would have bothered to notice.

But there was another person there who wasn't dancing.
Amid the increasing clamor in the room, Rocco stood in a corner, involved in passionate political discussion. The couples
danced around him, sometimes stepping on his toes, but he did
not even notice. He was talking about how, now that they had
obtained the land, they would need to form cooperatives in order to farm it. The party would have to assume an important role
in this process, and not simply limit itself to taking possession of
the land. Look at Reggio Emilia, for God's sake, their cooperatives really worked. People had to open their minds and forget
their self-interest. They needed to change their agricultural
methods and introduce crop rotation, because on a small plot
wheat impoverishes the land. And in Reggio Emilia, people
actually lived on the land . . .

. His interlocutors took turns listening to him respectfully because he was the teacher, and he was talking about serious matters they could barely understand, in correct Italian, without
cursing even once. His interlocutors kept changing but he did
not even notice, so passionate was he about what he was saying.
He would pause for a moment and then continue where he had
left off.

When Bruno Arpaia tired of playing the barrel organ,
Mimmo brought out an old gramophone. He vented his frustra-
tion by cranking the handle, and put on a waltz. Only a few
people knew how to dance the waltz, a handful who had learned
during their military service. The dance floor cleared as people
went to cool off with a glass of wine and a sweet pastry.

The notes of the waltz seeped into Rocco's political consciousness, bringing with them a wave of intense, painful mem-

ories. He interrupted his speech about mandatory education and stood up, looking for a way out.

He saw Alba sitting near the wall, and at that moment he suddenly noticed that Mimmo's sister had grown up. He hadn't seen her since the distant day when she had imprinted a clock face on his arm with her small, sharp teeth. He asked her to dance.

He spoke to her in perfect Italian, and perhaps that was why she did not say no. She had already noticed him; he seemed different, which in her mind was a mark of honor. He took her tiny waist, placing his open palm on her lower back, and they began to turn and glide gracefully among the clumsy couples.

As they danced, Rocco told her about the time he had gone to Paris with her brother Mimmo, to fulfill the pact they had made as boys. Three days by bus, and then three glorious days in the city. They had seen the Eiffel Tower. When they asked a man for directions to the Bastille, he had said, "*Coupé, coupé,*" and made a dramatic gesture with his hand. Paris. The city of *Vogue . . .*

She spoke less than he did. She reluctantly told him that she had been in boarding school and that she liked mathematics. Rocco did not give this much weight. He was far too stirred by her lightness.

Standing behind the gramophone, Mimmo happily cranked the lever. One by one, the other couples stopped to watch them.

One two three . . .

How feminine she was.

One two three . . .

He felt that he was holding something very fragile and very valuable in his hands.

One two three . . .

Was this that thing people talked about? Was this love?

One two three . . .

The complete extraneousness of her life captivated him.

One two three.

He had been to Paris. The city of *Vogue*.

The vases of flowers whirled around them. In 1950, transitional law number 845/50 redistributed the land in the towns of Montescaglioso, Irsina, and Grottole.

Their feet become interwoven, Rocco's dream becomes reality: the government builds farmhouses on the newly redistributed land, but the farmers refuse to leave the towns. They continue to plant wheat in the fields, as they always have.

The dust is swept up by a breeze. A restless soul wanders through southern Italy, awakening suspicions from all sides. He is Adriano Olivetti. It is hot. Olivetti founds a model cooperative in Corleto Perticara. He buys tools, pays his workers, builds roads.

The air is hot, steamy, unbreathable; her dress is tight. Olivetti has suspended his funding for the cooperative; it is ready to become autonomous. "What am I, a fool? Why should I work without pay?" the laborers ask. They give up on the whole idea. After leaving the Communist Party in 1956, Rocco runs the community center in Grottole, lending out books to farmworkers. During the first two years of his married life, he dedicates every free moment to this activity.

One two three, one two three . . .

"Why is it never truly clean?"

Time presses on. Olivetti goes into politics, opposed by the Communist Party. The community center in Grottole is empty. In Corleto Perticara, the weeds grow.

One two three . . .

Almost all of the redistributed fields are abandoned, and the farm laborers have gone off to work in the factories of Turin and Switzerland or the mines of Belgium and France. Adriano Olivetti dies alone, on a train to Switzerland.

Point, counterpoint. Two and three. Two and three. One and

two. Mara is gone, disappeared, wrapped in her overcoat. A new rapture, a mournful passion, built out of incomprehension and self-deception. Irreducible differences: her angular hips and sharp bones, her full chest, her narrow waist and long neck, shiny eyes black as coal.

Other easier and more alluring loves fade away because they are not yours. In the end, this painful love is stronger. How can you love the thing that makes you suffer the most? Perhaps you can if that thing belongs to you and you belong to it, but still, you try to elude its grasp. How can you not love that which has brought you life?

The waltz was becoming vertiginous. Rocco held Alba tightly and went round and round, and he felt a weight in his heart lighten with the dance. Alba kept moving her feet, short of breath. Perhaps this was the love her friends spoke of, that Gioia had described to her in the schoolyard, the love that would surely come one day for each of them, their immutable destiny, the love one recognizes at first sight with no possibility of error, that grabs you and sweeps you off your feet, leaving you breathless. Her dress was tight, her head was spinning, and all around her the walls, and the flowers painted on them by her grandfather, exploded with color, leaving smears of pistachio green and petunia pink . . . And then suddenly everything went black.

Rocco discovered Alba in his arms, limp and light as a rag doll. He decided at that moment that she would be his wife.

In mezzo a questa piazza
c'è una lepre pazza . . .

In the middle of the town square
there was a crazy hare . . .

Chapter Seventeen

Alba's pregnancy progressed in a half slumber filled with dreams and visions. Already in the second month the doctor had told her she would have to stay in bed if she hoped to keep this baby, and she had been forced to comply. From morning to night, she lay in semidarkness, relishing the refreshing crispness of the muslin sheets her mother changed once a day. She felt her skin stretching over her fragile bones, pushed powerfully from within. This internal activity so sapped her energy that she felt her consciousness extinguish. The people around her saw it as a sign of docility in the gestating mother, and did everything they could to spare her any disturbance.

The house was enveloped in a dreamlike silence. Even Rocco was kept away. When he came in to say hello to his wife or to pick up a change of clothes he was told to tiptoe, scolded at every turn by the women who presided there. His mother, Lucrezia, his mother-in-law, Candida, his sister-in-law Ninetta, and his other sister-in-law Clelia shuttled from room to room, murmuring, furtive as witches. They kept out even the sun and prepared concentrated broths that were like magical potions, made out of turkey, doves, and tiny, newly born birds taken from the nest.

In the evenings Rocco ate with his mother, who had finally reclaimed her son. They sat in total silence, interrupted from time to time by Lucrezia's comments; she claimed that even if Alba was able to carry the baby to term she would never be able to breast-feed. They would have to find a wet nurse . . . Rocco listened distractedly, responding in monosyllables.

Alba had dreams. She dreamed of colored lights unlike any she had seen in real life. Of her body blowing up like a hot-air balloon, floating over the nearby hills; of people running to see her as she floated by, waving. She dreamed of becoming as tiny as a chickpea and floating around in a walnut shell, like the man in the fairy tale, experiencing adventures and misadventures. She dreamed of the being inside her, always in a different form: a fish, or a dinosaur like the ones depicted in schoolbooks. Or a monkey, or a beautiful girl. In her dreams, Alba tried to speak with that being, but somehow she never could. She felt that nothing was more foreign to her than this thing that was growing inside her body.

The being also had dreams. It dreamed of deserts and drought. It dreamed of the sea parting to let it through. Of mountains collapsing beneath its steps. Of marshes that threatened to suck it down. Of passages from light into darkness and from darkness into light. It dreamed of everything, because it wanted to exist.

It dreamed of a hunger greater than itself that devoured everything around it. Of a journey in search of food. Of a new land. It was filled with the terror of wanting for food, of wasting away, of dying. That was how the dream ended. The being absorbed its mother's blood.

Sometimes it felt so exhausted that it longed to retreat into the soft walls of flesh that surrounded it, to merge with them once again, but it could not. It had to break free. And so, without knowing it, it resented this body that both nourished it and pushed it away, the body of its mother. The subtle resentment grew as it grew.

In the being's prolonged, enervating dreams there was a woman whose rage and impotence made its blood boil. And a man who masked his fear with silence, who no longer knew who he was. There was laughter that began quietly like a summer storm and then exploded, irrepressible and deep. There was a wind. A light spring breeze that suddenly turned dry and cutting and blew the leaves from the trees. Envy was everywhere, powerful and omnipresent, seeking out ways to survive through time. In the dream, the being sensed a bovine docility, a heartrending sadness, the eyes of men and women, incomprehensible phrases. A melody that surfaced and then disappeared again, like the faint music that Gioia had irradiated whenever she walked in the street, causing the workmen to turn and gaze after her on their scaffoldings, lingering in the memories of those who met her long after they had forgotten her face.

Some images rose to the surface and stayed there. Scenes from the lives of men and women. A girl kisses a younger girl, in secret. The door opens. A gluttonous child sneaks into the kitchen in the middle of the night and eats everything within reach: sauces, sausages, meats. To cover her tracks, she goes to the pantry and replaces what she has eaten.

A man prepares to journey across the ocean. The being does not know the ocean, but it does know fear. This is what it feels toward the unknown world that awaits it.

It perceives a faint taste of lemon. It does not know what lemon is, but the bitterness is familiar. It knows sacrifice and loneliness, desire and determination.

It could be one of many things, and each of them is a false

start. Its cells subdivide and multiply, and it is subsumed in its mother's dreams.

It is a monkey captured by a Dutchman in the African jungle, imported to England and exhibited in London's theaters, wearing the uniform of Queen Victoria's guard. A university professor buys it for research and falls in love; because of this, the captured monkey discovers love and tenderness.

A pointless, eccentric dream; this is not what the being will become. And yet something in the story resonates, perhaps simply a sense of lost possibilities.

The road that leads to what it will become is a maze filled with paths leading nowhere. There are countless possible incarnations, countless more or less distant approximations. Even the things that it will never be are part of it. It learns to know itself by comparison. Its own identity is made up of that which others are not. At times, though, it feels as though there is no substantial difference. They are shapes built from the same materials. At the least, the differences seem irrelevant.

Suddenly it dreams of a horror without which it could not exist. Extermination, destruction. A horror that is reproduced through time and space. It is the victim. And the perpetrator.

Patiently, it formulates the questions that it will encounter in the ensuing years. Difficult questions, for which it will not always find answers.

It knows many things that it will forget at birth. A great fear, a storm, a struggle to the death for existence, survived only by life itself.

Sometimes it experiences a great wave of cold. A feeling of emptiness, of nothingness, of nonexistence. Like a snail that retreats into its shell, a desire to cease existing, or at least to exist in another place. But existing in another place is the same as not existing. It must accept what it is.

Alba tosses and turns in the bed. Her forehead is beaded with sweat. She is afraid. She has suffered yet another narrowly averted miscarriage.

The hours go by slowly, vacantly.

The being germinates. Like a plant.

It begins its voyage prematurely.

The place where it lives has become intolerable. The love that nourishes it is suffocating. It is too great, or too slight, a pernicious love, like a poison.

The earth moves beneath its feet. Something gives way and a great void opens before it, a void it will carry inside forever.

On August the fifteenth, Alba went into labor. Her water broke two weeks early, as the procession for the Assumption of the Virgin marched down the Via Nuova. "*Evviva Maaaria, Maaaria evviva!*" "Long live Maria and her Creator!" The women's singsong rose up toward the blinding light.

At her mother's house, they were setting the table for the midday meal. The antipasto consisted of boiled eggs and sausage.

Clelia assisted at the birth. She had recently passed the competitive exam to become a midwife in Grottole. It would have been pointless to attempt to rush Alba to the hospital in Matera on the Feast of the Assumption.

Little Clelia, the ninny.

Alba's baby was crouched in a strange position. She was like a small animal that does not want to be dragged out of its den.

"Cleliayoustupidfool! Take your lizard hands off of me! Leave me alone, don't touch me!"

Clelia extracted the little girl. It was her first delivery. Her hands trembled, and she was sweating, even more than the mother. Gioia's hip was dislocated, a condition that would affect her throughout her infancy. Alba finally had a real reason to hate her sister-in-law.

Chapter Eighteen

Swallow. Come on now. Swallow. One more bite, just one more. Come on, it's the last one. She hasn't eaten for two days, for goodness' sake. She just chews and chews, and then spits it all out. I can't stand to watch!

Alba leaned forward desperately, holding the spoon to her daughter's mouth, as her daughter watched her, cheeks filled with balls of food like a hamster. Here, drink a little bit of water and swallow. When I was little I went for days without eating, just like her. The less I ate, the less I wanted to eat. She'll starve to death. Alba was growing visibly thinner, drained by this impossible task, surrounded by the vapor of pasta rings boiling in broth and the smoke of grilled meats. She whisked sole into a paste, extracted the juices from the leanest cuts of beef, and secretly added puréed banana to the baby's orange juice. Look at the twins, with their pink and white skin, they'll eat anything! They would eat me if they could. Bless them, they'll even eat dry bread, they dream of sauces, and they wolf down meat. Lucky things. My God, everything turned my stomach when I was a little girl, and my daughter is even worse, she's not interested; I remember as if it were yesterday, the less I ate the less appetite I had. She'll starve. She's too thin, I told you! What do you expect, with a mother like that? She must have a worm in her belly, they say she doesn't eat but it's not true, I took her a fresh egg and she didn't want it, but she has her own food, homogenized, with semolina and cream and I don't know what else, but still, she's too thin. Lucrezia complained to her son about the wife he had chosen.

Despite her lack of appetite, Gioia was growing up full of energy and mischief. She sat on her high chair as if on a throne, watching all the members of her family pass by: grandmothers, aunts, cousins. Sometimes they wore masks to amuse her or made funny faces or did improvised tricks that worked every time; Mammalina made a mouse out of a handkerchief that scampered across her hands and disappeared up her forearm. Or the trick where you pretend to pull off someone's nose, and then, there it is, wiggling between your index and middle finger. And the coin that appeared and disappeared, or the silly hare from the town square, hopping around the palm of your hand.

Her mother had chosen the name Gioia, against everyone's wishes, in honor of her vanished friend and as a sign of distinction, because she didn't want her daughter to be lumped in with the other children in the town. From her friend, the child seemed to have inherited the red highlights that glinted in her hair under the sun—Alba conveniently forgot her great-aunt Angelica's copper tint, which was not visible in the black-and-white photographs. She also refused to note the child's obvious resemblance to her grandmother Lucrezia, for whom she should have been named.

A photograph of Gioia in the first grade: she stands in a perfectly ironed, immaculate pinafore with a starched collar, her tomboyish face framed by two pigtails that are so tight they seem to pull her scalp away from her head. All around her stand little girls, lice visible in their matted hair, with crooked eyes and protruding ears.

When Gioia was a bit older, her grandmother Lucrezia would bring her swallows from the fields, their wings and beaks snipped. She would tie their legs to the balcony rail so that Gioia could watch them flitter about clumsily, trying helplessly to fly. In August Lucrezia brought cicadas, which she would place under an overturned glass. They would sing until they ran out of air and died of asphyxiation. And she brought lightning bugs, which filled the darkness above the chest of drawers in Gioia's room with a delicate, greenish light.

At the age of four, Gioia killed a swallow and cut it apart with her fingernails. Her mother found her rummaging in the bird's stomach. She screamed in horror. "Your clean dress! I just changed you!"

On afternoons in early spring, when the sun was warm but the air was still sharp, Alba dressed Gioia in beautiful, starched, embroidered white dresses and took her for walks beyond the wall. There, she met her friend Gianetta, who, like her, was overcome by the burdens of motherhood. People stopped in the road to say hello. Oh, what a pretty little girl, what a little princess . . . Large women would give her sticky kisses. Gioia furtively wiped her cheeks with her hand. She feared her grandmother Lucrezia's kisses even more. They were voracious and insistent and she was afraid they might swallow her up.

Whenever Luigino La Ciminiera saw her he would invite them into his butcher shop. There were puddles of blood on the floor and quartered animals hanging from hooks. Lamb heads dangled, their eyes opaque with terror. Luigino would give her a piece of candy wrapped in silver paper. If she threw it on the floor it made a loud sound. She ate it with a slight sense of disgust. "Come on, give Luigino a little kiss," her mother would say. His skin was dark and smelled of blood.

Gioia on the subway. She sits there as people stand all around her, dangling from the metal bar; they shift from side to side and it seems they might fall on her at any moment. There is a black woman wearing a gaudy dress and carrying a chubby-cheeked baby in a sack. Two Arab girls. Three Asians. Gioia doesn't notice. She stares at a distant point, light years away from the crowd. A beggar gets on. Gioia stares directly in front of her, at an imaginary point in the distance, as she learned to do long ago. She has been living in Rome for some time. She has no history. None of the people around her have a history.

As a child, Gioia enjoyed running around her grandfather's shop. She weighed herself on the scale and measured how many centimeters she had grown, just as her mother and uncles had done before her. She played with copper sulphate crystals, mixing them around; she poured streams of grain and lentils through her fingers, caressed fabrics, and went through people's trousseaux, which were no longer handmade as they once had been.

In Grottole, the sixties were the golden age of the trousseau.

IN 1959 the big news broke: they had discovered methane in the valley of the Basento.

At Cugno del Ricco during the excavations a young engineer from Turin had found a blackened object. He cleaned it off. It was a silver pocket watch with two F's engraved on the lid. God only knew whom it had belonged to, and how it had ended up there. The clock marked five-thirty.

The following year thirty-two methane wells were inaugurated in Ferrandina, Salandra, Pomarico, and Grottole. The one in Grottole was the last, and its opening was marked by an all-night celebration. There was an orchestra and street performers—including a fire-eater—but the main attraction was the huge flame that shot up into the darkened sky before the amazed eyes of the farm workers. In its flickering light, many of them swore they had seen the specter of poverty finally leaving the town, echoing the words of a television announcer who had come to document the event.

Pozzi, Agip, and Anic opened branches in the area and hired all the available workforce from the towns in the valley. The land that had been obtained through the agrarian reforms was soon abandoned. For the first time in the history of the town, money began to circulate, and the farmers, who had now become industrial workers, immediately invested it in that which to them most clearly represented a brighter future: in other words, trousseaux. Factory-made linens became all the rage, and Colino's shop was crammed with boxes in neat piles on the shelves. Instead of buying three pieces of fabric and sewing them together to make sheets, one could buy them already made, with flashy psychedelic designs, in strange new fabrics that were incredibly, sinfully smooth and that, if you rubbed them, produced a joyful burst of sparks, like fireworks. During those years, new fabrics appeared and disappeared, lasting a season or two, like abortive experiments on the road to evolution. They resembled satin or silk, and had intriguing names that usually included at least one *y*, as well as strange collateral effects that led to their quick disappearance from the market. One in particular, Terital, triumphed over all the others. You didn't have to iron it; it was indestructible and inalterable, like the petroleum it was made of.

When the methane companies began to build a pipeline to carry away the gas, a great cry rose up. The methane is ours! You can't take it away! Rocco led the insurrection; they decided to kidnap a technician from the Società Nazionale Metanodotti company. They took him for lunch at Settecapozzole's trattoria, whose cuisine he enjoyed, and then set him free toward evening. Rocco paid the bill out of his own pocket and insisted that he should try the *crostata*. Meanwhile, at home, Alba scrubbed the bathroom tiles and waxed the dining room floor. That time, they got their way.

GIOIA'S HIP DEFECT did not keep her from playing with the other children. She scratched about in the dirt looking for shiny rocks, played hide-and-seek, climbed up on things, lit fires. She was the bravest of them all, even as a little girl; she would go anywhere and if she fell she would sing to herself to keep from crying. Candida shook her head as she consoled her: "Tell Grandma, when will you get some sense?"

Gioia ate a banana. "What is it?" A banana. Gioia eats a banana and throws the peel on the floor. A little girl picks it up. "Don't you eat this part? It's good." She scrapes the white part inside the banana peel with her teeth. At the time, many people emigrated to Germany; later, they went to Turin.

Gioia was sick.

They kept her inside, like a fruit in a greenhouse, protected from the wind. Why was she always sick?

A blond doctor with a Christlike beard came to see her. "Give her milk and honey," he said. "That's all?" "Milk and honey is all she needs." Fine. Miraculous. Milk and honey for a cough. Milk and honey for a stomachache. Milk and honey for a back ache. How odd! He was arrested in Grassano because he had no medical degree. Such an affectionate man, and he didn't charge much.

Every so often, a truck came to town trading plastic for copper. Plastic is nice. So colorful, so hygienic. Let's get rid of all the old stuff, throw it away. The old copper pots hanging in the kitchen. Old furniture. Gone. We want plastic, nylon, rayon, Moplen. We want factories. Clelia cut her hair and got a wave.

When Gioia was six years old she had her tonsils removed, because they were just a bit of extra flesh that nature had put there for no reason, a receptacle for germs and influenza. To help her forget her sore throat and the unpleasantness of the anesthesia and the chair with the straps, her grandmother Candida spent three days and three nights by her side telling one story after another, never stopping even for an instant.

Caterina Caterina dammi la gamba con tutta la scatolina . . . Caterina, Caterina, give me your leg and the little box . . .

"Tell me another one." "No, that's enough, I'm tired." "Just tell me the one about the barrels." "All right, but then you have to go to sleep." "I promise."

Candida told her the story about Grandma Concetta who was poor and Grandpa Francesco who was rich. The one about the barrels filled with coins hidden in a wall. And about Aunt Angelica and how beautiful she was. And the seamstress who made dresses you could not move your arms in. She would tell these stories once, twice, three times, always the same stories, with a few variations, a new detail here, a new word there. As she told them, a door opened through which Gioia could escape without being scolded.

Later, Gioia sought out other stories, printed on paper. She found Uncle Mimmo's library in a cupboard with glass knobs. She read everything she could get her hands on, from Dostoevski's novels to Brother Indovino's calendar, in order to block out the babbling of the women as they knitted in a circle in Candida's bedroom.

Sometimes they fell silent when Gioia came in. She would catch a phrase here and there, but could not decipher the meaning. Even so, she sensed an air of intrigue and secrecy, the same atmosphere that suffused the novelettes her grandmother read. In real life, it felt completely different. After a while, she realized that all these phrases, looks, and allusions referred to one person.

"Did you see the boots she bought?"

On this subject, her mother was the most dogged of them all. Even her voice changed.

A salesman had come to town selling a novelty, knee-high boots. "How awful, I would never wear them, even if they paid me!" And trousers. "Plaid trousers, can you imagine?" Alba said. "My brother is too lenient with her, and that's an understatement. He has only stood up for himself once in his life, and guess against whom? That's right, you guessed it. When she was a girl, his wife was a dumpy little thing. She had no dress sense at all, and her father used to make her wear sleeves down to her elbows! Look at her now, she thinks she's the cat's meow and she's even gone and cut her hair! She's crazy! She's a fool, but don't pay her any mind. She thinks she's somebody because she makes money, but have you seen her house? Have you noticed how long it takes her to wash the dishes or do the laundry or dust? And of course she has no idea what it means to really clean . . ."

Not to mention her daughter, who, in her opinion, had been damaged by this woman.

"And you, don't get dirt on your new dress! Just look at you, there's a stain already, for heaven's sake, you'll drive me to the grave."

The person they were talking about was Aunt Clelia.

She had become a different person after she married Mimmo a few years earlier. Little by little, she had developed a sense of entitlement, until eventually she became the complete opposite of what she once was. Where once she had been taciturn, timid, and insignificant, she was now increasingly eccentric and strident, always defending absurd causes and saying things that defied common logic, going on interminable tirades that the other women mockingly listened to while exchanging ironic glances behind her back. Candida would sometimes put up a tepid defense of her protégée, but without much conviction—it was not her nature to work up a righteous indignation. Meanwhile, her gossipy daughters-in-law and daughter continued to whisper, like a crackling flame burning in the embers.

Clelia reached the apex of her unpopularity when she began taking the pill. She said that she did not want any more children after the twins, because work made it impossible. Those poor boys were always being dragged here and there and left to fend for themselves, their fat little cheeks always dirty. "Why is it that they eat, and my little girl refuses to?" Alba wondered. "My little girl won't eat a thing."

Aunt Clelia's house was not glacially immaculate like the others in town, where there was never even the slightest trace of dust on the furniture. The doilies starched stiff. The marble tile floors polished until they were slick and shiny as glass. The twins could run around like wild animals and never had to worry about scratching the floor. They spilled sauce on the tablecloth and on themselves and dropped crumbs on the floor, and if they didn't feel like finishing their food they simply left it on the plate, but this hardly ever happened because they were ravenous as wolves, gobbling up everything within their grasp: soap, coins, knick-knacks, jewelry . . . Their birth was shrouded in secrecy, as if a god had descended from Olympus and taken human form and was somehow implicated in the affair.

Clelia discussed topics that Gioia had never heard anyone else even mention. She had an unnatural passion for the bidet, which she mentioned at least once in every conversation, her eyes sparkling like a love-struck girl. She explained to Gioia how it was used, miming each gesture as she straddled a chair, and then afterward asked her to repeat everything to make sure she had understood. On Sundays she skipped Mass and expected her husband to stroll around the piazza with her. Mimmo would have done anything to make her happy, but here he was forced to draw the line. People already talked enough . . . At home he even helped with the dishes, praying in his heart that no one would ever know . . .

Often, Clelia asked Gioia what she thought of her outlandish clothes: palazzo pants, miniskirts . . . "Don't I have nice legs?" she would ask. Gioia stared at her in disbelief, but Clelia was not discouraged. She asked Gioia if she wanted to try on her clothes. Gioia said no, but tried them on anyway, and got the giggles. She enjoyed Clelia's company. When they were together, it was as if the line that divided the adult world from her own, and that between men and women, began to dissolve in the psychedelic swirls of Clelia's rayon blouses.

ALBA ERASED ALL TRACES. She cleaned furiously, as if trying to eliminate the evidence of a savage crime. She wiped away footprints, streaks, smudges, and particles of dust, until the surfaces in her house were smooth and polished and appeared as untouched as the surface of the moon before Neil Armstrong set foot there.

Alba loved the moon. On July 21, 1969, when the lunar landing was broadcast on television and Alba saw those expanses where no man had ever set foot, where there was no gravity and bodies were freed from their earthly bonds, she wondered for a moment whether that was her true home. She would travel there in her mind when she was cleaning, polishing tiles, dusting furniture, washing the floor. She dreamed of that weightless place, on the edge of infinity, in which headaches, filth, and needs did not exist.

When summer came, after a busy winter occupied by the reading center, the party office, the club, the hours spent tutoring students who failed their exams, the heated political discussions in the piazza that lasted well into the night, and his own preparations for the schoolmaster exam, Rocco drove Alba and Gioia up north for a week to visit churches. He studied the churches closely, inspecting each column, every arch, and afterward invariably declared that all that money would have been better spent building houses for the poor.

When they drove through Grottole in their Volkswagen, the neighbors rushed to the side of the road, in part because the road was narrow, but also to watch them go by. They waved as they passed. Rocco loved to explain, with great pride, that Volkswagen meant "car of the people."

In the summer of 1968, during the Feast of San Rocco— which was when the Grottolesi living abroad came to visit from America, Germany, and the north—the festivities were particularly pitiful, with an orchestra made up of orphans whimpering off-key in the piazza. Cataldo had an idea. In a cheeky jab at Don Arcangelo, who had always presided over the ceremonies, Cataldo and a few friends, along with his younger brother Francesco, organized a celebration that did not honor any saint, but rather a scandalously pagan divinity: youth. They invited a band called Marilù and the Dynamics. Marilù arrived in a miniskirt that took your breath away and tall white boots that showed off her plump thighs. The Grottolesi had never seen anything like it.

She opened the set with the song "Ma tu vuliv a pizz" ("But you wanted pizza"). The crowd made her sing it seven more times. The young men stood at the edge of the stage, jostling for a strategic spot from which they could just make out a tiny corner of paradise, Marilù's blue nylon panties. In the ensuing years, and even in the new millennium, any band that came through town was asked to play "Ma tu vuliv a pizz," but no one, no one could play it like Marilù.

NINETEEN SIXTY-NINE. Waves of popular unrest. Many roads were blocked by protesters because the Basento valley had not received any federal funds to promote local industry. "Factories! We want factories!" they yelled. "No more emigration!" This would be Rocco's last protest, but at the time he didn't know it.

On Sundays, women still went to Mass, even if they no longer believed. The men strolled in the piazza and then went to the club. Sometimes they held a political meeting. Gioia was three years old. She learned to say, "*Adda vení baffone*" with her fist held high. At six, she celebrated her First Communion with a bruise on her nose from a fall, and she learned to embroider using the stem stitch. At seven, she embroidered her first handkerchief with tatting and read Gramsci's book of fables *L'Albero del Riccio* (The Hedgehog's Tree), a gift from her father. When she was eight, one day she stood for a long time next to her grandmother, staring at the statue of Christ descended from the cross. "Grandma, I have to tell you a secret," she said. "I don't believe in God." Here we go, thought Candida. "What do you mean? Look at him there, our Lord, look what they did to him. He sacrificed himself for us." She made the sign of the cross and prayed to her beloved friend Christ for the millionth time, asking him to protect them from the problems that were coming. But He must have been distracted, or perhaps He was just tired.

Zzzzzzzzzz Zzzzzzzzzz Zzzzzzzzz. A noise like a helicopter. A green beetle flies around and around; one of its legs is tied with string. Can I try? No, no, no! Fine, it's your loss! I know something but I'm not telling. What is it? Not telling.

Springtime. The children have perpetrated a massacre of baby birds. They have swept their nests out of the roof gutters. Featherless chicks with big, yellow beaks. Tonight we'll fry them. No, I don't want to. They're so little, look at them, they're crying! Don't be silly. You stupid girl. No, I don't want to, I don't want to! If you don't want to eat them you don't have to. Gioia cried all day long with great sobs that shook her whole body. It was an avalanche of sadness. Toward evening the house was filled with the fragrance of fried birds; it penetrated every room, even the room where Gioia lay on the bed, tightly clutching her talking doll, the one they had given her when she had her tonsils removed. An evil, tempting, irresistible fragrance. The little birds were crying. "Can I taste?" In the end, she ate most of them, with ravenous pleasure, tears falling with each bite.

Chapter Nineteen

At the age of nine, Gioia discovered that the Promised Land did in fact exist, and was not, as the Bible claimed, located at the source of the Tigris and the Euphrates, but rather less than one hundred kilometers from the place where she had been born, on the Puglia coast.

After putting it off for years, busy as he was with his political activities, Rocco finally took the competitive exam to become a school principal, and placed well, and from the list of available spots, he chose Monopoli, where Alba had gone to school and where some of Colino's relatives still resided, a rather forlorn branch of the family. They had a houseful of girls, all named after queens, who, with the help of their husbands, had squandered the fortune built by Minguccio the Merchant. Rocco and Alba's few visits to these relations had provided a rich store of anecdotes and imitations, whose retelling for many years had become an integral part of the general pandemonium during Easter and Christmas lunches back in Grottole. After the initial visits prescribed by tradition and good manners, the two branches of the family never frequented each other again, but the mere presence of these distant relatives made Rocco feel that they were not living in a place that was completely foreign.

In Monopoli the olive trees did not look like skeletal structures contorted by suffering, the sun did not scorch, and the countryside was not parched. Monopoli had the sea, the rocks, and the beach. Women wore colored dresses. There was a train.

"Can we come back tomorrow?" Gioia said, standing open-mouthed at the train crossing. "If you're good, we'll see." Their new building had an elevator. Gioia rode it up to the fourth floor, then ran down the stairs and rode it again until she had spent all of her money, ten lire.

Rocco no longer discussed politics in the piazza with the other men, nor was he involved in party activities. Politics were a distant echo, one of the many subjects discussed in respectable drawing rooms, interrupted by plans for outings, vacations, and dinner parties. Politics were like the good intentions that paved the road to Hell, drowned out by the bonhomie of opulence. At night Rocco was sometimes awakened by certain thoughts, which disappeared without a trace during the day.

Rocco and Alba went out with other couples their age. There were lunches, dinners, and parties at which canapés and vol-au-vents from the Grand Café were served. They all insisted on paying the bill, pushing their way forward and arguing; sometimes they almost came to blows. They went to Bari to buy clothes and shoes. In the summer they went to the beach and in the winter they went to the movies: *The Knock-Out Cop, The Anonymous Venetian, Amarcord* . . . "What does '*amarcord*' mean? Do you know?" They enjoyed themselves but were slightly ashamed, because they had always thought that fun was something allowed only during one specific period in life: the passage from adolescence to young adulthood, when a man seeks a wife, and a woman seeks a husband.

Alba observed this new life diffidently. She always said no at first, and then dove into the novelty at hand with the enthusiasm of a child. She learned new recipes. How many recipes are there in the world? Seafood salad, *pasta alla sangiovannella*. "Did you remember the capers?" On summer nights they danced in their friends' living rooms. First they put on records, and then Professor Cavallo would play the mandolin and the couples embraced and danced the tango: *Changez la dame* . . . The olive trees were so thick that a man could not reach around the trunk with his arms. In the empty lots, crickets sang. Their friends brought bags of cherries, big as sorb apples. There were also almonds, jars of capers, cups of juicy prickly pears. One time, someone brought chocolate-covered oranges. "Try them, they're delicious! One of my husband's patients, the politician's wife, gave me the recipe; such a nice lady . . ." Alba sometimes went out alone, or with her women friends.

One rainy afternoon Alba went to pick up Gioia from her piano lesson, a source of exasperation for both of them, because Gioia did not want to go, and Alba was determined that she should. As a prize for agreeing to continue her studies for another month, Alba had promised to take her to the movies. It was a film that had given Alba pause; Gioia was probably too young for it, but she insisted, and Alba wanted to make her happy. It was a love story about two factory workers, played by Giuliano Gemma and Stefania Sandrelli, with a tragic ending. Alba had called the theater to make sure there were no overly risqué scenes, because you never could tell. A while back she and her husband had gone to see a movie with a romantic title, which sounded quite promising. It was *Last Tango in Paris*. They left without even seeing the first part, eyes lowered, not knowing where to look. Was it really necessary?

Now, in the confusion and the rain, Alba almost collided with an elegant lady in a fur coat. The winters in that area were mild, and furs were not necessary, but chic women wore them anyway. Alba opened her eyes wide and shuddered as if she had seen a ghost. She and the woman stared at each other, suspended together in a moment of silence. Many years passed before their eyes. Then, at once, they both cried out: "It's you!"

They smiled. Awkwardly. There was another silence, as if neither knew what to say. "This is my daughter," Alba said finally, pushing Gioia forward. "Pleased to meet you, I'm Gioia," the lady said. "What about you?" Alba asked. "Two, a boy and a girl. They're older." "That night . . . ," Alba suddenly blurted out, and then paused. "Yes?" the lady asked, but Alba had already decided not to go on. An older gentleman arrived. "My husband." "Pleased to meet you." "And you." "She's an old friend. Let's keep in touch, all right?" She left, leaving behind a trail of perfume.

AMID THE WHITE HOUSES with Moorish domes near the harbor, Gioia had quickly ceased to be the difficult child she had been in Grottole. After four operations her limp was almost gone, when she walked, she pitched slightly side to side like a little boat in the current, swaying her hips. It had become almost a charming affect in her walk. She strengthened her muscles with corrective exercises. Her teacher probes her adolescent body to explain the work she needs to do to become stronger. Meanwhile, her breasts develop, firm and beautiful, and she contemplates them at length on Sunday mornings in the misty bathroom mirror.

Rocco and Alba nursed secret, personal dreams for their daughter, dreams that did not coincide. He imagined her at a university, as a professor, and when he was feeling particularly grand, in Paris. The only external manifestation of this desire was his acquisition of a series of French lessons on 45s: *"Le premier jour d'école est toujours une aventure . . ."* Alba would have liked to see her on a stage in an evening gown, sitting at the piano. But Gioia had no intention of spending all day at the piano, practicing. So Alba consoled herself with the thought that her daughter would be dealt the same lot she had and which was rightfully hers: marriage. And children. So it had been for her mother and grandmother, and so it would be for her.

Up to a point, Gioia tried to fulfill these dreams, just as her parents had once tried to adapt to the clothes made for them by the local seamstress. But every week she made up new names for herself because she no longer liked her own, and she still turned up her nose at her mother's soups, and she still placed a faith in her father's words that almost nothing in her life had yet challenged.

Some days, Rocco seemed distracted. He was thinking about his mother, Lucrezia. At Christmas, he persuaded her to come visit. He had to force her, almost. She did not want to leave Grottole. He picked her up one cloudy afternoon, arriving at the house unannounced, packed her only spare dress, closed the glass-paned door behind him, and carried her away from her troubles, her disputes with the neighbors, and the teasing of the neighborhood kids, determined to give her the fragment of happiness to which she was entitled. They made a bed for her in his office. Lucrezia spent the days sitting in a chair, her back to the window, with its view of the sea. Wrapped in her brown shawl, her lumpy shoes peeking out from under her black dress, she looked like an uprooted tree.

Gioia plunges her hands into the dirt of an empty lot near the beach. She and her two closest friends, Porzia and Madia, have planted beautiful, stinky onion flowers there, which they sprinkle with salt water. When the plants dry up there is no time to be sad. The girls have made a pact: they will live on this vacant lot together after they are married. Gioia had met her first love. A little blond fellow with tender eyes and a Morini motorbike who, for an entire year, had tried unsuccessfully to gather the courage to tell her he wanted to kiss her.

He holds her tight. They are dancing slowly to music from *The Godfather.* He whispers in her ear that he needs to tell her something. He feels as if he were about to jump off the high dive. Their skin is so hot that it vaporizes the freshly washed fragrance of his white cotton shirt and her powdery perfume. "What do you need to tell me?" The only answer is the sound of his labored breath. Shivers run down her back from her ear to the base of her spine, making her believe that happiness is eternal. He holds her even closer. "I can't guess." Her voice grows even softer and more velvety. "Why don't you tell me over the phone?" She enjoyed keeping him on a string.

But it was too much, because their kiss was not to be.

O sorcio mi pelat
e si mort nda la pignata.

The mouse lost all its fur,
and landed in the frying pan.

Chapter Twenty

On March 16, 1978, the news circulated that Aldo Moro had been kidnapped. Gioia was standing on the steps of the Liceo Ginnasio E. Duni in Matera, on her way to recess. She asked her friend to repeat what he had said, because she couldn't believe it. The others also thought it was a joke, but it was true. Gioia was overcome by a strange, dark euphoria; it was as if the rules had suddenly changed without warning, or as if suddenly there were no more rules, and anything was possible. She experienced a feeling of bewilderment and power. She laughed as the bell marked the end of recess. Reluctantly she returned to class, but not for long because a few minutes later the custodian came to fetch her.

"What? When? Who told you?"

"*O frat mí, o frat mí, o frat míííííí . . .*" ("Oh, brother of mine!")

Colino's coffin lay in the parlor, the one with the flower frescoes on the walls. The people of the town had been filing by since morning, and women pulled at their hair and beat their chests as they told stories from his life.

"*O frat mí, o frat mí.* He was a good man, a clever man; when I think of everything he did for me, *o frat míííííííí.* That year, that terrible year when we had the cold snap in May, I went to the shop to get chickpeas and flour, but I couldn't pay and you gave them to me and didn't say a word, Colino, you didn't say a word. And when I said, 'Colí, I have a daughter, Lucietta. How will I make a trousseau for her? She'll be an old maid, that's what she'll be, an old maid.' And you said, 'Quiet now, quiet, quiet,' you said, 'that's enough, go on now, get out of here,' and you measured the fabric for the sheets and the bedclothes, and you said, 'Here, take them and go, not a word!' A good man, *cumba* Colí. By the time I paid my debt Lucietta had three children, three children I'm telling you. Who can forget such a thing? The good Lord has made a mistake, he's taken the wrong man. Why couldn't he take a scoundrel instead of you? You were a good man. May you receive as many blessings as you bestowed on all of us, Colí."

O frat mí, o frat mí, u cerson, my oak tree.

Candida was slumped dejectedly on a chair, lifeless, then she would suddenly stand up and go over to the coffin, as if possessed by a superhuman strength.

"The rag doll, the doll you gave me. It's still there, but now you're gone . . ."

The farm laborers came in from the fields to tell stories of how he had sold them pasta on credit, and the small landowners told how he would give them fertilizer and collect payment only after they had sold their harvest. The women who sold Colino eggs came to the house, as did the women who cleaned the soapwort and *lampascioni* for the shop. Everyone had a story to tell, going as far back as the war, when Colino could have gotten rich off the black market, as so many had. He wasn't interested in getting rich, but he never hesitated to sell a handful of wheat or ricotta under the table, saving many from starvation.

"*O frat mí, o frat mí.*"

Lucrezia came, beating her chest and crying out, "Why wasn't it me instead of you? It should have been me. That way I would be out of everyone's way and everyone would be happier."

There was not a single citizen of Grottole who did not come to pay his respects. In the weeks, months, and years thereafter farmers continued to knock on Candida's door, to settle their debts, even though they could have gotten away without paying, since only Colino could decipher the shop's ledgers.

IN A CORNER, Gioia watched the mourners with amazement. She had been away from Grottole for a long time because after they left for Monopoli, she had not wanted to set foot there.

Two years earlier, they had moved to Matera.

Rocco was retired and wanted to be closer to Lucrezia, who was getting older but still refused to leave her house.

Gioia would have preferred death to leaving Monopoli, their apartment on the fourth floor of the teachers' condominium, with balconies overlooking an orange grove, the sea in the distance, her friends, and the waves that scattered seashells on the beach in winter. Alba did not want to go, either. Finally Rocco had said that if this continued he would go without them.

In 1974 there was a referendum on the abolition of divorce, and Alba voted no. The no vote won, and divorce stayed on the books, but she herself would never have been able to stand the shame. Divorce was something for women who lived far away, in the huge, frigid cities of the north, for unfortunate women who were beaten by their violent, alcoholic husbands. Her husband would never have dreamed of beating her. She followed him to Matera.

Gioia cried until she had no tears left, for a love that had not even begun, for the end of summers spent on the back of friends' mopeds, for the vacant lot where she and her friends would never live, and for her father's betrayal. For a long time, Rocco hoped the storm would pass, just as, when she was a little girl, she had eventually recovered from her colds, influenzas, and tantrums. As he had back then, in order to console her, or rather to distract her, he had come up with nothing better than to buy her a book that was being discussed in all the papers, and was flying off the shelves. It was called *Porci con le ali* (*Pigs with Wings*), and it started with the words "*Cazzo, cazzo, cazzo*" ("Fuck, fuck, fuck"). For a moment she smiled, almost despite herself, then it became yet another stone she could cast upon him.

"*O frat mí, o frat mí.* The doll you bought for me . . ."

Gioia saw her grandmother's eyes fill with passion like an adolescent girl, with a carnal passion for the man who was leaving her. Luigino La Ciminiera came by as well, and for a moment Gioia was afraid he would ask her for a kiss just as he had when she was a little girl.

Clelia was there, standing near the coffin. Gioia rested her head on her shoulder.

After the coffin was lowered into the ground, nothing was ever the same again.

IT WAS CATALDO, known as Dino, the only one of Candida's children who hadn't gone to school, who inherited the shop. For a while he experienced a period of unbelievable prosperity. He got rid of much of Colino's junk and slowly began to phase out the items that he felt were superfluous. Soap, pasta. What was the point of selling those things? You could make a lira or two, but who cares? You can't just sell everything like in the old days. He got rid of the fertilizer, the seeds, the olives. "What do you think this is, Mamma, a bank?" He no longer gave credit, and gradually people started to go elsewhere.

In the early eighties, Cataldo's daughters were always dressed to the nines; no one in town had ever seen anything like it. They wore designer clothes bought in Bari, Rome, or Milan, with the labels emblazoned on them, as if they were inside out. Armani, Missoni, Krizia . . . The girls seemed to know these and other names better than those of their closest relatives. A supermarket opened in the valley; it sold everything, as Colino's store once had, but neatly divided on the shelves, and there was no buying on credit. Cataldo and his wife spent their days doing crossword puzzles in the empty shop. They became fat as rhinos. Even their oldest customers stopped coming. They barely sold trousseaux anymore. Everyone had a car now. They could go to Matera or Bari to do their shopping. But Cataldo's girls were still dressed in high style, in fact they became even more fashionable, and their refrigerator was stuffed with food; meanwhile their debts grew day by day and they had to mortgage the house. The girls' fashionable clothes inspired envy and nasty gossip among the few people who still lived in the town, but even that was not enough to fill the days.

The youngest, Isabella, slept later and later in order to make the days pass more quickly until finally one day she didn't get up at all. The eldest, Concetta, known as Tina, left town in search of a better showcase for her wardrobe. She wandered around the party scene in Milan, wobbling on her high heels, long enough to get mixed up—she did not even know how—in a cocaine bust that cost her family a fortune in lawyer's fees. In her small way, she too played a part in the bankrupting of the family business.

Cataldo ended up working as a caretaker in his brother's building in Ancona, and in a way, the bankruptcy was a relief to the whole family. Isabella was forced to get out of bed in the morning to go to work, and Tina resigned herself to marrying a neighbor who had courted her for years, in vain, and who turned out to be an excellent husband. Cataldo and his wife managed to avoid drowning in a sea of cholesterol that would otherwise have killed them.

AFTER THE FUNERAL Gioia and Clelia went for a walk alone beyond the wall. Behind the stone parapet, the sun was setting over the valley of the Basento. The chimneys of the Anic refinery pierced through the red and purple clouds. They walked hand in hand, not like an aunt with her niece, but like two friends in primary school. Instead of psychedelic blouses, Clelia now wore vintage rags that she bought at the flea markets in Rome, where she and her family had moved. People turned to stare at them, but they didn't notice. They talked for a long time about many things, some of which had never occurred to either of them before that moment; they made them up then and there for the simple pleasure of confiding in each other. Gioia said she had only one desire: to leave Matera. Clelia talked about erogenous zones, about self-awareness, and about the exact location of the clitoris. Gioia nodded, as if she had always known these things. When they returned, people were worried; someone had been sent out to look for them.

That night they ate together, standing in the kitchen. They brought down the *capocolli* that hung from hooks in the cellar. It was the last time. Slowly, the house emptied out.

Sons, daughters, daughters-in-law, and grandchildren no longer filled the house, there were no men standing in the front room discussing politics, no women in the bedroom sharing gossip, no children chasing one another from room to room.

Candida wandered alone in the empty house, cursing the high ceilings that swallowed up the heat produced by the radiators that had recently been installed and praying uselessly for the Good

Lord to call her to him. On the increasingly rare occasions when her children came to visit on Sundays and official holidays, she no longer handed out packages of pasta, fabric, money, or advice. Now that she no longer had her husband at her side, and despite the fact that even when he had been there it was she who made all the decisions, her opinions no longer mattered. The only thing she did not lose was her impertinence. She still reacted vigorously when life tried to force her hand, even when that was all she had. It was Alba who had taken her place without even desiring to, just as in a pack of animals, where there is no such thing as free will.

WHEN IT WAS OVER and done with, after the silent embraces and handshakes, Rocco, Alba, and Gioia returned to their cement fort.

This was how Gioia secretly referred to the house that Alba had selected after the move. It was a small house surrounded by what had once been a little garden, which Alba had cemented over because of the dust that came in.

Alba had been driven crazy that June by the dust that coated the furniture with a depressing patina; even a river of Vetril wasn't enough to get rid of it.

On their return from Grottole, Rocco went to bed. Alba and Gioia stayed in the kitchen for a while longer. That night, Alba tried to talk to her daughter for the first time in years. They did not look alike, but in photographs one could see that they were surrounded by the same aura. It was impossible not to know that they were mother and daughter.

"What did your aunt have to say?" "What do you mean?" "She's a bit . . ." "What?" "Nothing . . . when you were little, you wanted to be a ballerina, do you remember?" "No." "You wanted a tutu . . ." "I don't care anymore." "Did you see that the twins . . ." "What about them?" "They have the same mole as Uncle Vincenzo; don't tell me you haven't noticed!" "*Basta!* Leave me alone!"

When Rocco came into a room, it filled with silence.

No one was involved in politics anymore. It had become simply a topic of conversation in the piazza on Sundays when Rocco drove to Grottole, something to discuss with his brothers-in-law. They had endless conversations about what might have been. And what should have been. Arguments with Mimmo, who had left the Communist Party after he moved to Rome and joined the Socialist Party, which was led by an aggressive young man by the name of Bettino Craxi. This was the same Mimmo who had refused to leave the party back in 1956 after what had happened in Hungary and had tried to convince Rocco to stay by arguing that in these difficult times it was important to show confidence and consistency. Now he made strange, sophisticated arguments in which he used the word "modern" each time things didn't quite make sense. In any case, no matter how you put it, to Rocco it still tasted of betrayal.

Since they had moved to Matera, the years had begun to pass ever more quickly, and increasingly Rocco felt as if time had left him behind. At first it bothered him, like the first time one discovers a wrinkle or a gray hair, but then he gradually came to accept the situation and gave in to old age without a struggle. The enthusiasm that had sustained him through each of his projects, even those undertaken late in life, disappeared. Nothing seemed worth the effort.

He became irascible. He lost his temper over small things, surprising the people who had always known him to be a thoughtful, mild man. And his temper worsened over the years, until people stopped paying attention to him at all.

One day, he was driving back from Grottole, where he had gone to visit Lucrezia, as he did three times a week, each time spending two hours with her in perfect silence. Without knowing why, he turned off at La Martella, one of the rural villages that had been built in the fifties after the land reforms. Suddenly he remembered the happiness he had experienced in those days: the celebrations, the farm laborers, the dance at Mimmo's house where he had met his wife. Now only a few of the houses were inhabited. The streets were as deserted as the ghost towns of the American West. The arcades, designed by the architect Ludovico Quaroni, were stained with mold, and in the courtyards that had been built for community activities weeds grew in the cracks in the walls. It was raining lightly. Rocco realized that he did not feel like going home that night. Nor the next day, nor the day after that. He did not feel like going home to any place. He wanted to lose himself in the silent countryside, amid the undulating lines of the hills.

He drove his Volkswagen in a straight line for a while longer as he found peace in this dream and his gaze wandered over the pale-green fields. When he came to a small parking area, he turned around and drove out of town, but it was as if a part of him, perhaps the best part and certainly the part of him that was most alive, had stayed behind, roaming the deserted streets of La Martella under a light rain in the frustrated hope of meeting someone, one of the inhabitants of those houses, who would approach him and quietly reveal that he was truly happy.

AFTER A LONG PERIOD of tears and sleep, Gioia awoke one morning apparently transformed. She tore up the photograph of her friends from Monopoli: Giovanni, Francesco, Porzia, and Madia. It was a kind of photomontage created through a trick of perspective that made it appear as though she were holding her friends in the palm of her hand as they stood near the harbor in the morning sun. She stopped straightening her hair and refused to wear the white blouses her mother carefully ironed for her or the blue turtleneck sweaters she had once draped over her shoulders. She let her blue loafers grow moldy in the closet, threw away her strawberry-flavored lip gloss, and gave up on her dreams.

For a while, she spent her time just as she had as a little girl, leafing through the books she found in her father's boxes, which had miraculously resurfaced after the move, like remnants from a time no one could remember. Trotsky, Engels, Gramsci. They made her head hurt. Sometimes she would pause when she read a line she particularly liked and write it out in block letters in her school notebook, the one with illustrations by Benito Jacovitti.

Instead of answers, she found more questions. Only one thing seemed certain: her father had done everything wrong. She swore she would never be like him and dreamed of a life completely different from that of her parents. A life in which everything would be invented from scratch. She began to spend time in certain graffiti-covered houses in the Sassi district of Matera, frequented by other young people who were viewed with suspicion. They came from the poor neighborhoods to which their parents had been relocated in the fifties when the new urbanization laws were passed to clear out the Sassi. Their grammar was bad and their conversations were filled with obscenities. They borrowed Gioia's things—sweaters, books, bracelets—and never returned them, because she was a rich daddy's girl.

When she came home, Alba would check her eyes with a pocket flashlight, not, as when she was thirteen, to see if she was wearing makeup, but because of a dangerous substance she had heard about on television that at first makes you feel happy and calm, as if you were lying in a field next to a brook with the person you love, and then kills you a little bit at a time. For some time, it seemed that her daughter had changed beyond recognition.

If Gioia had been given a chance to go back and revisit every fork in the road, taking the opposite path from the one she had chosen, she would most likely have arrived at the same point. The little girl who had tried to capture the moon in Grottole's town square when she was four, who had cried when her uncle gave her a toy iron for Christmas when she was seven, who made a pact with her cousin when she was ten which she tried in vain to break many years later, and who still prayed at night in bed, could have taken a false path at any point in her life and lost her way. Perhaps what seemed like detours were in fact the most direct path, the only path she could have taken, to her destination.

"When will you get some sense?" her grandmother had asked.

ON ONE OF THE MANY DAYS when she skipped school, she met Alex in the Sassi district. He was skinny, with a checkered shirt and a mustache, like so many men at the time. His hair was raven black, with a touch of dandruff. His muscles were like steel. He had wolverine eyes. The girls in the movement didn't stand a chance. The two of them walked for a long time in silence amid the rocks and weeds. Every so often he would kick a rusty can as he told her a story, which she did not know whether to believe. He told her he had certain contacts in Rome. That he was in hiding and needed to find a secure spot by nightfall where no one could find him. He asked her to find him a sleeping bag. She didn't know whether to believe him, or if all these stories were just meant to make him sound interesting. She decided, as she often did, not to think about it too much. She let herself be drawn in by his words and the possibilities that they revealed. That was all.

She led Alex to one of the many abandoned houses in the northeast facing Sasso Caveoso. She particularly loved this house, and had often dreamed of living there one day. It was an intricate maze of rooms and anterooms, of ancient parlors and storage depots, caves, and cellars. From a window one could see the rocks of the steep cliffs over the Gravina, which turned pink in the setting sun. Most of the rooms had no floor. There were nettles growing underfoot and pellitories sprouted from the walls. The ceilings were quite high. In a corner that had once perhaps been a chapel, there were remnants of a fresco depicting a girlish Madonna. Gioia told Alex that he could sleep on a trough there, and he nodded distractedly. He seemed to be lost in his own thoughts, as if his situation no longer interested him.

When they were about to leave, he held her back. His wolfish expression intensified, and she felt trapped. She tried to move away, filled with a kind of revulsion, but he cornered her. He pushed her against a wall. Gioia protested, but he was already on top of her. He was panting. Gioia turned her head away. She said no. Alex had already pulled up her skirt. His hands were moving up her thighs. Gioia felt powerless. A burning shiver ran through her pelvis, pinning her to the wall. She felt her body melt and a pulsing, galloping sensation in her belly. Her neck and lips were burning, and she felt as if she were dying and coming to life, losing herself and finding herself. The sense of disgust grew stronger, and so did the attraction. She said no again, but more weakly. Alex said that she was just being bourgeois; it was obvious from the way she dressed, from her attitude, from the way she did her hair, that she was completely bourgeois. She felt shame as he put his fingers in her cunt, moving them up and down, and everything became wet and hot. "Just bourgeois fear," he said. Shame and desire. The clear evidence of her excitement belied her words. Alex's mouth on her ear, biting, licking, blowing, and plunging inside. Gioia loses herself in an infernal paradise. Bourgeois. He feels her breasts, squeezes her nipples. Gioia sighs, pants. Alex smells of sweat. He is wearing a coarse cotton T-shirt that rubs against her skin. He presses against her body, forcing her against the wall. He pulls her down to the ground. Her legs are bent and open and her skirt is pulled up. Gioia is afraid that someone might come in. She tells him. Alex doesn't listen. He is somewhere else. Between her legs. He pushes, panting. Gioia is afraid. Her tangled hair forms a final defense. Alex murmurs something that Gioia does not understand. He seems upset. In the tangle of arms and legs, he once again introduces his hand. He does his best to pull away the dampened pubic hair. He pushes, enters. Gioia cries out in pain. There are pebbles under her thighs. Her tangled hair pulls against the damp, rough-edged rocks. There is blood.

"So you were a virgin?" Alex asks, amazed. He looks as if he has just returned from a free trip; his eyes are liquid and placid. Virgin. Bourgeois.

Gioia ran away from home the day she turned eighteen. She left a note: "Don't look for me." Rocco searched for a long time, up and down stairways in the Sassi, in abandoned houses, criss-crossing deserted neighborhoods.

When Gioia was born, along with a great joy Rocco had felt a slight disappointment that he could admit to no one, not even himself. He had been hoping for a boy who would fish with him for carp and tench on the Bradano. When he was older they would discuss politics, argue. One day he would realize that the boy knew more than he did, and he would feel proud. The initial disappointment increased little by little as Gioia grew older and, instead of playing the game of the wolf and the three piglets with her father, spent more time with her mother discussing women's things that had nothing to do with him. Over the years, she grew distant from him. But as time passed his love for her also grew. A passionate love, different from anything he had experienced before. The less he understood her, the more he loved her. The more he thought he understood her, the more he loved her for the wrong reasons, and the more he loved her, the more he saw her as something other than what she was and wanted desperately to give her all the happiness he had not been able to give her mother. He wandered for a long time in the Sassi, searching for her in every shadow, all in vain.

"*O frat mí, o frat mí, o frat míííííííííí . . .*"

Part
III

There were gelid winters that hardened the earth and split the skin of people's feet with chilblains. The tulle in the wedding gown was eaten by moths, and verdigris corroded the copper pots. Pino the Idiot ran down into the river after a girl with blonde hair who had appeared in a dream. They found him a few days later, his belly bloated, his white flesh eaten away by carp. A boy learned to play games with the wind: he let it blow over his head, wrapped it around his wrist, or flung it far away and then pulled it back, now filled with forests, mountains, and highways. From that moment there was nothing left to say. "Ay, ay, ay," murmured the witches of Salandra . . .

Chapter Twenty-one

They are between fifteen and thirty years old, a crowd of them, walking toward the lake. They advance blindly, crossing narrow streets and clusters of houses as they eat ice cream, wurst, and watermelon with their hands. They throw food at each other and pass bottles of champagne, drinking straight from the bottle. Some of them are naked, others are draped in a light-blue damask cloth.

Among them there is a dark-skinned girl whose hair turns a fiery red in the sun; she laughs and shakes her head. She too is wearing a light-blue curtain, wrapped around her like a Roman peplum. The curtain is from a train they assaulted that morning. The boy next to her is also laughing. A middle-aged couple on the sidewalk watch them, shaking their heads. The boy wears the curtain around his hips; his hairless chest is bare. He wears a batik scarf—singed by his marijuana pipe—wrapped around his wrist. How can one choose between them . . . ? They look like they've known each other forever, but then a group of Neapolitans carrying an enormous "confiscated" watermelon catches up and separates them. Gioia takes a piece, digging her fingers into the ruby-colored flesh. The juice drips down her tanned back. A boy wearing a top hat smiles and licks her shoulder. She glares at him, then smiles back. A hand covers her eyes. Nooooo, it can't be! I knew we'd see each other again! Sweet, sweet, sweet. They embrace, so tightly they can't breathe, turning round and round. Can you believe it? Remember that guy? Which one? The one whose mother came to get him? They had lost sight of each other in a piazza, they can't remember where . . . I knew I'd find you again, sooner or later! Were you in Perugia? The dust blows in the wind. They are happy, happy and sad, happy and paranoid, happy and *basta*. Then they dive, naked, into Lake Trasimeno. Umbria Jazz, 1978.

A short-lived season of freedom and belonging, of losing herself in crowds in piazzas across Italy: Rome, Bologna, the Ponte Vecchio in Florence. She sleeps with a Swiss boy whose skin is as smooth as a girl's, and then with a comrade from Calabria. She yells out slogans like *"P.38, ti spunta un foro in bocca!"* ("With a P.38 pistol, I'll blow a hole in your mouth!") and is moved to tears by the sight of red flags. She uses the flagpole as a bludgeon, masks her face with the red cloth, and raises a clenched fist as she did when she was three and her uncle encouraged her with slogans: "Come on, now, let me hear you say it: 'Victory to the red flag!'" "If you want Lamas, go to Tibet. We want everything, and we want it now! Fuck your mother!"

UTOPIA IS A PLACE that doesn't exist. It is the only state in which Gioia can live.

Part of Gioia is back in Monopoli. She's married, with a little girl. Her husband is a doctor, head physician in the pediatric section of the hospital in Putignano. They were in the same class at the classics high school, in the legendary Terza B section. She teaches art history. She spends her Sundays in the same houses where she once listened to the songs of Francesco De Gregori with her friends and felt warm skin through cotton shirts. She still listens to Francesco De Gregori. Her clothes are moderately more original than her friends'. She doesn't use the word "chic," but her friends do. She would like to visit Paris but hasn't had the chance. She's happy but she doesn't know it.

"The piazza is ours, and so is the city!" Their voices rise up. "Enough protests against inflation / proletarian expropriation!" "Long live armed struggle!" A sudden wind lifts up waves of dust. "Forget Comrade Enrico Berlinguer! / We need real Communism!" The crowd roars. "The police shoots us, but don't you worry, we'll win in the end, and they'll be sorry!" "No more daughters, mothers, wives / down with the family, get out of our lives!" "Sa-cri-fice, sa-cri-fice." "Stuuuuupid, stuuuupid." The clamor grows, becomes deafening.

Gioia and her husband's house in Monopoli, in the life she might have had: an apartment on the fourth floor with balconies overlooking the sea, not far from the elementary school she and her two best friends attended as children. They are still best friends and live only a few blocks from each other. One of them has two children, the other only one; she would like to give her baby a little brother or sister, but so far hasn't been able to. Open-format living room, with an arched doorway, kitchen connected to the living room by an alcove that sometimes becomes a nook for floral arrangements. A hallway and two bedrooms, one for Gioia and her husband and one for their daughter. Her husband's office, a storage space, and two and a half bathrooms. Guzzini flatware, teak furniture, custom-made curtains. The fine table service—a wedding gift—neatly stacked in one of the cabinets in the dining room. The lace-edged towels, sewn by Candida, Albina, and Concetta, all part of the grand trousseau that welcomed them into their happy married life.

This is not 1968, but 1977; we have no past or future, history is killing us.

On the church steps, Gioia burns a ten-thousand-lira bill with her cigarette lighter. Her comrade Salvo, from Palermo, watches her with admiration. He admires her curly, lustrous hair, and something inside him feels like he is about to break into tears.

Somewhere, in a time that might have been, Gioia walks by the sea with her thirteen-year-old daughter, Alba. What a pretty name, her friends at school say. Gioia has a truly special relationship with her, which is not spoiled by the usual small skirmishes that arise between a mother and her adolescent daughter, but rather is rendered even more intense. Gioia does not have to say no two times out of three, as her mother did, when her daughter asks for a pair of designer jeans, a brightly colored or perfumed T-shirt, or other silly things. When she was a girl, she too liked those things. She had a T-shirt with a giant strawberry right over her small breasts that gave off a strawberry scent, and all the boys wanted to sniff it. Come to think of it, it had the word "sniff" written on it. Gioia married well. She can say to her daughter, "When I was your age . . . ," but the truth is that the slight belt-tightening made necessary by the recession of the early seventies never affected her much. Austerity plans, "cycling Sundays," "if you don't feel like walking, buy a mule"—none of this kept her from frequenting her rich friends with their villas, mopeds, and charming manners. In fact, she married one of them, her second boyfriend. Gioia's father, Rocco, adores the little one. When he's not picking her up at school or taking her to dance classes or piano lessons, he passes the time with a group of retired schoolteachers who meet in the country houses where they once went to dance; now they exchange stories about their grandchildren's imperious natures. Since Alba was born, he no longer goes to Montescaglioso, a small town in the province of Matera, to visit the widow of a Communist militant friend of his, as he used to at least once a year. He never stopped visiting Lucrezia, until she left them a few years earlier. On All Souls' Day the whole family visits her tomb in the small flower-filled cemetery in Grottole.

"I speak strictly in a personal capacity, in the name of the Elfs of the Fangorn Forest, of the Colorful Nucleus of Red Renegades, of the Dadahedonist Cells, of the Workers' Orgasmic Committee . . ."

These are the words of the founder of the absurdist Indiani Metropolitani (Urban Natives), Gandalf il Viola, speaking at the Foreign Press Association, in Rome.

The air in the room is thick. Gioia is a tiny lilac speck in the back, or perhaps she's that cloud of lace and frills, that giant flowery skirt, that dress of transparent, rose-colored gauze, barely visible on film. But in fact she was never there, she didn't make it, she was too late. As the slogan said, SPARATE AL TEMPO. Kill time.

What might have been: Sunday lunch at Candida's. Gioia is there; she drives down from Monopoli with her husband and daughter. Beneath the frescoed ceiling, the long table is set with a tablecloth used only for special occasions. Candida, Alba, and Gioia do not stop moving even for an instant; they clear dishes, bring more dishes, everyone tells them to stop and sit down, come on! Behind them hang photographs. Graduations, weddings, christenings. Gioia with her husband and little Alba. And one of Gioia shaking her professor's hand. She is the first woman in the family to get her degree.

Another slogan:

WE ASSERT OUR RIGHT TO BE IDLE!

The following paid ad appears in the Communist newspaper *Lotta Continua*: "An end to squalor, to folly without words and to words without folly, to the suburbs that grind you down, to your bourgeois fears, to your broken promises, to your dreams that are not mine. You were sweet when I was a little girl, but now I'm taking back my life. Don't look for me, Daddy."

At home, Rocco reads these words. He and Alba talk only when they need to compose the shopping list for the supermarket. Alba demarcates her territory with ever more powerful solvents.

On the Ponte degli Angeli in Rome, Gioia sells earrings made out of bread crumbs, painted blue. She smiles and people buy them. They don't know that after a few days they will begin to disintegrate. Life is easy, it requires no effort at all.

For months, Gioia wandered from place to place, living among squatters and in communal apartments, sharing rooms with students or sleeping in a giant penthouse filled with African knick-knacks. She battled with ticks, played atonal Chinese music on Radio Onda Rossa at two in the afternoon, slept in an occupied building on Via del Governo Vecchio in her grandmother's nightgown, and stuffed herself with cream pastries in the morning to make up for sleepless nights. Her life belongs to her, happiness is within reach, all she has to do is grab it, peacefully or by force. She is convinced of this, even though she can hear a muffled sound, a trembling underfoot. Gioia thinks it is the sound of change, and it's true, the world was changing, but not in the way she thought; the party was over and no one had told her, or rather the party was just beginning. All around her it was Saturday Night Fever and she didn't even know it. "Listen to the ground / there is movement all around" . . . A scrap of paper blows in the wind and then floats back down, a blond boy asks if he can kiss her; he stares at her with his sweet hazelnut eyes, and then suddenly it's all over.

"Figlia mia," the other Gioia says, "you have no idea how much I love you. You'll only know how much when you become a mother yourself. I want to give you this necklace made of red gold. It belonged to my great–great–grandmother, Concetta. They say she was buried in all her jewelry, but somehow this necklace was left behind. Perhaps it slipped off her neck. So my grandmother Candida took it, and then she gave it to Alba, my mother, and now I'm giving it to you."

Gioia is walking in a suburb of Rome. Her silhouette is outlined on the asphalt in the intense light of the early afternoon. She looks around and then enters a building, climbs up to the fifth floor, and knocks on a door. Somewhere above her two women are talking on the landing. Her heart beats hard, then seems to stop. She delivers a package and leaves without looking back. She has no idea what is inside. She has no idea why she said yes when they asked her to do it, it all happened so fast. She has never shrunk away from danger.

EVERYTHING'S BACKWARDS

She has no money left. With her last coins she buys five tokens. She inserts them into the telephone and dials. As the first token falls, she begins to sob into the receiver. The next day, Rocco is in Rome, looking around confusedly at the train station. Gioia spots him from far away. She hasn't seen him for a long time. He looks smaller and older amid the grimy marble walls of the station. He seems to be waiting for someone to come and take him by the hand, more than she does. She slows down.

Gioia enrolled in the Department of Drama, Arts, and Music at the University of Bologna. Are you a dancer? She studied semiotics and wore black. In this same city, she had seen shepherds walking by the Church of San Petronio with their flock;

she had seen the stones turn flame red; she had read her future written in hieroglyphics on a table in a bar in Pratello; she had dispensed kisses, calling herself Alice, and walked through the Margherita gardens hand in hand with a young drug addict with almond-shaped eyes. The city was now in mourning. In the park near Via del Guasto, the veterans of the Movement shot up heroin. Leaning against walls that were still covered in colorful slogans and beneath the porticos on Via Zamboni, drugged-out youths begged for a hundred lire. In the kitchen, a comrade—nobody knows his name—wraps himself in a sleeping bag and turns toward the wall. He's covered in sweat. He took some pills, Rohypnol. The police show up. Do you remember that guy? What was his name? Lucio? Alessandro? No, Alex. They found his address book, full of phone numbers and addresses. Gioia knocks on a door. Her heart is beating hard; she can feel it beneath her shirt like a frightened bird, and then it seems to stop. She hands over the package and leaves. I will say all the no's you did not say. I will say all the no's in the world. They left for Paris that very night. In the train, a nonsense rhyme buzzed in Gioia's ears as she watched Italy recede farther and farther into the distance: "*Ambarambà cicí cocò, tre civette sul comò, che facevano l'amore con la figlia del dottore . . .*" Where is the Bastille? *Coupé, coupé.*

Chapter Twenty-two

How much can a man lose and still be himself? He can lose love, money, stature. He can lose someone dear to him. His dignity. He can waste his talent or miss his big chance, his appointment with destiny, the moment he has been preparing for all his life. He can lose his ideals, his dreams, and in the end, even his memories.

And what if a man were also this? All the lives he could have lived and all the things he has lost?

This is the story of Spiros, who in 1980 climbed over the wall of the barracks in Athens where he was doing his military service to be with an eighteen-year-old girl called Eleni, and make love to her at her seaside villa, which was closed for the winter. He got caught and was sent to serve in the special forces, headquartered about ninety kilometers from Thessaloniki. It did not take long for him to realize that neither his personal warmth, the effect of a privileged, spoiled childhood, nor his family—no matter how influential—could save him in the long run from the constant martyrization of the spirit and, worse, of the body, to which he was exposed day and night. The only salvation he could see was escape, and escape he did soon after, with Eleni, who in the meantime had emptied her parents' safe-deposit box.

With that money they went to Paris and lived the high life for about two weeks. As a deserter, Spiros could not return to Greece.

In Paris, after the first few years, Gioia had rented a studio on the rue des Rosiers, in the heart of the Jewish neighborhood, the Marais. Many of those who had left Italy with her had since returned, but she had not; she was accused of being part of an armed group and was awaiting the big trial, in which she was a minor defendant. She had decided not to turn herself in. If she was found guilty, she would stay in France forever.

Rocco tried in vain to convince her to change her mind. She must return, confront the situation, resolve things. Finish university, earn her degree. In the evenings, he and Alba watched the same television shows in separate rooms of the house, he on the old black-and-white set, and she on the color television they had recently bought.

The apartment on rue des Rosiers was a garret on the seventh floor in a building with no elevator, with a spiraling staircase that she climbed swaying slightly; as she felt the old ache reawaken in her hip it filled her with a rage that helped carry her to the top, twenty square meters beneath the eaves, from which she could enjoy her view of the slate roofs of Paris. She loved to gaze at the sky. Those vast northern skies in which colorful clouds chased after one another and the wind rustled, slicing at her hands and face in the days before she learned how to keep warm. In her second Parisian winter she bought one of those Russian hats lined with fur, which framed her mischievous countenance, the irreverent face of a veteran of the Red Brigades. She had finally learned never to go out without gloves, or to forget her datebook, or the map of the Métro. She learned to wear long coats that reached down to her feet, to turn her head discreetly when she saw a beggar dying of cold, and never to say she was free the first time a man asked her out.

Every corner of the city was full of memories, even if she had never been there before.

By her third winter in Paris, Gioia could even walk around nonchalantly in a light snowstorm; she drank vodka and knew all the Métro lines by heart; her teeth chattered only when she wanted to call attention to herself; and often she felt happy. She loved Paris like a creature of indeterminate sex, in whose mystery she lost and found herself, a vast mirror in which she and her dreams were reflected.

ONE DAY, after a series of part-time jobs she took in order to pay the bills, she was offered a small role as an Italian refugee in a costume drama. "I'm hungry," she was supposed to say.

She said it with such conviction that the director noticed her. He took her to dinner and later tried to take her to bed. She didn't accept the offer, but this was how she got the idea of becoming an actress. She remembered how, when she was a child, she had made faces in the rearview mirror of her father's Volkswagen Beetle: the poor, unjustly persecuted girl; the woman in love; the daring explorer of subterranean worlds. She imagined her family watching her on-screen. She thought of everything she had wanted to do or be, the things she had done, and all that others had wanted for her—too much, she now realized. This line of work seemed to finally fulfill all these possibilities, allowing her the privilege of living innumerable lives while living only one, and making sense of all the times she had changed course. It was the happy ending that sooner or later she had always hoped to find.

A photo of her, wearing an intense expression, was included

in the catalogue of an actors' agency. They called her "*la petite italienne.*" And, hearing herself speak, she felt a bit exotic. It wasn't unusual for her to be chosen from among the girls in the green-room who were dying for a part, thanks to her sunny smile, or maybe the nonchalance with which she entered and exited her roles, as if she couldn't wait to be someone else.

As she walked along the Seine she was as happy as an angel, which, being incorporeal, has no age and does not experience carnal love. She became very beautiful. Men would often stop her in the street to tell her so, and she was surprised when she caught her reflection in a shop window. Her restlessness, now tempered by the northern frosts, produced a liquid light that escaped through her dark eyes like volcanic lakes and her body seemed to have been sublimated.

By some strange, late-arriving miracle, the little girl who had once stained and torn her doll-like clothes, pushing her mother to despair, had become a young woman who was as perfect as inorganic matter, untouched by the unpredictable effects of time. Speaking in this language without memories, each morning she could invent an entirely new past that resembled her old dreams and carry it with her for the rest of the day—to the supermarket, the post office, up and down escalators.

She was free. More than her mother, her grandmother, or she herself could ever have imagined. But for what? she asked herself one morning, while she was getting ready to go out. And who could she tell?

Now that she could be everyone, she was no longer anyone.

She continued to do the things she'd done before, as if she'd never asked herself this question: screen tests, parties, openings, walks in places so enchanting they seemed unreal, but they no longer had the same effect. She began to feel out of place in drawing rooms and sitting at café terraces. She got tired of eating elaborate dishes and explaining to everyone that she came from a place called Basilicata, pointing to the instep of her foot to explain where it was. Too many things needed explaining, and she had no words for the most important things. In an attic room of her memory she stored up streets, objects, and faces that only she knew, and they stayed there in a pile, gathering dust. Some days she felt like a rock from a remote geological era, so hardened that it seemed as if at any moment she might simply shatter.

Her relationships with men changed, too. But soon that would change for everyone. In any case.

Gioia had not been with an Italian since she had arrived in Paris. She had been involved with (in no particular order) an unspecified number of Frenchmen, including Corsicans, Bretons, and members of other ethnic minorities, with whom she had perfected her amatory abilities. After they made love, each of them had told her, in more or less the same words, that she was the most beautiful and fascinating woman on earth and the love of his life. They said this again and again until their erotic exploits began to bore her. There was also a series of Englishmen, all of them graduates of Oxford or Cambridge; they didn't amount to much in bed, but on the other hand she was charmed by their crystalline *th*'s and the suffocating rigidity of their collars. Then there were a couple of Canadians, one of whom was so tall and heavy that he was afraid he might crush her when they made love. Several Americans, and a Portuguese man born in Madagascar whose name was Nuno, or "no one." There was a Colombian in his sixties with the spirit of a child and the strength of an adolescent. A Mexican who made love to her on the hood of his wife's car, after driving her home from a dinner party. A South African stuntman. A student from Prague. Then a

Turk, a Chinese man who amazed her, and a female Finnish model, but never a black man. Then she stopped completely.

Gioia's chastity came from far away. She, who had always applied herself enthusiastically between the sheets, began little by little to lose interest until one night in the arms of her latest lover she fell asleep at the critical moment. From that day a barrier formed between her and men, a detachment without rancor, populated only by a few fleeting memories. Her body stopped aging. It became soft and pale, as if she were made out of foam rubber, and began to emanate a fragrance of dull serenity like the young nuns her grandmother had once dreamed of emulating, as she lay in the warmth of her happy conjugal bed.

BECAUSE HER SCREEN TESTS were no longer leading to many roles and the rent still had to be paid every month, one morning Gioia decided to respond to an ad in *Libération* for an erotic call center operator. These call centers were popping up here and there, along with Minitel and a new illness that resembled an ancient plague that God had put on earth once upon a time to punish men for their sins.

A while back, someone at the agency had told her excitedly about a rock star who had to be confined to a sterile room because the slightest cold could kill her. Gioia had assumed it was just one of those crazy stories actors like to tell to make themselves interesting, but then suddenly the illness exploded, terrorizing everyone who had avoided it so far with its four initials, branding whoever contracted it with infamy, cutting down homosexuals, drug addicts, promiscuous types, and hipsters, and putting a definitive end to the age of sexual liberation. Doing it on the phone was safer.

"Please take off your clothes and touch yourself. I want to see how you touch yourself." The man, wearing a jacket and tie, peered at her impassively from behind his glass desk in the high-tech offices of the call center, whose windows looked out on the Sixteenth Arrondissement. A bit farther, the Eiffel Tower was visible. "Why? I just have to talk, right?" "Do you think I enjoy this? I've seen hundreds of girls, much prettier than you. So, are you ready? I don't have time to waste." "Where?" "Right there, on the floor." The floor was wood, polished to a glasslike shine.

Meanwhile, the other Gioia walked along the seafront with her daughter. There is a light spring breeze. "Mamma, will you buy me an ice cream?" "What flavor?" "Strawberry."

"What flavor?" "Strawberry."

JUST BEFORE SUNDOWN, the bushes were covered in dust, the air turned cool, and the sound of hooves grew quieter. The horse that had been following them caught up. They were passing the field at Cugno del Ricco. A lark flew into the air. A dull, persistent buzzing of insects began all of a sudden, then sank into the background. Don Francesco Falcone felt a final shudder. He was remembering that afternoon in March when Concetta had shown him his infant son, and the joy he had felt at that moment. Where was it now? As life left his body through his half-open mouth, he felt that someday someone would find it again, someone he didn't yet know.

One morning in March, as Gioia returned home from her shift at the call center, she had an intense feeling of nostalgia. For what, she wasn't sure. She crossed the esplanade in front of the Beaubourg. She zigzagged among the wandering musicians who were beginning to set up on the square, passing the Gypsy selling flowers, the lady with her dog, the two sailors, the mechanical organ. The phrases she had repeated all night contrasted with her thoughts: *"Oui mon chou, oui mon poulet, oui, fais-moi tout ce que tu veux."*

She chased these words away.

Breathing the pungent air, she was suddenly filled with an energy and hope that she hadn't felt for ages. She felt that she could see far into the distance, beyond the horizon. Raising her eyes, she saw a minute click on the clock counting down to the end of the millennium. Eleven years, 6,127,233 minutes. She tried for an instant to imagine everything that each of those minutes would bring.

She kept walking, following the smell of butter, coffee, and croissants just out of the oven, blending with the fragrance of her thoughts. She felt happy, almost euphoric, like a time when she was little and she had slipped out of the house unseen and walked all the way to the piazza by herself.

But as soon as she turned into the rue Rambuteau, a different, acrid smell hit her. On the grate of the Métro, a bum was sleeping with his mouth half open in front of a boutique. She wasn't able to change direction or look the other way in time. Another line, a slogan from 1977, slipped into her thoughts. Better a desperate end than endless despair. Better a desperate . . . The sky was clear, the light radiant. She was surprised to find herself thinking that her joy had betrayed her, that her dreams would be revealed to be illusions, that her life would continue to spin, and the truly beautiful things would escape her grasp. A bit of oily paper, lifted up by the wind, flew against the edge of the sidewalk, and fell down again.

The stoplight was about to turn red. Her thoughts continued to multiply, ever more numerous, as the car sped toward her. *Oui mon chou, oui mon poulet.* And then the slogan. *La di-stru-zione-è-libe-razione.* De-struc-tion is liber-a-tion. Tell Grandma, when will you get some sense?

The squealing of brakes. Gioia is thrown a few meters and the Citroën spins around and around on its axis. Miraculously, no one else is in the street. A man gets out of the car. He is tall, dark, with olive skin and black, kind, Levantine eyes. It is Spiros.

The shade of the oak trees extended across Don Francesco's inert body. The first stars were visible in the pallid sky. The crickets had not yet begun to sing. It was quiet all around. A spasm contracted his body. He let himself go.

Nothing happened. Spiros took her to the nearest hospital to make sure she did not have a concussion, but, except for a banged-up arm, a few scratches, and a big bruise on her leg, she was fine. He insisted on taking her for a cup of coffee nearby.

A great sense of peace. The crickets chirped, fell silent, and began again. The stars were out.

At first, Gioia barely noticed him. The *petit crème* in front of her completely absorbed her attention. She stirred in the sugar and looked out the window at the people passing by on the sidewalk. She was trying to put together some pieces that didn't quite fit, but she didn't tell him that.

He didn't tell her that he had taken his final dose of methadone that morning, that he was married to a woman who supported him, that they had a daughter, Sabine.

What he told her made her laugh.

THE CITROËN BACKS UP. "What's that?" Gioia asked. He turned around to look. Down on the quay of the Seine, a goat grazes on some weeds growing between the paved stones. How did it get there? They say something, then fall silent. She turns toward him, and suddenly she sees him.

The car is parked near the river. The water is very close. It is dark out. The darkness is so deep that they cannot make out each other's faces. A pale glimmer reflects against the lens of his glasses and hers, which are sitting on the dashboard. They have driven for a long time to find this spot. They have talked and laughed all afternoon. Suddenly, she realizes that she is in a car with a stranger, in a dark, isolated spot. He could rape and kill her. No one knows they are together. He might kiss her. She moves as far away from him as she can, pressing against the door. She doesn't dare interrupt him as he tells her about his family. The story seems to go on forever and becomes entwined with the story of the heroic resistance of a radio station during the rise of the regime in Greece and the feats of a woman called Maria. Gioia is ashamed of her thoughts. How could she think he wanted to kiss her?

They have been in her garret apartment for hours. Sometimes, while they are making love, she says something. He answers, and the rhythm of their lovemaking slows down. They tell each other a thought, a fantasy, a memory. They enjoy slowing down, as if all this did not have to end. The first kiss lasted forever, half an hour, three-quarters of an hour, an hour; when it was ending it began again, like a wheel that touches the ground and goes up again, a circle. They have found each other, and kissing is their way of expressing it.

His heart beats so hard in his chest that he feels it is about to burst.

He makes love to her, and the pain stops. What pain?

One day he gazes at her body on the bed, her lines, touches her belly. "Where are you from?" he asks. "I don't remember," she says, laughing. "I've always been here, with you."

Down at Ai Mar, a frog began to croak, and others followed. Something rustled in the wheat.

She understands what he feels, what it is like to be so far from home. A dry land, near the sea. In his body, she can see the tortured trunks of the olive trees, their strong wood, the roots that dig into the rocky soil.

He reminds her of her grandfather as a young man, the way he appeared in photographs, of her uncles, of the father she would have wished for, the brother she might have had, a cousin, her school friends, the boy with whom she used to dive from the tallest rocks. She remembers the dry stone walls, the sea, winter afternoons, summer nights, novelties, sadness, and joy.

Their skin is similar.

They would like to know each other, if that is possible in a room with no one else but the two of them. Just them and the things they tell each other.

Spiros told her his story during a long afternoon in her apartment. He told her about the night he deserted from the army. And about the country he could no longer return to. One day Gioia decides she will not let him in. How would this story end? He waits. "I'll stay here until you open the door."

Who are you? Who am I? Who are you? Who am I? I was lucky to meet you; you want to hear my story and maybe at the end you will be able to tell me who I am, and I will hear your story and at the end I will tell you who you are.

Their story is a poker game, an earthquake, an appointment postponed.

She is an expert at postponing appointments.

Their stories seem to complete each other; one gives meaning to the other. By intermingling, they become a single story. The only possible story, in a city where no one knows them. A love story.

Somewhere high up in the trees, an owl shrieked in the darkness.

Gioia believed that she and Spiros were two rivers that had veered off course, their currents weakened and bogged down as they meandered through foreign lands. Their muddy waters had been diverted into hundreds of tiny rivulets until all hope of reaching the sea was lost. She hoped that by coming together, their waters would feed each other and that they would again be able to flow placidly toward their destination. But it was not to be.

ONE DAY HE DISAPPEARS. She waits for him all of Tuesday, Wednesday, Thursday, and every day of the following week and the week after that. She realizes now that she knows everything about his past but almost nothing of his present, only what they have shared in her apartment one day, one minute at a time.

She does not have his phone number. Without him, she no longer knows herself.

Can I slap you? She would like to slap him the next time she sees him. Why? So that she can forgive him. Not too hard. Not too soft, but not too hard. Take off your glasses. That's right. Good.

She looks for him in the streets of the Latin Quarter, in the tourist restaurants where they sometimes go to lose themselves in the crowd. She looks for him near the Hôtel de Ville, where she met him, on the Île Saint-Louis, where one evening, after a tiff, he had looked at her strangely and she'd asked him what he saw. A woman locked inside a child, he'd answered.

But she doesn't find him.

One day the phone rings. Gioia picks up the receiver; her heart beats hard, as it does every time the phone rings since his disappearance. Her agent is on the line. A famous director wants to give her a leading role in his film. It will be shot in Spain and Normandy. Gioia hesitates for a moment, then says yes. It's her chance, her salvation.

During the days, hours, and minutes that she waited for Spiros's return, Gioia evaluated each word she would say the next time she saw him. She had time to imagine every sentence, pause, comma, and implication. She missed only one detail. One day, he reappears out of the blue. He knocks on the door. She assumes it is a messenger bringing new scenes and opens the door distractedly, not bothering to comb her hair. Spiros is on the doorstep. They stare at each other. He says something and she laughs, and suddenly all the words she has imagined saying, everything she told herself, the film, the director, her future, even the slap, have no meaning.

Spiros does not explain his absence, which suddenly shrinks and becomes irrelevant. He has come back with an idea that fills him with enthusiasm. He wants to take her south, to the Côte d'Azur. Didn't she once say that she'd like to go? There are olive trees, and the sea, and dry stone walls. The beaches she dreamed about. Cliffs. Oil, garlic, and onion. The blood once again begins to flow in her veins. Gioia says yes without hesitation. She doesn't even mention that shooting starts the following day. That is not her story. The story she is about to live with Spiros, rightly or wrongly, is her story. Now she is sure of it: with him, and only with him, can she be herself. As authentic as a gold coin.

They make an appointment to meet the following day in the Place de la Bastille. Gioia wears a dress she has bought for the occasion. It is bright blue, and it suits her. She is beautiful, and one or two people stop to tell her so in the street. It is a sunny day, one of those rare days where the sky is limpid and open. The workmen on the building site of the Opéra Bastille turn to stare at her. Spiros is late. As she waits for him, Gioia glances at the obelisk in the middle of the square and remembers the anecdote her father and uncle used to tell. How did it go exactly? But she has neither the time nor the inclination to remember. Another endless minute passes, and still he hasn't arrived.

She likes seeing his hands on the wheel, his graceful movements, his decisiveness, his tenderness. In the car they talk, laugh, touch each other. In this world, they have always existed. When they have almost reached the coast he mentions, half joking, half serious, that they should go away together. To the United States, perhaps. Far away. As far as possible. She has no doubts. There, with him, happiness awaits her; but she says nothing, simply puts her hand on his thigh as the car takes a hairpin turn.

It is late when they arrive. The restaurant on the promontory is a lonely beacon in the darkness. There are only a few customers left, and the waiter says that the kitchen is about to close. He sets the table for them outside, with a faint smile. Beyond the cemented waterfront lies the sea.

During dinner the wind begins to blow, the Mistral. It sweeps up the tablecloths and napkins, knocks over glasses. They talk. They discuss banal topics, the movies they've seen in the past months, the books they've read, a crime story that has been in the news, their favorite animals.

The wind blows harder and becomes almost like a hurricane. Dishes and glasses are flying, then chairs, and finally even tables. The two of them continue to talk through it all, as if nothing is happening, as if it were possible for them to have a life together, as if this were their path to salvation.

After paying the bill, Spiros gets up to go to the bathroom. Gioia waits for him. She watches the maritime pines bending in the wind. Everything is perfect. The landscape, the moment, the circumstances, the strange yellowish hue of the sky, the situation that has brought them there, thirty kilometers from La Ciotat. Here, on the Côte d'Azur, a place that had seemed unreachable to her as a girl.

She feels so happy that she decides to go and find Spiros. She wants to tell him that she will go with him to America. To talk about the two of them. She descends a stone staircase with a balustrade made of branches tied together with rope. She catches a glimpse of him around a corner.

He is talking to someone, leaning against a black Saab that Gioia remembers seeing arrive a moment before. There is a blonde woman inside; Gioia thinks she recognizes her, an actress perhaps. Gioia hears her laughing at something Spiros says. He is smiling. Spiros hands a suitcase over to a man in the car. The wind carries bits of their conversation to where Gioia is standing. The car drives away.

Spiros's white shirt cuts through the darkness. Now he will turn around and see her. She could pretend she has just arrived. They could kiss beneath the portico. They could leave for America. Begin again. Be happy. Pretend that the secret that has brought them together is not an age-old devotion to failure, and that their happiness is not like the warm breeze that caressed them for a moment, only to become a wild tempest that disappeared into the darkness.

He turns, their eyes meet, and everything is over in that moment. There is nothing more to say.

This is Gioia's last image of Spiros. The contrast of his white shirt against his tanned skin is imprinted on her brain as if it had been burned there with napalm. The image of the silver ring on his index finger, in the shape of an eye, digs into her heart, along with every minute they have spent together, every gesture, every image and word, like shrapnel from a bomb blast.

The birds began to make a terrible noise in the forest of oaks next to the field and then fell silent again. The sky was beginning to grow lighter. A group of men on horseback was approaching, searching for the corpse.

At that moment the wind began to blow, a refreshing breeze from the Capucin mountains, bending the still-green wheat stalks in its path. It would be a clear day. The wind played with the blood-caked hair around Don Francesco's unrecognizable face, lifted up some leaves, and continued toward Ai Mar.

On her way home from the Gare de Lyon the next day, dazed after a night on the train, Gioia thought she saw her grandfather Colino from behind, walking down the rue de Rivoli. She hurried to reach him, hoping secretly that he would turn around and embrace her, pick her up as he did when she was a child, even though she knew very well that it could not be him. And in fact his face looked nothing like Colino's. She stood on the sidewalk. As people passed her without turning around, she thought of certain afternoons spent on her grandmother's porch, of the taste of olives, the coolness of bedsheets, and the bitterness of words. Only then did she realize she was fleeing, that she had done nothing but escape all these years.

Ten years later Gioia received a letter from Spiros, who had somehow found her address in Rome. By telling her the story of his life, he wrote, he had understood what he had to do. With the money from the business deal in which she had unknowingly taken part and with the help of certain contacts he had made during his disappearance, he had been cleared of the charges against him and was able to return to Greece. He had left his wife, daughter, and everything else. He was happy.

There was no address on the envelope. Gioia would have liked to thank him, because by losing him she had found something she had been seeking for a long time without knowing it.

Chapter Twenty-three

It is not easy to tell this story to someone who does not know the Basento valley, the sky as blue as a colored pencil in a children's set, the hills that turn green in the spring and yellow in the summer, the bush fires, the oil wells, the dying towns on the hillsides, the flight of the kite bird.

What all this has to do with me I can't quite say. It is like the look I see on my face on certain days, when I catch my reflection in a mirror. Like certain moods that suddenly come over me, so deep that they seem to emerge from a time before I was born. Like the questions I ask myself and the answers I stumble upon. Like unexpected events. Like my constantly upended plans. Like everything which has meaning, no matter what that meaning is.

In certain lives there are moments when things take an unforeseen turn. A kind of derailment. You begin to wander through the days as if you were lost in the streets of an unknown city. You see things and people that should seem familiar but are not. You do not recognize events or the small actions they are made of.

You ask yourself when it happened. How it began, and how you reached this point. You reflect on the events, moment by moment, that have brought you here. The forks in the road, the detours. And without knowing it, you become lost in history. In your own history, which you piece together little by little and tell yourself every day in order to exist. Only when you turn toward the past do you understand that time is not a circle but rather a spiral, and that the effort you expend to embrace the past projects you forcefully into the future.

IN MARCH OF 1989 the newspapers reported—as they had been reporting for some time—the news that the Communist world was crumbling. *L'Espresso* published a series of letters to the editor that had appeared in *Ogonek*, a popular magazine in Russia during the Gorbachev regime. One of the letters said that the great famine of the thirties in Ukraine, which had killed countless children and old people, had been orchestrated by Stalin in order to force the farmers to join communal farms. Another described the privileges accorded to the members of the nomenklatura; another, the falsifications of history that were taught in school and the concealment of data indispensable for scientific research; others spoke of the abuses that took place in army barracks, of the lack of personal liberty. Alba read these letters on the train. Her husband read them at home, alone, and his world faltered. Even his memories were shaken.

On March 19, 1989, it was hotter in Paris than in Matera.

When Alba got off the train at the Gare de Lyon, her bones stiff because she had refused to ride in the sleeping car, the first thing she saw was a giant poster proclaiming: *"Liberté, égalité, marron glacé."* Paris was celebrating the bicentennial of the French Revolution. There were images of Marianne, Danton, Marat, and Robespierre on every wall. The tricolor flag, white, red, and blue, was displayed on gadgets in shop windows: hairpins, ties, lighters, coffee cups, underwear, plates, dolls, datebooks, calendars, ashtrays, statuettes, busts, pajamas, and scarves. "*Le bonheur de tous*," happiness for all, the ultimate goal of the Declaration of the Rights of Man of 1789, was for sale everywhere for a modest price.

Alba's taxi passed the Place de la Bastille. There was no Bastille. It had been torn down in 1789. Alba did not react; her mind was empty.

Her daughter's apartment was just as she had imagined it: a mess. From the window one could see the roofs of Paris. She had always wanted to go to Paris, but she never imagined it would be under such circumstances. She did not dwell on this thought. She inspected the apartment with scientific detachment. A moment later, she dove in.

There were books and clothes everywhere. Stuffed in the back of the closet, all wrinkled and gray, Alba found her grandmother Albina's crocheted sheets. She remembered when Gioia had insisted on taking them with her, stealing them from her future trousseau. After all, she had no intention of getting married, she had insisted. Alba had resisted as long as she could, and she had been right to do so. Just look at the state they were in; not even a gallon of bleach could make them white again.

She set the clothes aside because she would take them with her. She would have to wash them all before putting them in the suitcases. She packed the books in boxes. She would leave them there, and they could decide later what to do with them. Alba was horrified by the state of the carpet, which was stained and so clogged with dust that it was obvious it had not been deep-cleaned for decades. She swore never to have wall-to-wall carpeting in her house. Then she began to clean it with a special foam she had bought. That night her back hurt so much she could barely move, but the rug had turned a different color. It took her three days to put everything in order. When they left, the apartment had a sinister gleam and Gioia's clothes were folded neatly in the suitcases—ironed perfectly and fragrant with fabric softener. Albina's sheets had been torn up to use as rags. Gioia was driven by taxi to the sleeper car.

The first week, Gioia did not say a word. Her mother fed her, just as she had when Gioia was little. She cooked the same things, mashed concoctions that she patiently fed to her daughter, blowing a few times on the spoon before holding it up to her mouth. But most of the food went cold on the plate.

Rocco went into his daughter's room at least a dozen times a day. He never stayed for more than ten minutes. He would stand there, frozen, looking for something to say, then leave. Then, after a little while, he would come back.

Gioia could hear the sound of televisions coming from the neighboring houses, which had been built closer and closer over the years. Alba, too, flipped from channel to channel in the evenings until she fell asleep on the couch, her mind filled with sequins and dancing girls.

One day Gioia did what she had done when she was eight months old: she spat out her soup in her mother's face. Then she said she was leaving. "Where?" Alba asked. "You can barely walk." A week later, Gioia left.

In Grottole, Candida made a bed for her in the room beneath the storage space, guarded over by photographs of her grandfather Colino, her great-grandmother Albina, and her great-great-grandmother Concetta, and by the portrait of Don Francesco Falcone, which had been moved there. Candles burned through the night. The muslin sheets were the same ones she had played in as a little girl, imagining that she was in a little house. They were cool to the touch. In that house, time stood still, as in a bubble that turns round and round, but always ends up where it began. Gioia began to feel better, slowly at first, then more quickly. She gained weight, and her menstrual cycle returned. She regained her color. The ruins inside of her began to breathe new life.

"When, in a hundred years, you go to meet your maker," Candida told her, "you can tell him that you've been to France, Spain, and England. 'I've been here and there, up and down, I've seen this, that, and the other.' And God will say, 'How silly of me, I've been up here the whole time.'"

Recently Candida had started to resemble her mother, Albina, and also her grandmother Concetta. When they were young, they were very different from each other, but with the years they began to look alike, and by the end they were virtually identical, as if the proximity of death had brought out their true essence. Candida spent her days at Gioia's bedside, completing what would become her final task.

She had started it almost ten years earlier, when she turned eighty, but over the years she had stopped hundreds of times. Her eyes were tired. It was a long bedspread with an extremely complex design, made out of the finest cotton anyone had ever seen. Candida talked as she moved her crochet hook without looking down at what she was doing; she could barely see, and her hands were deformed by arthritis. Her experience was all she needed.

Starting in the morning when she went to Gioia's room, she told stories, as she had when Gioia's tonsils were removed as a little girl. She told the story of Uncle Mimmo swearing on the altar, and the one about Grandma Concetta and her kindness toward the poor, and the story about the lady from Milan, and the one about Don Francesco's barrels of money. Gioia had heard these stories thousands of times, but in the past few years she had forgotten them. Now that she was hearing them again they seemed to merge into one, like the designs on her grandmother's doilies, which began as simple stitches and spaces—arches of chain stitches, rhombuses, and columns—but then became part of a larger pattern, with no particular meaning except for the time and love that had been put into their creation.

As the days progressed, Candida became more and more absorbed in her stories. She began to confuse the past with the future. The present shrank to almost nothing, like a membrane that is about to rip.

"I feel like I've been here a thousand years," she said one morning after her coffee. "I've had it! *Basta*, always more of the same! But the layabout upstairs, he can't seem to remember my name, he doesn't want to call me to him! I'm ready for a change. Just look at me! Who would have thought I'd still be here, poor unfortunate soul that I am."

And still, she watered the plants and when a flower opened, her eyes sparkled.

"Everything is different," she said another day, looking around with curiosity. "Everything. The world used to be easy, simple; now who can understand it? What was in the sky is now on the ground, and what was on the ground is in the sky. Nothing is the same. I've lost everything, everything, my girl.

"Where are you? Why did you go off to the shop without bringing me my coffee?

"And what about this house? What will become of it?" She would open the doors, peer into the bedrooms, the parlor. Some of the rooms had been divided, with lofts where the children had slept when the house was full. Candida wandered from room to room, like a fly looking for a way out. "Sell it, if you can find someone who wants it, and if you can't, just give it away, who cares? What do you want with this place? You know what will happen when I die? It will crumble to the ground. Let it crumble, who cares?"

Sometimes she would peer at Gioia as if she had never seen

her before. She would make an effort to remember. "Whose daughter are you, my dear? What's your name? I can't remember a thing. Lucky for me, this time I only forgot your name. Write it down on a piece of paper and I'll put it in my pocket."

There were scraps of paper all over the house, to help orient her in space, and, more importantly, in time, holding the dead at bay; more and more, the dead consorted with the living. It was becoming difficult to keep them apart.

"Last night, I heard the children calling to me. Where is my husband? Where is my father? Where is my mother?"

One night before going to bed Candida decided she wanted to talk to Cicia. They hadn't spoken in years. She dialed the number from memory and on the other end of the line her friend picked up after a few rings. She had gone a bit deaf but her mind was still sharp. They talked, without giving in to nostalgia, about what they had eaten for lunch, about the weather, and about their respective aches and pains. Then Candida said good-bye.

One morning Gioia felt that her strength had returned. The woman who came to cook and clean had not yet arrived, and Candida was nowhere to be seen. Gioia pushed herself up and climbed out of bed. She still felt a bit light-headed, but it was good to breathe deeply. She could feel the air in her trachea as it went down into her lungs. She walked barefoot and the floor, with its flower pattern, was cool under her feet.

As she walked by the sitting room she saw a light under the door. It didn't look like daylight. Inside, the shutters that opened onto the valley were still shut, and the ceiling lamp was on. The table had been opened to its full length for the first time in years, and someone had laid out the embroidered tablecloth that was used only on special occasions. Each of the twelve plates contained an antipasto of sausage and hard-boiled egg.

Gioia turned out the light and shut the door slowly behind her. She stood still for a moment. She took a deep breath and walked over to the bedroom, which was still enveloped in semidarkness. Candida was tiny in the middle of her huge double bed. Gioia went to her and took her hand.

"I want to wear my new dress, dear, it's hanging in the closet," Candida said before leaving this world forever. It was her last bit of coquettishness.

When Candida closed her eyes, Gioia let go of her hand and went over to the window. She opened it. Outside, the sun was shining.

She felt an inexplicable happiness, unlike anything she had experienced before. It was a dazzling sensation that started at the point where her feet touched the ground and climbed through every cell in her body. It was made of the brilliant blue sky above, the silence of the stones bleached with lime, the cries of the swallows, and the almost painful intensity of the colors of the gaudy flowers that grew along the roadside—periwinkle, pink, purple, yellow, bloodred. It was an ancient happiness that she had forgotten, but that had remained intact in some hidden part of her. She would feel it again in certain moments of her life when she was distracted and let herself be surprised, or when she was in love, and in moments when she was bored or in despair. Then, the feeling would suddenly rise up from some hidden place and wink, and she would smile for no apparent reason.

In these moments she would remember a time when she had been a queen in her kingdom, a kingdom of things, of people, and of events, all of which existed somewhere else in time and space. Only within her could this kingdom become the present: spring afternoons, wildflowers, Luigino La Ciminiera and Cacacespugli . . .

In the street, standing on a crowded subway, or waiting in line at the supermarket, she would suddenly remember the rusty coins she had played with as a child, the flies in her grandmother's house, the laughter, the kisses, and all the rest. She would think of Don Francesco's treasure hidden away in stories, regrets, and dreams that had survived through time and now belonged to her. "I am Gioia," she said to herself as she closed the window.

She stayed with her parents for a few months longer, until she was completely well again. In November she left for Rome to attend the first hearing of her trial. On the morning of her departure, both of the televisions in the cement fort were on, filled with live images of the events taking place in Berlin. It was November 10. The Wall had fallen. In the kitchen, Alba was frying a cutlet to put in a sandwich for Gioia to eat on the train. Gioia did not have the heart to remind her that she had been a vegetarian for years.

Before she left, she looked at the only tree in the garden, a frond-filled mimosa; she had watched it grow over the course of her convalescence. On television, people were celebrating their rediscovered freedom, walking to the other side of the Wall, not knowing what they would find. Gioia shut her suitcase without forgetting anything, kissed her parents, and said good-bye.

On the train, her compartment was empty. She put her suitcase on the seat next to her, sat down, and looked out the window.

The undulating countryside that had nourished her nostalgia—her nostalgia for bitter suffering, for tears, for unsatisfied curiosity, for captivity—had lost its virginity. The harmonious line of the hills, which changed color uniformly with the seasons—yellow, green, then brown—as unvarying as the emotions that lay within the unilateral hearts of the inhabitants of that land, capable of only one feeling at a time, had been deflowered.

Cement buildings, pylons, and billboards introduced angles and colors never before seen in that landscape. "None of it makes any sense," she thought, remembering Candida's voice, which gradually dissolved into the sounds of the train. Gioia felt her heart breaking apart like this landscape in which the eye could wander only for a brief stretch before crashing into something and turning back on itself, like a fly trapped in a room. The nucleus that had remained intact for centuries or even millennia had broken apart in just a few years, but no one seemed to notice. In her own life she had battled against it but now she mourned its loss, and observed its funeral in silence, without tears.

Acknowledgments

I would have liked to thank all the people who, through their help, made it possible for me to write this book, but as things progressed in the six years it took to complete it, they became even more numerous than the characters who populate the book, and so it has become impossible to mention each of them by name. First of all I would like to thank those who, with their stories, inspired me to write this book, especially my family, and my grandmother Emilia most of all. Then, all of those who answered my questions as I attempted to reconstruct stories, traditions, and local idioms. My family, once again, and other inhabitants of Grottole and the surrounding areas. Some of these people are now gone. Signora Luisa, who provided information about Reggio Emilia. My father, who did some of the research. The librarians in Matera who provided me with books and documents. All those who read the book and gave me their opinion. Those who read it and helped me find a publisher. Those who selected it and ushered it to its final version, becoming impatient only a few times along the way. Thank you all.